KILLER ADDICTION

MIKE DOWSETT

DowCorp Press

Published by DowCorp Press 2020.

This book is a work of fiction.

ISBN: 978-0-6488474-3-4

To my amazing wife, Liz—thank you for all
the love and joy you bring to my life and
your incredible support and belief in me.

CHAPTER 1

Sally and I walked together along the shores of the Potomac River in West Potomac Park, Washington, D.C. The late afternoon sun was shining on us as bright as the love we had for each other. We passed the memorials of Thomas Jefferson, FDR, and Martin Luther King Jr., then stopped in sight of the Lincoln Memorial and the Washington Monument in the distance. In another time I might have paid attention to these heroes and icons of the USA's history, but right at this moment I was oblivious. My sole attention was on my darling Sally and the anticipation of what was to come.

Sally was a glorious vision of colour in her splendiferous ensemble of a bright pink tank top, lurid yellow skirt, purple knee-high boots and green hair that she had been showing off for the past week. I looked down at her as we walked side-by-side, enjoying the closeness we loved to share. Ever since we met a little more than a year ago, we had been inseparable, together every day. I had never felt such an intense and desperate love for anyone in my life, and I knew Sally felt the same for me.

I took off my backpack and pulled out two picnic blankets. I laid one out on the soft grass of the riverbank and we sat down, looking across the Potomac to the Lady Bird Johnson Park. We laid back on the blanket and Sally rested full stretch on top of me, reached up to my cheeks and kissed me long and hard on the lips, her tongue flickering and exploring inside my mouth. I responded with an urgency of my own, looked deep into her eyes, felt her breath panting on my face and sensed her longing.

I could tell she was ready. She rolled off me; we lounged back on the grassy slope and covered ourselves under the second blanket. Now safely out of view of the prying eyes of passers-by, I removed my belt, excited with anticipation. Sally did the same.

Then I laid out our works on the blanket in a nice neat line—belts, alcohol swabs, cotton ball, water, citric acid, spoon, lighter, syringe, and finally, my baggie of heroin.

Sally's eyes widened, and her lips parted even more while she eyed the works laid out between us. I prepared the gear, lightly heated the heroin solution, careful not to let it burn and smoke because it wasted the precious drug. I prepared one hit each—our his-and-her ticket to paradise. Today's choice was to mainline between the toes, since all our available arm veins had collapsed. We each pricked our needle under the skin between the toes, looked with love at each other, kissed longingly and then simultaneously drove home the plunger of each of our syringes.

As the heroin started coursing through my wasted, tired veins, I laid my head down on the soft blanket and the rush hit me like a sledgehammer. I gazed crookedly into Sally's drug-hazed eyes and she said, 'See you on the other side, Simon. Love you, babe.'

It was the last time I would ever hear her voice.

CHAPTER 2

The harsh beeping of the alarm clock blasted its way into Leonard's consciousness as he awoke, exhausted, from yet another fitful night's sleep. He wearily got out of bed, walked the three steps to the desk and turned off the alarm. He had learnt long ago that the alarm's snooze function was a recipe for oversleeping, so had moved the clock to the other side of the room, forcing him to get out of bed to silence the racket.

Leonard walked to the bathroom and started his mental preparation for the day ahead by adhering to his rigid morning regime. He started with toilet, shower, and shave, then plastered his hair to his head with old-fashioned Brylcreem. Next were his wire-rimmed spectacles, which were almost unnecessary because his eyesight was not bad. He only had a low power prescription but liked to wear his glasses for the added sense of superior intelligence he felt they portrayed.

After his regular bowl of oatmeal, Leonard put on his suit pants and crisp, white business shirt, both immaculately laundered and pressed by his maid, followed by his shiny black business shoes. He inserted his plastic pocket protector and one each of a black, blue, and red pen in the left breast pocket of his shirt, then put on his tie and his best tweed jacket complete with brown leather elbow patches. He then picked up his slim gunmetal briefcase and headed out of his apartment looking the very picture of bookish intellectualism.

Despite being over six feet tall, Leonard walked in precise, small steps, a study in minimalism. It was his way of blending into the background and not making an impact or attracting attention. Unfortunately, it didn't always work. As he walked into the lobby of his apartment complex, the building manager spotted him and said, 'Good morning Mister Price, you're looking mighty fine today.'

Leonard grunted in response and muttered under his breath, 'Unlike you, you insufferable moron. And that's *Doctor* Price to you,' treating the man with the same disdain as he did all the other idiots in his building.

Leonard walked out of the historic Colonial Village residential complex on to Wilson Boulevard in Arlington County, Virginia for his short walk to the Court House Metro Station.

The peak hour crush was in full swing by the time Leonard reached the subway. Tens of thousands of commuters were making their daily pilgrimage into the power centre of Washington, District of Columbia, or just 'DC'. The trains on the Orange line of the Metro included a smattering of early bird tourists keen to check out the famous landmarks in the immediate area. Popular choices included the imposing Pentagon, Arlington Military Cemetery and the gravesite of President John F. Kennedy for the more morbid observers.

Leonard tuned out of the commuter mayhem for the next eleven minutes on his train journey that took him under the Potomac River. He absorbed himself in his well-worn copy of *Ulysses* by James Joyce, one of his favourite books to read in public because of the intellectual gravitas he felt that it portrayed to the other passengers.

Flowing along in the human crush with thousands of commuters, Leonard got off his train at Farragut North Metro Station. The famed Golden Triangle extended from the White House across to Dupont Circle in Downtown DC. He took the direct accessway into the swanky Washington Square Building at 1050 Connecticut Avenue NW, past the specialty shops selling cigars, shaving gear, and Victoria's Secret lingerie. He passed the Washington Square Post Office, the restaurants and bars, without a second thought to being a stone's throw away from the seat of the most powerful man in the world at the White House.

Leonard strode haughtily through the foyer and the building security guard greeted him as usual and said, 'Good morning, Sir.'

Leonard responded with his usual flick of the eyes, not even a grunt or a nod, and muttered, 'Imbecile,' under his breath.

After a brief wait in the lobby, Leonard stepped into the elevator and punched the button for the top floor. After his quick ride, he exited the lift and entered the expansive foyer of Langhorne and Cartwright Insurance Brokers. He made his usual stop in the kitchen and poured himself the regular batch of filthy coffee that somehow once again achieved the unlikely combination of lukewarm temperature but burnt flavour.

Leonard made his way to his own private hell of a ten-foot by ten-foot office cubicle formed by dull grey partitions. There was no personalisation to make it his own—such individualisation was strictly against company policy. He logged into his computer and started his work as an insurance actuary; a daily grind of risk assessments, claim reviews and calculating the value of human life. His mood slowly improved as he lost himself in numbers and disconnected from the human interactions that had occupied his morning.

His day of calculations to assign compensation for lost lives, missing body parts and various diseases finally ended. Leonard headed off to the one-and-only social activity he attended—his local Mensa meeting. Leonard's Mensa gatherings were a haven for him. He could stimulate his genius mind and communicate with his peers on an even footing, far away from the stupidity of the populace that he dealt with daily.

He craved the attention and admiration of his clever compatriots, all of whom had scored in the top two percent of intelligence testing. They recognised Leonard as one of the intellectual elite where the members were defined by the number on their I.Q. scale rather than their personality, an area where Leonard was sadly lacking.

After a delicious meal at the club meeting, Leonard left early as usual and made the trip home to his apartment, feeling drained and exhausted. He removed his clothes and dumped them on the floor, saying silent thanks for his maid Esmerelda. The old Portuguese woman visited his apartment every day and took care of everything for him. She cooked, cleaned, shopped, washed, and ironed. Leonard had gotten so used to Esmerelda running the apartment he took no notice of whatever was lying around, knowing that by the next night everything would be clean again. Esmerelda's daughter filled in for her on Sundays and on her two weeks holiday per year, so Leonard was looked after constantly. He never needed to occupy his brilliant mind with such trivial matters as doing laundry or buying toilet paper, let alone cooking or cleaning.

Leonard fell into bed early. In less than a minute, just at the onset of sleep, he experienced a hypnagogic jerk. The violent spasm jerked him awake, an uncomfortably common occurrence that troubled Leonard often in the transition zone between the worlds of consciousness and sleep. He was disturbed but relieved it wasn't another panic-inducing episode of sleep paralysis, where he was aware of his surroundings but totally paralysed and unable to move or speak just as he was about to doze off. Leonard sighed, rolled over and fell asleep within seconds, exhausted.

CHAPTER 3

Blood pounded in my ears, intense beams of light pierced my eyelids, my tongue rasped in my mouth like sandpaper, and bolts of pain shot through my skull as I re-entered the 'normal' world after my heroin high.

Sally was nowhere in sight, which was weird. Normally after we shot up, we woke side-by-side, sometimes even holding hands. But I couldn't see her anywhere. The early morning joggers and dog-walkers pounded along the banks of the Potomac River, ignoring the homeless people and junkies laid out along the grass and under bridges, anywhere they could find shelter. I gave up trying to push through my recovery, closed my eyes and laid my head down once more.

Once the bright morning sun had eased in intensity and the stream of human activity had slowed down, I finally summoned the will to wake up properly. Still there was no sign of Sally, which really was highly unusual—we were always joined at the hip, intensely in love and constantly by each other's side. She wouldn't have gone anywhere without letting me know where she was going. I rolled over on to my stomach, crouched on my knees and slowly, awkwardly, drew myself up to a standing position, swaying slowly and unsteadily.

I carefully extended up to my full height of six feet, four inches and looked in every direction but couldn't see Sally anywhere. I knelt, stuffed our blankets into my backpack, and then gingerly walked up the hill to the top of the riverbank and surveyed the scene. There were homeless people dotted around the place, but none with Sally's quirky wardrobe combination.

I looked down at my filthy hands, emaciated arms and stained clothes and shrugged my shoulders. I simply didn't care about my appearance; I had more important things to worry about, like finding Sally. I grabbed a page of a newspaper from a rubbish bin and headed back down to the patch of grass where we had spent the night before. I retrieved a pen from my backpack and wrote Sally a note in the newspaper's margin saying, 'Missed you this morning babe, gone looking for you. If you read this, stay here until I get back.' Then I poked a stick through the newspaper into the dirt and set off on my search.

I had a sudden urge to take a dump and knew I needed to hurry. I was nowhere near a toilet and had shat myself way too many times coming down off heroin to want to do it again, so I quickly ducked into some nearby bushes, dropped my pants and emptied my load. As I reached out to grab a handful of dry leaves for the clean-up, I heard a noise and looked up to see a little kid, maybe six years old, staring wide-eyed at me with a dopey, gap-toothed expression, not moving. I smiled and said, 'What's the matter kid, never seen a grown man shit in the bushes before?'

I wiped my ass with my makeshift toilet paper, pulled up my pants and scurried off in the other direction away from the curious kid, chuckling to myself as I heard his mother calling out to him.

Hours later, after talking with more crackheads and homeless people than I cared to count, I was still no closer to finding Sally. I circled back around to our spot in the park five times throughout the day, but there was no sign of her. I went the whole day with no food, although this was not unusual. Eating never seemed to help—only smack could fill the emptiness inside me.

As the daylight slowly faded, I gave in to the ever-increasing fear that something terrible had happened to Sally. Since the day we met, we'd *never* been apart for this long without some connection. And to make it worse, my drug cravings were already kicking in; I had stomach cramps, alternating hot flushes and cold sweats, my skin was crawling and itchy, my eyes were tearing up, my nose was running, and I was restlessly shifting my weight from foot to foot, trying to keep my shit together, for Sally's sake. God knows what I must have looked like to passing observers, but I was oblivious to them.

I reluctantly made my way to the nearest police station and stopped out the front. My inner voice screamed at me not to go in, but I summoned every ounce of will and forced myself to walk up the steps, in the door and approach the front counter. The desk sergeant stared at me with dead-fish eyes over his reading glasses, scowling at me as if to say, 'How dare a street-filth junkie like you contaminate my station?' He stared at me silently with an unblinking gaze and no trace of sound or recognition, waiting for me to speak.

'Um… I need to report a missing person,' I mumbled quietly.

'What's the name, how long have they been missing and what's their address?' he immediately shot back at me.

'Uh… it's my girlfriend, Sally Heineman. She's been missing for the past twenty-four hours,' I explained.

'Ha-ha-ha-ha!' cackled the desk sergeant in a most unexpected display of mirth. 'You must be joking! A junkie missing for twenty-four hours? Well, let's hold the phones, pull out all the stops and send out an APB, because some street whore got lost on her way to get a fix from her dealer!' he barked sarcastically.

I recoiled from his tirade and responded, 'But it's not like that—she wouldn't leave me without telling me where she was going. Something terrible has happened to her!' The pitch of my voice was getting higher by the second in my panic.

Now returned to a manner devoid of any trace of humour, the desk sergeant dismissed me with a wave of his hand and growled, 'Get out of here, you scumbag, and stop wasting my time. And don't come back, even if you find her dead somewhere. I don't need the aggravation.'

CHAPTER 4

Ryan had been a night owl for as long as he could remember, sleeping by day and roaming by night—never seeing the sun, like a vampire or nightcrawler. He awoke in the late night and felt a thrill of anticipation; tonight would be special—when he could witness the aftermath of his kill of The Junkie, as he had labelled her. He got out of bed full of energy and quickly dressed in his usual all-black ensemble of jeans, T-shirt, leather jacket, and cowboy boots with the shiny silver tips. He slipped on his black leather driving gloves with holes cut out for the knuckles and to top off the look, donned his trademark Ray-Ban Aviator sunglasses, even though it was dark outside.

As usual, Ryan didn't eat in the apartment but made his way to his regular bar down on the corner where he chugged a beer and wolfed down his usual order of loaded chilli fries.

With his tousled hair, confident swagger, and an air of mystery and danger about him, Ryan was the life of any party and a regular at many nightspots around the city. Men wanted to hang out with him, and women wanted to sleep with him. His walk, appearance and manner screamed, 'I'm a badass motherfucker, so stay out of my way.'

After some light-hearted banter with the sexy waitress who he had bedded the week before, Ryan promised to come back to meet her by the end of her shift. As he made his way into the cool night air, his pulse quickened, and he felt a stirring in his groin with the promise of what was about to unfold. He walked the short distance over to his studio, opened the gate, then straddled his classic 1977 Harley Davidson FXS Low Rider and started it up. The engine roared into life and he peeled out into the street in a thunderous roar of exhaust and tyre screeching.

Ryan parked his big bike out of view at the rendezvous site he'd meticulously arranged the night before, then strode down to the Potomac River and found the spot where he had kidnapped The Junkie. The place was deserted in the late hours of the night. He quickly walked over, sparked up his big Zippo lighter and surveyed the scene, spotting the newspaper with a note scrawled across the top. With a soft laugh to himself, he said with a smile, 'Ha—gone looking for you, babe? How about I help you find her, buddy?'

Ryan pulled out a plain piece of notepaper from his pocket and wrote *I'm at the old factory where the C and O Canal meets Rock Creek. Come look for me*. He laid out his note next to the newspaper and impaled it into the ground with a syringe, then retreated to a vantage point among a small clump of trees. Hidden from sight and with an excellent view of the surrounding area, he settled down to wait.

Ryan's anticipation was building with every passing minute until at last he saw a dark figure scurry over to the patch of ground where he had left the note. A lighter flame flickered, and Ryan could tell the figure was a man, who in the dim light appeared to resemble the boyfriend of The Junkie. The man bent down, picked up Ryan's note and held it up close to his face, then flicked out the lighter, stuffed the note in his pocket and lurched forward, setting off at a quick but unsteady walk. Ryan followed, keeping his target in sight by the light of the moon and the occasional streetlamp.

Across the park they went, under Interstate 66 on Theodore Roosevelt Bridge, under the elevated arteries that fed the city's road network, past the John F. Kennedy Center and alongside the Watergate Complex made famous by President Nixon's fall from grace. The man made his way across the Rock Creek Bridge, oblivious to Ryan's stealthy pursuit. On the last stretch, they headed up Rock Creek until they hit the historic Chesapeake and Ohio Canal. Ryan's heart was racing, and the blood was pounding in his ears as he watched the man frantically searching, looking through the windows of the old building, yelling out, 'Sally! Sally!' in words dripping with fear and panic. Ryan's excitement grew until he could barely contain himself—the voyeuristic act of seeing the impact of his kill on a loved one was proving to be almost as much of a thrill as the killing itself.

Finally, the addict's manic searching stopped—he'd seen something!

CHAPTER 5

'Sally! Is that you?' I yelled as I peered through the grime of the enormous warehouse window. Through the faint wash of moonlight, I thought I could see a body inside. Oh, please God, please don't let it be her. I found a door, but dammit, it was locked!

I picked up a rock and hurled it through the window, shattering it with a deafening crash as the old glass split into hundreds of tiny shards. Desperately, without thinking, I put my hands on the windowsill, ignoring the pain and the gush of warm, sticky blood on my palms and fingers as I jumped through the opening.

I ran across the room and skidded to a stop next to the dark shape on the floor. It *was* a body! Through rising panic, I tried to pierce the dim light and identify the facial features. But there was something strange about the eyes that I just couldn't make out in the dark. I pulled out my lighter and flipped the striker and suddenly wished I hadn't, as the sheer horror of the grisly scene unfolded before me in the flickering light.

I could tell it was Sally, but only just. Spread-eagled on the dirty floor, she'd been stripped naked and tied with a thick rope at the wrists and ankles back to steel beams and pieces of heavy equipment. Someone had turned her into a grotesque syringe pincushion, stabbing her at least twenty times with syringes that were just left there, sticking out of her. But the most horrific part of the scene was her eyes—each one of her open eyes had a syringe sticking out of the eyeball, with the needle driven down to the cylinder.

The horror of the scene hit me with me all its force and I collapsed back on my haunches and screamed with every ounce of air I had in my lungs until I could make no more sound. I collapsed forward on my knees, racked with grief, and the sobs came pouring out of me in spastic convulsions as the truth dawned on me. It was my fault!

'NOOOOOO!!! Sally, I'm so sorry! What did I do to you? It's my fault!' I yelled to the rafters and my screams reverberated in the cavernous space, mocking me as they echoed back. Drained and exhausted, I collapsed onto the floor beside Sally, my body still convulsing with sobs at my loss, her suffering, and my guilt for the part I had played in her hideous death.

My sobbing slowly eased, and silence settled over the scene like a hangman's black hood to match the darkness of the room and my heart. Seconds ticked by and then the sound of a big motorbike coughing into life and tearing off down the street outside flooded into the building.

CHAPTER 6

Barely able to control himself at the ecstasy of the scene that had unfolded exactly as he had hoped, Ryan was at one with his machine as he blasted his way over the Theodore Roosevelt Bridge, back to the bar and his appointment with the hot waitress. The thrill of his first kill had been an incredible rush, but to witness firsthand the impact it had on The Junkie's boyfriend had been another high altogether. Ryan knew with absolute certainty that murder was the thrill he had been seeking for so long.

He parked the Harley at his studio and then walked across to the bar, bursting through the door full of adrenaline and energy. The place was dead, with just a few regular drunks still in attendance along with the manager and Ryan's favourite waitress finishing the closing.

'Hey, sugar,' she oozed in her husky tones, the development of which had been assisted by her twin vices of a major cigarette habit and high alcohol intake. 'I thought you'd forgotten about me.'

'No way, Randy. I'm ready and raring to go. Kick these losers out and tell the manager you'll finish up, so we can have the place to ourselves,' responded Ryan.

A few minutes later with the bar clear and all the doors locked, Ryan went over to the jukebox and cued up some heavy rock tunes including Guns N' Roses, AC/DC and Metallica—not exactly the romance of Barry White, but perfectly matched to Ryan's mood.

The entire bar was dark, apart from the flashing lights of the old Wurlitzer jukebox and the globes over the pool table. Randy emerged from the shadows and sauntered over to Ryan as the heavy rock vibes burst forth from the old speakers. She wrapped her arms around his neck and kissed him forcefully on the lips, immediately threading her tongue into his mouth. Ryan responded instantly, the surge in his groin almost too much to bear after his exciting build-up. He reached down to her generous ass, planted one hand firmly on each cheek and lifted her up off the floor.

Randy wrapped her legs tightly around Ryan and he walked over to the pool table, resting her ass on the cushion. She looked deeply and desperately into his eyes, and they kissed hungrily. Then she pulled away, smiled and languidly laid herself back down on the pool table, arms stretched back over her head. Ryan admired her in the soft glow shining down from the pool table lights. She had a few years on the clock but was still in good shape—what she lacked in youth and smooth skin, she made up for with experience and enthusiasm. Randy was a real firecracker.

Ryan leaned forward and stretched his hands up under her tank top, reached behind and expertly undid her bra with one hand. 'Smooth move baby, you've done that a few times before!' she said with a smile as she removed her bra and top.

'Nah, it's my first time—just got lucky,' replied Ryan. 'Enough foreplay, let's get down to business!' Randy responded, reaching down and undoing Ryan's belt, unzipping his jeans and grabbing his rock-hard cock in her hand as he lifted her miniskirt and pulled down her panties.

Ryan reached inside her, feeling her wetness and heard her panting and knew she was ready—she guided him into her and immediately groaned with pleasure as he thrust hard and deep. Ryan reached under her ass with his right hand and pulled her close and hard into him, reaching up with his left hand, feeling her firm tits and pressing her nipples between finger and thumb.

Randy raised her knees and brought her feet up to the pool table, then drove her stiletto heels into the side cushion. This gave her the leverage she wanted to drive Ryan even deeper inside her. The thrusting intensified as they both approached their peak. Ryan groaned louder and louder and Randy screamed in pleasure until they climaxed together in a cacophony of noise mixed in with the raging sounds of Axl Rose screaming *WELCOME TO THE JUNGLE, WE GOT FUN AND GAMES!* accompanied by Slash's ear-splitting lead guitar.

CHAPTER 7

Finally, my grief spent, I stopped crying.

I looked at Sally and somehow, like some unseen force took over my body and mind, a part of my former life came back, and an unexplainable feeling of calm came over me. My past life broke through the drug torture I had put myself through over the past year, my training took over and I started taking in all the details of the crime scene around me. With the words of my teachers at the FBI Training Academy at Quantico ringing in my ears, I detached from the emotional connection I had with 'the victim' and committed to studying everything, missing no details, no matter how shit I felt right now and how desperate I was for a hit.

My first task was to contact the authorities. I exited the scene, leaving Sally untouched. I crossed the canal and strolled into the lobby of the swish Four Seasons Hotel, hoping the late hour would mean some slack security. Thankfully, my hands had stopped bleeding, but they were drenched in blood along with my arms and clothes. I was filthy and reeked with a stench I'm sure didn't grace the Four Seasons too often. I made it through the front door and over to the house phone, called 911 and reported the crime scene.

I left just as the night manager spotted me from across the other side of the lobby and was making a beeline for me. I was sure his next task would be to disinfect the phone I had just used.

I made my way back to my poor Sally and re-entered the warehouse. I knew I had little time left before the cops turned up and before my withdrawal symptoms got so bad that I could no longer function, so I got to work. The darkness made it difficult—all I had to go on was my trusty old Zippo lighter casting a flickering light on the grisly surroundings. I squatted down on my haunches, peering over what until just yesterday had been the woman I loved with all my heart. Desperately trying to detach myself, I studied the body, the wounds, and the bindings for any clues, careful not to touch anything that I hadn't already. Unfortunately, the ground around Sally was a mess of footprints, blood, and scuff marks from my earlier activity, but I still tried to preserve as much of the area as possible.

As I examined the body, the thing that struck me most was the careful placement of the syringes. What had initially looked like just random stabbings turned out to be very strategic applications of the surgically sharp needles. The killer had inserted a syringe in various critical parts of Sally's body. They had stabbed major organs like the heart, lungs and liver; I couldn't see her kidneys because she was lying on her back and I didn't want to disturb the body. The killer had stabbed both her eyes—I felt a fresh set of my tears burning when I looked at her face again.

I noticed a syringe poking out of each of her ears and one protruding from her suprasternal notch, the large hollow in the centre of her throat between the collarbones. There were more syringes along the neck, plunged into the jugular veins and carotid artery. Moving down the body, I noted her killer had stabbed each of the shoulders at the subclavian arteries and then also the femoral artery of each of her legs.

It was then that I noticed with a fresh wave of horror a glistening from around her vagina. I looked closer and realised with a shock that she had even been stabbed with syringes around her vagina. This new violation was just too much for me—I could no longer remain detached, and a wave of nausea hit me like a freight train. It took every effort I had not to vomit directly over Sally, and it was probably only because I hadn't eaten for over thirty hours that I could turn aside and throw up a few feet away from the body.

Amid my retching I heard movement, so turned towards the sound and an intense beam of a flashlight blinded me. A shouted instruction came, 'Put your hands on your head and get down on your knees! NOW!'

I briefly considered putting myself out of my misery and committing 'suicide by cop', but I quickly dismissed that thought from my mind, knowing I couldn't avenge Sally if I was six feet down a hole somewhere. I stopped retching, put my hands on my head and got down on my knees.

While still being held under the flashlight beam and I assumed also by a gun, another pair of hands roughly grabbed my wrists from behind and wrenched them down behind my back. As the handcuffs clicked into place, I felt I was safe for now from a stray police bullet, because they had neutralised any potential threat from me.

'Take it easy guys, it's okay,' I pleaded. 'I'm the one who called you. I know this probably doesn't look great, but I didn't do anything! I just came here and found her.'

'Shut up, dickhead. Not interested,' came the deadpan response. 'Keep quiet until the detective gets here, then you can tell him your sob story.'

We didn't have long to wait. A few minutes later, another torchlight bounced its way into the room and made its way over to the uniformed cops. After a brief discussion, the man newly arrived on the scene walked over to me and shone the bright flashlight up close, right in my face. As I squinted in protest, my fleeting mental clarity suddenly deserted me and all resemblance to my past life evaporated under the bright light and I was back to being a pathetic, strung-out smackhead.

The light moved up and down on me slowly from head to floor, and I could only imagine what conclusions the observer was coming to already, even before seeing Sally's corpse laid out on the floor. 'What's your name, Boy?' he snarled.

'Simon Winter.'

'My name is Detective Frank Delaney. And your ass is MINE,' he snapped at me, thumping me in the chest with the bright end of his flashlight to emphasise his point.

'We've met before, Delaney. A long time ago in another life when I visited your station house from Quantico,' I responded. I'd met him back in the day on an academy field trip to the local police force; he was a tough-as-nails local detective who I knew would be a giant pain in my ass.

'Well, well, well,' chuckled Delaney in a tone full of derision as he looked down at me, still on my knees. 'How the mighty have fallen! I remember you now; a snot-nosed, smartass kid who thought he knew it all. I heard you were some kind of genius, Son. Doesn't much look like it now, does it? Did you put that super brain of yours on holiday when you became a fucking junkie? A one-fifty I.Q. and you think it's a good idea to become addicted to heroin? Fucking dipshit.'

I was not looking forward to the impending interrogation.

CHAPTER 8

The bright lights blazed down on me in the interrogation room at the DC police headquarters on Indiana Avenue NW. With knees hugged to my chest, I was rocking back and forth in a flimsy plastic chair, coughing, wheezing, sniffing and muttering under the unblinking stare of Detective Delaney.

In a shaky voice, I said again, 'Look, I already told you guys a hundred times, I had nothing to do with Sally's death! I loved her! We shot up together, then I woke up alone. That's it, end of story. Why the hell would I come INTO the police station looking for her, if I was the one who killed her? That just makes no fucking sense at all. And then I called you after I found her! Someone killed her and wanted me to find her—that's why they wrote me the goddamn note!'

'Yes, we read the note you had in your pocket, so that stacks up,' responded the impassive Delaney. 'What else can you tell us you haven't already?'

'Look, that's it!' I said, exasperated, frustrated and seriously in need of a hit. 'You've had me here for hours, and meanwhile Sally's killer is roaming around free as a bird! Like I said, the only thing I can tell you is that I heard a big motorbike, like an old Harley, take off down the street just after I found Sally, but whether that's related, I couldn't tell you.'

I was losing it now, with tears running down my cheeks and my voice cracking under the strain and starting to whimper. I felt like I had bugs crawling under my skin, eating my flesh from the inside, so was scratching feverishly at myself all over.

'Jesus Christ, Winter, look at you! I can't believe what you did to yourself. Yes, you were a shithead, but you were smart, I'll give you that. *Now* look at you, a pathetic strung-out junkie who doesn't know what day it is,' said Delaney with a sneer as the disappointment and accusation dripped from his voice. 'You're right—only a complete idiot would alert us like you have if they had been the killer. Fine, you're off the hook for now, but don't leave town. You're still a person of interest in this case. Now you can go write yourself off somewhere, you absolute waste of a human being.'

And with that, he turned on his heel and stormed out the door.

CHAPTER 9

Leonard parked his grey Toyota Prius and made his way into the office of his psychiatrist, Doctor Ellen DeMarco. In her early forties, Ellen was attractive, but distant, almost aloof, as if she were hyper-aware of keeping the therapist / patient wall an impenetrable barrier.

'Hello Leonard, how have you been this week?' asked Ellen.

'Hello Ellen,' replied Leonard. 'My hallucinations and visions have eased a bit since we last spoke, but they still flash at me just as I'm about to go to sleep. I have these violent spasms and short, shockingly vivid dreams that haunt me just between that awake and asleep phase. I'm constantly tired, and I even had another blackout last week—a short period when I couldn't remember anything. But I feel like these sessions with you are helping. Even though this is only our third session, I feel like I'm improving and getting more awareness about what's happening. It really has been trying, these past twelve months with all these problems I've been having.'

'Thank you, Leonard. I'm glad to hear that you feel the sessions are helping. Last week we were just about to talk about your parents. Let's continue from there,' said Ellen.

Leonard, who'd never had a conversation with anyone about his parents, took a deep breath and started talking. 'Well, I guess the logical place to start is my father. I don't really remember much about him, because I was so young when he died; I was only five years old, so I only have a few dim memories of him, and those that I do I could not describe as significant. From what I gather, he was an unremarkable man—he was a nondescript, middle level sales rep for a soft drink company, working the regional routes of Virginia and Maryland. He died of emphysema caused by smoking two packets of cigarettes a day for thirty years from when he was only twelve years old. Not much to tell, really.'

'Okay, we'll come back to your father later once we've covered some more territory,' said Ellen, who was leaning back in her chair with a notepad on her lap. She appeared attentive, but not leaning in and engaging; she was the picture of professionalism without close personal connection.

'Well, my mother's story is different to my father; quite a bit more information on that front, I'm afraid,' said Leonard. 'After my father died, my mother and I had ten years together. To be honest, she was a miserable wreck. She fell apart his death and sought solace at the bottom of a whiskey bottle. She had an impressive capacity for alcohol consumption and embraced the mess and chaos that came along with it. My mother was quite the barfly.'

'That must have been difficult for you, Leonard; growing up like that with no father and a drunk for a mother. You mentioned you had ten years together—did she leave you?'

'No, she didn't leave. She's long dead. It was only a matter of time, with the abuse that she unleashed on herself. In fact, I'm amazed she even lasted ten years. There were many times growing up that I thought she had died. I was fifteen when she finally went.'

'How did she die?' asked Ellen, in a gentle, supportive tone.

Leonard's head snapped around to attention and he locked his eyes onto Ellen's. Reacting to her vocal softness, he responded in a voice with a hard edge and menacing undertone. 'Save your sympathy, Miss Therapist,' he snapped back at her. 'She was a pathetic retch. A miserable shell of a human who retreated from life, abdicated her responsibilities and deserted her only child. She left me alone, with nobody to care for me and nowhere to go. Neither my mother nor father had any siblings and all my grandparents were dead or senile, and to top it off we had no genuine friends. It was just me and her, and she was goddamn useless—an empty sack of skin.'

The pain and hurt in Leonard's voice were clear for Ellen to hear, speaking the truth that his blank face tried to hide.

'I'm sorry, Leonard, I understand this must upset you, but it's an important step in our work together,' said Ellen. She reverted to the detached professionalism that was a more natural communication modality for her precise, ordered patient. 'How did she die?' she asked again, this time in a neutral tone.

'It was simple, really, and not altogether surprising. After yet another marathon drinking session, she staggered out of a bar in the middle of a foggy winter night. She tripped down the gutter and fell face first into the street, right in front of an eighteen-wheeler. The truck drove over her head and her cranium exploded like a watermelon,' answered Leonard in an even, matter-of-fact tone.

Ellen involuntarily sucked in a breath through her teeth, disturbed at the casualness of Leonard's response. She felt there was a lot going on here that they would need to work through. The detached, business side of her mind quickly realised how much she could earn from the many sessions that lay ahead of them.

'I'm so sorry to hear that, Leonard, it must have been a terrible shock for you, being just a teenager,' said Ellen.

'I didn't find out until the next night,' said Leonard. 'I was home alone, but that wasn't unusual. It had been happening regularly since I was about ten years old, when her drinking got more and more out of control. She often wouldn't come home, she would pass out drunk somewhere, or spend the night with some stranger she picked up in a bar. She entertained many men, but thankfully did me the service of keeping them out of our apartment.'

'Go on,' prompted Ellen.

'I quickly learned that I needed to look after myself. I survived on cereal for breakfast, sandwiches for lunch, and macaroni for dinner most days between the ages of ten and fifteen. Frankly, I'm amazed I didn't end up with malnutrition or scurvy.'

'So, what happened after your mother died?' asked Ellen.

'Well, that was a whole other problem,' said Leonard, with a hurt tone in his voice. 'I went through six foster homes in three years until I turned eighteen. Each home was just as depressing, boring and pointless as the one before it. I wasn't abused, but I was sure as hell neglected. My foster parents were only interested in their pay checks—they certainly didn't spend the money looking after me.'

'How did you survive those years?' asked Ellen.

'I packed bags at a grocery store and got myself through high school. I was just marking time until I could reach adulthood and look after myself. I was a recluse in the years after my mother died, throughout the rest of high school. I had no family and no friends, I kept to myself and didn't bother anyone. Let's just say the girls weren't knocking down the door to get me to the prom.'

Ellen was in full data collection mode, furiously taking notes as Leonard downloaded his childhood story. So many of her patients agonised over sharing their story, and Ellen didn't want to break the flow of data by asking questions just yet—she wanted to collect the facts now and would go deep on the questioning later. For now, she just wanted to keep him talking. 'What happened after high school?' she continued.

'I have a genius I.Q., so I got a partial academic scholarship to attend Johns Hopkins University in Baltimore doing a degree in Applied Mathematics & Statistics,' responded Leonard, this time with a noticeable touch of pride in his voice, that Ellen immediately recognised and noted in her book. 'By the end of my first semester, I was already doing advanced second year work and by third year I was already starting on my Ph.D. I received my doctorate in only four years and could call myself

"Doctor Price" at the age of just twenty-two,' he finished with a flourish. This clearly meant a great deal to Leonard, and he wanted people to know just how smart he really was.

'How was college life for you? Any easier than high school?' inquired Ellen.

'Morons surrounded me at college. Idiots of sub-standard mind populated most of the campus. I found some people of an acceptable level of intelligence. But by-and-large they were an uninspiring lot, more interested in getting drunk and having sex with each other than developing their brains.'

Ellen continued taking notes as she formed a picture of Leonard's character from the revealing sub-text of his conversation. He had a superior attitude, loved his high intelligence and had a poor opinion of the vast majority of the population. 'Please go on,' she said, encouraging him to reveal more through those important formative college years.

'College was like high school; I kept to myself. I had no friends and didn't bother anybody. I merged into the shadows of the college halls like a ghost. People would look through me as if I weren't even there. But that suited me. Numbers were my passion, my escape, my muse. I embraced my studies, tested my intellect whenever and however I could, took on my lecturers and quickly surpassed them. I worked hard in two jobs to put myself through college and even with that and my partial scholarship, I still came out with a student loan debt.'

'That sounds like a very lonely existence, Leonard. Didn't you have anyone you could turn to or confide in?' asked Ellen, recognising that Leonard had finished his download and was ready for a heart question instead of a head question.

Leonard raised an eyebrow and looked pensively out the window as if to bring back the painful memory. 'I had one person I communicated with through my middle grades: a pen-pal. We wrote to each other on-and-off, but then after my mother died, he suddenly stopped writing to me, just when I needed him the most. I would write to him, but he never responded, like he had dropped off the face of the Earth. I eventually gave up, feeling that I would never hear from him again,' he said, almost wistfully.

'What was the name of your pen-pal?' asked Ellen.

'Ryan.'

CHAPTER 10

I stared down at my bare forearms, fixated on the pimply gooseflesh that had formed on them, just like a cold turkey, and thought of the appropriateness of the description for what I was about to do to myself—cold turkey withdrawal from heroin.

I'd had seven hundred in cash left from my last burglary, which I had allocated for my dealer. Instead, this went to several other recipients. Most of it went to the manager of a dingy motel for a room paid ten days in advance. Another fifty went to him in return for an agreement to leave me alone for the duration, no matter what. Next had been a stash of packaged food and a carton of Gatorade, enough supplies to last me through the brutal period that I knew was coming.

Understanding my potential to give up in the darkest hours and run again to my dealer, I'd bought a small safe with a combination lock from the local hardware store. I had asked the store owner to set the combination and only reveal the number to me in ten days when I called the store and asked him for it. He thought it was strange but agreed after I slipped him fifty bucks.

On this, my first morning, I locked myself in the room and locked the key in the safe. I knew I wouldn't be able to get through the bars on the windows and the heavy door to my room opened inward, so I couldn't easily kick my way out. I figured if I was aware enough to get out without the key, then I would probably be safe from a relapse.

I know I need to stay strong and will need every ounce of my willpower to get through this. It would be easier with help, but I feel this is something I need to go through alone. I want no medication to ease the pain and no comfort, support, or advice from anyone to help me on my way. I need to suffer for what I've done to Sally, and I have to get through this if I'm to find her killer. I'm determined to see my mission through to the end, whatever my personal cost. It seems only right that I should suffer for the path down which I had taken my darling Sally.

I looked up at the grimy mirror in front of me and my eyes teared up again for what seemed like the hundredth time. The picture of Sally that I'd stuck on the mirror captured her beautiful, smiling face adorned with bright blue sparkly lipstick under a mop of crazy red hair. It made me smile and filled my heart with love. Then my gaze shifted to the other photo on the mirror—a grisly image of Sally's corpse. It hit my heart like a hammer, making me gasp with a sharp intake of breath, even though I had looked at it so many times already. My resolve hardened once again to get myself through these torturous days of recovery.

Detox passed in a blur, as one day blended into the next. I was a blathering mess of convulsions, seizures, chills, hallucinations, and sweats. I was cold, hot, sweaty, chilly and a bundle of muscle aches and pains. I vomited and paced, paced and vomited. I was restless and twitchy as fuck, I would sit down, stand up, walk around, lie down in a mess and a haze of confusion, having no clue what time, or even what day it was. I was off the grid—no phone, no medical contact, I hadn't even told the police where I would be, despite their last message of 'don't leave town'.

I couldn't bear silence through my self-imposed ordeal, so the TV was my constant companion. Judge Judy, Days of Our Lives, Doctor Phil, or the Shopping Channel, it didn't matter, so long as there was some noise and action flickering on the screen; anything to take my mind off the hell that I was imposing on my body and brain. I was breaking all the rules that the rehab experts talk about, because they say cold turkey by sudden detox is dangerous and if you are irresponsible enough to do it, then you shouldn't do it alone. Every cell of my body craved a hit—I had been a daily user with a high drug tolerance, so had been running big doses to get the high I needed; all of which meant that getting myself off it was pretty fucking challenging, to say the least.

Finally, one morning I had my shit together enough to focus on what was on the TV. The date they announced on Good Morning America told me I had completely lost a whole week. So, it was day seven when I finally felt human again. I had resisted the worst of my detox. My personal prison had done its work, and I had kept myself in the room without escaping to track down my dealer. The massive drug cravings were still there, but the convulsions, sweats, chills and mind-bending hallucinations had eased off. Now that it was just me and my willpower, I was in a state where I could focus and be aware of what the hell was going on in the world around me.

I stuck it out for the next three days, treating them as insurance to solidify my detox. I had heard so many stories of junkies getting clean, only to relapse the minute they hit the streets again, so wanted to make sure I didn't suffer the same fate. Day ten came, and I rang the hardware store, spoke to the manager and got the code from him, then pulled the key out of the safe and unlocked the motel door. As I stood in the door opening, I looked back into the room and shook my head. It was a mess of Gatorade bottles, food packaging, dirty dishes and stained sheets. It was like a symbol of the filth and chaos of my previous life, one I resolved to leave behind for good. I didn't even want to clean it up, didn't want to touch it for fear of retaining the muck. I wanted to burn that image into my mind's eye as a reminder of the old life that I was leaving behind.

As I closed the door behind me, I turned and winced at the bright sun burning right through my eyes and into my brain, bringing on an instant headache. I knew this next stage of my life would not be easy. I would need to stay strong for Sally.

CHAPTER 11

Leonard's therapy session got him thinking about his past. When he had reached the age of twenty-one, he inherited the apartment from his mother's estate, completely paid off in full, with no mortgage. After college, he had returned to live in the apartment where he had spent the first fifteen years of his life, after a break of seven years.

Leonard looked back through his letters from Ryan. He had them sorted neatly in chronological order, starting from when they had begun in his middle grades. Leonard recalled that his mother had encouraged him to write to Ryan; it worried her that Leonard had no friends and also that Ryan needed someone to look after him, because he wasn't a smart boy and would get himself in trouble if Leonard, who was 'so much more intelligent', didn't help him. And he remembered his mother saying they should never meet, because Leonard was so awkward in person and Ryan wouldn't want to be his friend anymore, that Leonard should just let his true self shine through his writing on the page—she'd said it was better that way.

Leonard continued rifling through the letters, saw the long break when he had left the apartment and then when they had unexpectedly started up again just a few weeks after he returned from college. Leonard had received a letter that made it seem as if Ryan had been watching and waiting for Leonard to return to his old neighbourhood. It had unnerved him, like Ryan had been spying on him all that time, maybe punishing him by cutting off contact because he'd left the apartment.

Ryan's letters of adulthood had seemed different, darker, moodier and more sinister than the childhood ones. But Leonard had just wanted a friend, so ignored any concerns over the letters. He'd had nobody since Ryan left him and he was achingly lonely, couldn't explain to anyone how he felt. Desperate for contact, he had accepted the new Ryan and maintained their contact. He flicked through the letters in date sequence and recalled how they'd become progressively darker as time went by. Ryan had talked about his urges and how Leonard needed to help him, that if they could just fantasise in their letters about punishing people for their actions, then Ryan wouldn't have to do anything for real.

As Leonard looked back through the letters, he saw how he had become entwined and absorbed in Ryan's games, which had moved through random fantasies of hurting people to gradually becoming more and more focused on addicts, on people who couldn't control their urges, who would wreck their lives for the sake of their 'fix', whatever that might be.

Ryan would ask for advice in his letters and appeal to Leonard's superior intelligence and logical, analytical mind. He would ask Leonard for help on how to deal with a person he was having problems with, a barman who had pissed him off or a taxi driver who had 'given him shit'. Leonard smiled as he re-read some advice he had given to Ryan— conniving ways to get back at them, or masterful put-downs and insults he had come up with that Ryan could deliver the next time he saw them.

Leonard had long realised he enjoyed showing his superior intelligence by putting other people down, insulting the collective 'they' who lorded it over him but were so inferior to him intellectually. Ryan had become his weapon. It was his way of striking out against the world in a revenge delivered vicariously, in a way that Leonard would never have the courage to do openly. Leonard was hooked, realising he craved the attention and contact from Ryan, his only friend.

Leonard opened one of Ryan's recent letters, the critical one where Ryan had asked for Leonard's advice about the 'fucking junkie' that had bumped into him in the park one night and then had 'the nerve' to insult him afterwards. Ryan had explained that sometimes he fantasised about killing people, but that he would never *do* it; he wouldn't hurt anybody, but it would really help him if he could *imagine* doing it, if he could just play it out in his mind.

Ryan had asked Leonard the question, left it hanging on the page, dripping with potential, a delicate cry for help—a turning point where Leonard would either be in or out. Acceptance or rejection had been the fork in the road from that leading question; 'Help me Leonard, you're the only one who can. Use your brilliant mind to help me imagine how I could punish this drug addict, how I could think about a way to hurt them severely. Please.'

Leonard recalled reading that letter for the first time and remembered the pause, his sharp intake of breath, the reflection, and the moment of decision. The Pivot, he called it. The single thing that had changed him. When he dared himself to imagine what it would be like to take a human life, how you would do it, the statement it would make and the repercussions it would have, the ripple effect of that ultimate act. It had taken some time for Leonard to decide, but he'd understood that if he refused, he might lose Ryan forever and had realised that he felt excited by this fresh game they might be playing. And so, he had written back to Ryan and said, 'Yes, I will help you imagine what you could do, but only on the condition that nobody gets hurt. Tell me everything about what happened, who they are and where they are.'

And with that, their game had begun.

CHAPTER 12

It was after eleven at night when the knock came at the door of Ryan's studio. He paused from his latest artwork, stepped away from the large easel, walked over and opened the door.

'Are we *ever* going to meet in the daylight?' asked Gigi as she walked in.

'No, my dear, we are creatures of the night,' replied Ryan with a dramatic flair, his voice and body oozing with invitation, playing the charming artiste.

'Oh, give it a rest Ryan, you know that doesn't work on me,' laughed Gigi. 'We share the same taste in our sexual partners—nothing hanging between the legs, thanks.'

Ryan laughed loudly at the candid response from his art dealer. She was his meal ticket—his source of income. Ryan was erratic and compulsive with a strong sexual appetite that leaned towards the unconventional, but he was smart enough to know when he was on a good thing and wouldn't do anything to jeopardise that.

'What are you working on now, my dear? Let Gigi have a peek,' crooned the art dealer.

'Hold on, let me reveal it to you in the way it deserves,' responded Ryan. He walked over, reached his fingers up to her eyes and gently closed them, then guided her around to the front of the easel. He stood still for a moment, building the anticipation.

'Okay, open your eyes,' said Ryan quietly. Gigi complied and immediately squealed with delight and clapped her hands together as she caught the first glimpse of Ryan's near-completed work. She loved his dramatic paintings full of colour, passion, and a hint of danger.

'Oh, Ryan, I love it! It's another magnificent piece. The galleries will fall over themselves to get their hands on this one,' she said with a smile, already thinking about the nice juicy commission she would collect from the sale. 'I know we haven't been working together for long, but I can definitely see a long future ahead if you keep producing works like this.'

Gigi couldn't believe her luck, that she had stumbled across Ryan and his talent purely by chance. She had seen him drawing a miniature portrait of a woman on the back of a beer coaster in a club late one night as part of his pickup routine. Gigi was a student of human nature and liked to see the interplay of social interaction. After quickly identifying his talent, she had quietly observed him for more than an hour—he was the life of the party, confident, outgoing and sociable. His charm and talent did their job on his mark for the night and as they stood up to leave, Gigi had approached him, gave him her number and told him she might make a lot of money for him from his art. Ryan had called her from the bar the following night; she had visited his studio and immediately loved his paintings.

As Gigi soaked up Ryan's latest work, she reflected on its creator. Ryan was a challenging client, but worth it. Like many true creatives, he was unconventional, and he wasn't the sharpest tool in the shed. To top it off, he was disorganised, incapable of planning, illogical, erratic and volatile. But he was also attractive, charming, fun to be around and had a dangerous bad-boy streak that made her feel like anything could happen—he was unpredictable. Ryan operated strictly on a cash-only basis and was completely off the grid. He had no bank account that she knew of, no phone, no social security number, no driver's licence, no identification, nothing. He was a ghost, lurking in the shadows, operating only at night; they had never met in the daytime. She complained about it, but secretly liked the subterfuge, the sense of intrigue and danger that he represented. She loved the fact that she was his only conduit to the art world, that she was bringing this shadowy underbelly into the light of high society, displaying Ryan's dark art on the pristine white walls of galleries, high net worth private collectors and corporations. Gigi had to do some accounting gymnastics to explain the cash payments and a lack of formal paperwork, but her healthy commissions made it worth the effort.

'So, do we have a deal?' asked Ryan, already knowing the answer.

'Yes, definitely. There's a growing interest and appetite for your work. It's getting to the stage where I can start pushing the prices higher. I can give you five thousand for this one when it's finished,' responded Gigi with a smile, knowing she would more than double that figure selling it to the gallery that was hottest for his art right now.

'Sweet!' said Ryan with a smile. 'With the usual twenty percent advance?'

'Sure. Here you go. Don't blow it all at once,' said Gigi as she pulled out a thick bankroll from her pocket and counted out a wad of 50 twenty-dollar notes.

Ryan gleefully accepted his advance, reached it up to his face and gave the notes a big, loud kiss. 'Come and have a drink with me, doll. You work too hard,' said Ryan.

'Not tonight, buddy. I've got a late-night date with a cold bottle of wine and a hot woman who's probably getting very impatient right now. I'm out of here,' Gigi replied as she picked up her bag and made her way over to the door of the studio.

'Pleasure doing business with you as always, Gigi,' said Ryan and gave her a kiss on the cheek at the door.

'Ciao, Bello,' Gigi replied with a smile as she left.

Ryan washed the paint off his hands, grabbed his jacket, stuffed his pockets full of cash and headed out for a one-man pub crawl of his favourite haunts. By bar number five, he'd had a skinful of booze and was feeling particularly fired-up, more in the mood for violence than sex. But so far, nobody had really given him any grief. He wasn't one to pick a fight, but would respond viciously to the slightest provocation, believing that anybody who started something deserved what was coming to them, and then some. Tonight, the unlucky ones were three young men with a pack mentality and a nasty attitude, out late and looking for trouble.

Ryan eyeballed the men as soon as they walked in, recognising their swagger as the challenge it was, silently shouting, 'Hey, we own this place tonight, so stay out of our way.' The testosterone hung heavy in the air, like young bull elephants mounting a challenge. The group scanned the bar as they walked in, looking for trouble and spotting it when they saw Ryan staring calmly and coldly at them. With a nudge to his compatriots and a nod in Ryan's direction, the leader of the pack made his way to the bar, coming to a stop much closer to Ryan than needed.

'Hey baby, give us three buds,' said the leader to the barmaid who responded with a barely disguised look of disdain as she delivered the order and accepted the payment. 'Keep the change, honey,' said the man, puffing up his chest.

'Wow, thank you *so* much!' she responded sarcastically. 'A whole fifty cents. Imagine what I could buy with that! You've made my night, big spender.'

The man slammed both his hands down on the bar and snarled, 'You ungrateful bitch! Someone needs to teach you a lesson in manners!'

The barmaid realised she had pushed a hot button way too hard and quickly retreated, suddenly fearful of what this nutcase might do to her.

With both hands pressed on the bar, the man made to launch his way over, but a sudden flash of movement caught his peripheral vision and then he looked down in horror to see a switchblade sticking out of the top of his left hand impaled into the bar! The knife handle oscillated back and forth in front of his eyes.

As the man's nerve receptors caught up with the visuals, he screamed in pain and snapped his head to the side to look at Ryan, who calmly looked back at him and said, 'I've got a better idea, shit-for-brains. How about I teach you and your boys some manners instead?' and promptly smashed his fist adorned with brass knuckledusters right into the man's cheek. Instantly, the flesh split open and blood erupted from the man's face. His head recoiled from the blow and bounced off the bar in a sudden impact and his body collapsed to the floor, tearing at the hand still impaled to the bar, leaving it hanging above him like a corpse with a raised hand wanting to ask a question of the teacher.

Dumbfounded, the leader's two attack dogs looked at their bloodied partner on the floor, then at Ryan and each bellowed a roar, moving into action as one. But they weren't quick enough. In another blur of motion, Ryan reached behind the bar, having made it his business to know where the bar defence weapon was, and came out with a baseball bat.

Ryan bunted the first guy with a quick jab to the jaw, then spun around and swung a brutal home run right into the other man's ribcage, accompanied by the sound of ribs cracking at the instant of impact. With a crazy smile on his face, Ryan turned back to his first attacker and quickly jabbed him three times in the face with the end of the bat; bam, bam, bam! The hapless soul looked blankly back at Ryan, with his nose spread over his face, one eye already closing, and his top lip split in two, exposing his buck teeth. With blood splattered all over his face and scrunched eyes, he started sobbing like a baby. 'In the future, don't be such an asshole. Here endeth the lesson,' said Ryan with a smile as he surveyed his handiwork, feeling a powerful sense of satisfaction. It felt so good to educate people about how to act around women, he thought to himself.

He looked over at the barmaid who was shaking her head in disbelief at what had just happened in the blink of an eye. Ryan pulled five twenties out of his pocket and handed them over to the barmaid. 'Here's a better tip for your trouble. Thanks for serving me tonight,' said Ryan. 'See you next time.' He handed her the bloodied baseball bat, pulled his switchblade out of the hand on the bar and watched the crimson-tainted arm slide down to the floor to join its owner's body.

'Um, thanks,' mumbled the barmaid, still in shock at the violent firestorm that had flared and died so quickly, and watched Ryan walk out the door with a swagger of his own. A few seconds later, a big motorbike roared into life and took off down the street, fading into the distance.

CHAPTER 13

What's next?

I'm done with cold turkey, but I have nowhere to go. I have no plan, no money. All I have are the filthy clothes hanging off me. I know it's too soon to get in touch with my family or any of my old friends. I burnt those bridges long ago and none of them want anything to do with me; they know I'm a junkie and have stolen from them all before. In the past, I'd asked them for help and then shat all over them from a great height. Stealing, fucking up, shooting heroin in their home, you name it—it causes me physical pain just thinking about it now. I know they won't want to see me, because they won't believe I'm getting clean; they've heard it all before and will think it's just another junkie story. I'm on my own for now.

So, for one last time, I go back to what I know, because I have no other choice. I find an expensive house on a quiet suburban street, then case the place beforehand and wait patiently until the old couple go out for the evening. I use my lock-picking skills picked up from my law enforcement training and sneak my way into the house. I'm much more focused and aware than I've been in the past when breaking and entering, when I was often jittery and hanging out for a hit. But the problem is, this time I feel guilt, remorse, and fear; emotions foreign to me when doing this before, when all I could ever focus on was the high that was coming afterwards.

This time I'm much more careful than in the past. I'm wearing thin rubber gloves, take extra care not to break anything and am hyper-alert listening for anyone that might come home. I take only what I need and no more. I focus on cash, jewellery, small electronic items and two delicate display pieces, carefully avoiding items that look like they might have sentimental value. I'm in and out as quickly as I can, leaving the place looking tidy, pretty much untouched, and lock the door behind me.

I make my way straight to a late-night pawn shop and hock the jewels and other items, making three grand for the lot, at *way* under market value. Adding this to the thousand in cash that I had scored from the old couple's emergency stash in the zip-lock bag in the freezer (first place I looked), I have enough to keep me going for two months in a cheap motel, with some cash left over for food.

I swear this is the last time I will ever steal from anyone—it kills the soul.

CHAPTER 14

'Ellen, your five o'clock is here,' buzzed the intercom to the young psychiatrist fresh out of college and in her first year of practice. Ellen was keen to make a difference in people's lives. She was highly engaged with her patients and formed a strong emotional connection with them, despite the warnings from her mentors. Ellen felt that a deep connection made her a better therapist, but those more experienced in the field ('tired and jaded' in young Ellen's eyes) had learned of the dangers of getting too entwined in the lives of their patients.

Jane, a pretty, young eighteen-year-old, walked into Ellen's office, eyes cast downwards to the floor. As soon as the young girl looked up, Ellen could tell there was something very troubling going on in her life; her eyes were red and swollen and there were fresh tears running down her cheeks. 'How are you, Jane?' asked Ellen, as she came around from behind her desk and put her arm around the young girl. 'What's going on with you at the moment?'

'Oh, Ellen!' she wailed, and flung her arms around Ellen's neck. Such contact was strictly against recommended practice, but Ellen embraced her fully, comforting the sobbing girl. 'It's terrible at home, now that I've finished school. All my Mom cares about is getting drunk and her stupid new boyfriend! It's been the same ever since my no-good father left when I was little—Mom gets boozed up with her horrible boyfriends and just wants to be with them, she doesn't love me! But this time it's worse, because this jerk has moved in with us and thinks he owns the place. He says if I'm not going to college, then I need to move out. And he's a real

"

creep—he walked in on me in the shower today and just stood there looking at me totally naked! He didn't even *pretend* to look away, he just smiled like a dirty old man. I told my mom what happened, and she didn't believe me, said I was just being a stupid little girl. I can't stay there tonight, I just can't!' Her sobbing increased in intensity almost to the point of hysteria.

'It's okay Jane, don't worry, we'll work something out. It's not hopeless—let's sit down now, talk it through and find a solution,' said Ellen, directing Jane to the comfortable couch in the corner of her small office. While she had only been seeing Jane for a few weeks, Ellen knew that Jane was a troubled girl, had seen the self-harm scars on her wrists and arms and heard about her dark thoughts. But Ellen was idealistic about her profession and committed to helping her patients, however she could.

'Can you stay with any of your friends tonight?' asked Ellen.

'No, I've tried all of them and none of them can have me over. Not after what happened last summer.' Ellen let that comment hang in the silence, resolving to come back to it when Jane was calmer. 'I've got nowhere to go; I don't want to sleep in a bus shelter!' cried Jane. Slowly, she looked across at Ellen and locked eyes, fixing her gaze and pouring out all her sadness and pleading in her softest, childlike voice as she asked, 'Could I *please* stay with you tonight? Just for one night? I wouldn't be any trouble, I promise.'

It tore Ellen. She had seen this coming, and all her training told her to say no. She remembered all her professors telling her not to cross the line between professional and personal. But, she thought, that was just because they don't care and had given up after doing it for too long. Ellen was different, and Jane was different, and she needed her help. So, with a slight nod of her head, Ellen said, 'Okay Jane, but just for one night, while you get yourself together, then you need to find somewhere else.'

'Oh Ellen, you're the best! Thank you, thank you, thank you!'

squealed Jane, as she leapt off the couch and hugged Ellen all over again. Ellen felt warm inside as she received the embrace from her grateful patient.

The two young women gathered their things and headed out of the office, past the middle-aged woman sitting behind the reception desk, who shot Ellen a sharp look of concern and surprise. 'Um, Ellen dear, can I talk to you for a moment, please?' she said.

Knowing what was coming, Ellen cut her off and said, 'I'm sure it can wait until the morning Wendy, let's discuss it then. See you tomorrow.' And with that, Ellen and Jane walked together out the door of the waiting room.

They rolled through the clean suburban streets with immaculate gardens and children playing in the yards. Jane saw an idyllic lifestyle like something she had only ever seen on TV. The dream continued as they walked through the bright red front door into Ellen's house. Jane immediately felt the warmth and comfort of a cheerful home. She gasped as she saw Ellen's strikingly handsome husband and delightfully cute little daughter playing together in the living room with their own special private tea party.

'Well, hello there, who do we have here, Honey?' the man said in a smooth, friendly voice.

'Dan, meet my friend Jane. Jane, this is Dan, and this is my darling Lucy,' said Ellen with a flourish, the love and emotion evident in her voice.

Jane gasped again as Dan, incredibly handsome, tall, adorned with a healthy tan, sandy hair, striking blue eyes, and a warm smile, stood up and made his way over, put his arm on her shoulder, then leaned in and kissed her lightly on the cheek and said, 'Welcome to our home, Jane. It's wonderful to meet you.'

Jane's heart soared, her stomach fluttered, and her mind went into overdrive at his caring, gentle touch. Jane had been desperately lonely growing up. This image of a beautiful and caring home life seemed like an unobtainable nirvana for her.

The night progressed calmly and delightfully through dinner, followed by Lucy's bedtime, dinner clean-up and glasses of wine. Dan explained to Ellen his plans to take a trip to the lake and feed the ducks with Lucy the next day. Jane went off to bed in the spare room, just down the hall from Ellen and the deliciously dreamy Dan. Jane had never felt so cared-for and comforted. She spent the first few hours in her bed contemplating this turning point in her life and fantasising about her future. Reaching a decision and determining her course of action eased her troubled mind, and she finally fell into the deepest and most carefree sleep she had experienced for many years.

Domestic bliss continued in the morning as Ellen prepared herself for the day's patients and ran out the door, while Dan got ready to take Lucy to kindergarten. Jane had a hearty breakfast of waffles and bacon and then went off to fulfil her own plans.

Jane visited a friend who was a factory worker at a medical supplies company. He had always been desperate for her attention, but Jane had shown no interest until now. She turned on the charm and he immediately agreed to help her in any way he could, hoping it would increase his chances with her. Jane convinced him to steal two portable bottles of medical gas—one of anaesthetic and another of oxygen, along with tubing and a face mask. Jane left with a promise to be in touch soon and arrange going on a date together.

Jane returned to Ellen's house and made her way around the back. After spotting Dan upstairs, she snuck in through the back door, grabbed Dan's car keys and quickly made her way into the garage. She unlocked the car and then returned the keys to the house. She slipped back into the garage and then climbed in the back of Dan's SUV, well-hidden by the tinted windows and an old blanket that was laying in the back.

Jane's nerves were on a knife-edge during the half-hour wait for Dan, but she calmed down as soon as he got in and started the engine, leaving Jane undiscovered in the back. The quick drive to Lucy's kindergarten was uneventful and then joyful sounds emerged as Lucy jumped in the car, all bubbly and excited about her time at kindergarten.

'Do you want to feed the ducks at the lake, Honey?' asked Dan over his shoulder to Lucy.

'Yay! Duckies!' responded his daughter with an excited squeal of delight.

'I'll take that as a yes, shall I?' said Dan with a smile. He drove away from the kindergarten and after a few minutes made the turn off the main road towards the lake. Jane slipped on her face mask and hooked up her supply of oxygen, then poked the bottle of anaesthetic gas out from under the blanket and opened the valve slowly, careful to control the sound of the escaping gas. Soon after, Lucy's chattering stopped, and Jane could hear Dan yawning—she pictured his head nodding and him shaking it side to side to stay awake. He pulled into the parking area and stopped the car. Jane heard the gear selector go into park and the engine note change, but it kept running.

Jane poked her head out from under the blanket and saw that Dan had passed out before even turning the engine off. She left the valve of the anaesthetic gas bottle open and placed it on the back seat next to Lucy, then climbed over the back seat, still hooked up to her oxygen supply. She gazed longingly at Lucy, already thinking of her as her own. She took a deep breath, pulled off her face mask and then gave Lucy a tender hug and a long, delicate kiss on her soft little cheek. Then she replaced her mask and climbed through to the front passenger seat. She looked out of the car and noted the carpark was empty—the only signs of life were the ducks calmly floating on top of the lake, the surface of which was smooth as glass.

After another deep breath, Jane once again removed her face mask, then kissed Dan longingly full on the lips. She forced her tongue into his slack mouth, slipped her hands under his clothes and wondered at the feel of his firm, bare chest with a light matting of hair. Once she'd had her fill of the unconscious Dan, she withdrew her hands and lips, then put her mask back on and breathed once again. She reached down and moved Dan's seat back as far as it would go, then sat on his lap, squeezing herself in behind the steering wheel, loving the feel of his body and the flood of warmth inside her.

Jane took one last deep breath, then removed her face mask and placed it on the seat next to her. She turned for one more fond look at Lucy and a final, lingering kiss with Dan, imagining she felt a response. Then she turned to face forward, put the car in gear and gently pushed her foot on the accelerator to get the large car moving. She turned the steering wheel to direct the car towards the lake and then breathed deeply, taking in the anaesthetic gas that had flooded the car. With the vehicle now steadily moving ahead, Jane turned slightly sideways and nestled her head on Dan's shoulder, snuggling into his neck. She felt completely at peace, the happiest she had ever felt in her entire life, absorbing the tranquil, loving scene in the car. Finally, she had a perfect family all her own, and they would be together forever.

The big SUV effortlessly mounted the curb of the carpark, quietly rolled down the bank, then slowly slipped into the lake and submerged down into the depths.

A steady stream of air bubbles was the only trace left behind of Ellen's loving family and the troubled teen she had brought into their lives.

CHAPTER 15

I'd put it off long enough. It was time for me to confront my demons and say goodbye to Sally properly. I'd missed her funeral because of my detox. I had to reconnect with the world now after dropping out for the past eleven days while I got through the worst of my withdrawal.

I'd taken the first step and found myself somewhere to live; a crappy motel overflowing with the destitute but cheap enough to justify the clientele. Next step was my appearance—I had to get myself together if I would integrate back into society, get a job and try to find Sally's killer.

I took myself down to the thrift shop and went crazy with the little wad of cash I'd allocated for the trip. I got a great bicycle which sorted out my transport; who needs a car anyway, right? A stash of factory-reject Calvin Klein's solved my underwear, socks, and T-shirt problems. I got a full set of clothes in an eclectic mix of styles, from mothballed Miller western shirts to shiny track pants and ancient Nike pumps. I was treading a fine line between retro and down-and-out, but what the hell, recovering junkies can't exactly be the picture of sartorial elegance less than two weeks after they mainlined heroin between their toes.

I topped off my buying spree with an outlandish pair of bright gold pimp sunglasses, a pair of hair scissors and an old cutthroat razor with a pearl handle. Then on the way out I spotted a walking stick with a handle of a carved snake head glaring and spitting; I simply couldn't resist the urge to buy it. I figured I deserved a few ridiculous luxuries after what I'd been through. At the last minute, I spotted a Polaroid camera and some film, so tossed that in for good measure.

With my cash reserve somewhat lighter but exchanged for a great new selection of important items, I rode my bike back to my motel, lugging my shopping bags over my shoulder. I dumped everything in my room and then stripped off my filthy old rags and tossed them in the garbage.

I missed smack so much. Not feeling that rush left such a hole, so deep inside me, that I just felt like an empty husk. But my resolve was firm—I swore I would not be going back to that hell.

I stopped and looked in the mirror and shook my head in disbelief. It was the first time I had looked at myself naked in a mirror for more than a year. Gone was the big-chested, straight-backed, six-foot four-inch and 240 pounds of muscle-bound quarterback from my college days. In its place was a shell of a man, hunched over, round-shouldered and scrawny with bones protruding beneath pallid, yellowy skin. Long, greasy, matted hair clung to my scalp, and across my face meandered a scruffy beard. Milky, bloodshot eyes stared back at me in the mirror from deeply drawn eye sockets over enormous dark bags under my eyes. I figure I must have lost more than a hundred pounds of muscle; no surprise considering how severely I had been starving myself. A doctor would surely classify me as malnourished.

As I continued the visual stock take of my emaciated frame, tears welled in my eyes and rolled down my face, deeply saddened by what I had become and the depths to which I had sunk. It had all been in pursuit of that evil white lady, the vile bitch always crying out for more, never satisfied. I had become possessed, a slave to a substance that I would never have thought could have me in such a death grip. When I had been immersed deep in it, I was oblivious to what it was doing to me, but now, in the cold hard light of day after a period of abstinence, I could see the truth staring back at me like the zombie I was, one of the walking dead.

With my arms hanging by my sides, I turned my palms outwards to face the mirror and stared impassively at the ugly, red and inflamed track marks along my arms. My skin was blotchy with scars and poorly healed scabs and my dick and balls were shrivelled up like dried-out prunes. I had a shaky tattoo, intended to be an eagle, on my left shoulder that looked like a twelve-year-old had done it while having a fit. My arms, covered with street tattoos, stared back at me, mocking me in their hideousness. Hard drugs can seriously impair your decision-making abilities.

I turned around, back to the mirror, and looked over my shoulder at the ribs protruding beneath the skin. My gaze travelled down my body to what used to be my ass but was now just two flaccid empty sacks of skin hanging above my legs. My entire body ached and felt drained, like a giant industrial vacuum cleaner had sucked out my insides.

They say the first step to recovery is admitting you have a problem. Well, fuck me, I really had a problem. And it was time for me to sort my shit out. My first task was to record where I was right now as a reminder to never go back there. I took out my Polaroid camera, loaded the film, pointed it at my naked body in the mirror and snapped a photo of myself in the absolute worst physical condition I could have imagined. I resolved to use this as a tool on my road to recovery and rebuilding my life.

From the depths of my once brilliant mind, came a quote from the Chinese philosopher Lao Tzu—*The journey of a thousand miles begins with a single step*. And so, I turned away from the mirror and moved my feet to take that symbolic first step… right to the toilet, because I needed to take a giant shit.

So much for ancient Chinese wisdom.

CHAPTER 16

'Okay, everyone. Thanks for joining us tonight at our local "Quit Smoking America" meeting. It's great to see you all here, dedicated to kicking your habit for good, even at this late hour,' said the bubbly group leader. Ryan switched his attention from her and looked around the circle, studying the group of smoking addicts. There looked to be a few excellent candidates, but he would only know once he heard their story.

The first few addicts trotted out the standard lines—started smoking in high school, want to get healthy, save money; the usual crap. Nothing even mildly interesting about any of them.

Then suddenly, he knew. As soon as number five in the group started talking and Ryan heard the ugly, obnoxious loudmouth moaning and complaining, he knew that he was the one. The guy went on and on about how much he loved smoking, how the big tobacco companies had got him hooked, it wasn't his fault, blah, blah, blah. And how his bitch of a wife and her snot-nosed kids were constantly at him to stop smoking, and that he had to go to meetings, or she would kick him out on the street. And then where would he be? On welfare, with no job and no prospects. He reckoned that Philip Morris and the Marlboro Man had a lot to answer for, claiming no accountability for the part that he himself had played in his addiction.

The man's complaining outburst caused some discord in the group. The leader tried to get things back on track, but the guy kept going on and on, drowning her out. His vocal outburst got louder and louder as he revelled in the complaints from the group. He boasted about chain-smoking two packs a day and stealing money from his wife's housekeeping money to feed his habit, then babbled on about smoking expensive cigars with his friends around his big Texas smoker barbecue. Ryan said nothing; he was calm on the outside but boiling on the inside.

Finally, the meeting broke up in a rabble, with everyone feeling that one person had hijacked the whole thing and accomplished nothing. Ryan followed The Smoker out of the building and into an old beat-up Datsun. Ryan jumped on his Harley and started it up, then gave the car a few seconds to pull out and followed at a distance. Just a few miles later, the Datsun pulled off the main road into a side street and Ryan followed, noting the streets as he went.

As his target pulled into a driveway in the suburbs, Ryan came to a stop a block away, killed the engine, jumped lightly off his bike and made his way quietly down the street. Oblivious to the danger, The Smoker got out of his car and walked up the path to his house. Ryan stopped behind a large sycamore tree, sheltered from view, and watched the scene spread out before him, illuminated by the wash of light from the streetlamps.

The man fumbled around in his pocket and then cursed aloud and banged urgently on the front door until the bright porch light came on and a woman, presumably his long-suffering wife, answered the door in her nightgown.

'Jesus Christ, what the hell are you doing?' she cried out in frustration. 'You'll wake the kids! Where are your damn keys?'

'Shut up, woman! I forgot them, obviously,' he responded in a curt tone and then disappeared into the house, brushing roughly past the woman, leaving her standing in the doorway, fuming.

Sorely tempted to follow the guy into the house immediately and teach him a goddamn lesson, Ryan instead held his resolve and waited so he could do it properly. The build-up, the planning, and the waiting would make the ultimate act so much sweeter.

It was time to write to Leonard and plan The Smoker's final barbecue.

CHAPTER 17

I cleaned, scrubbed and exfoliated myself for what felt like an eternity. My skin was red raw, I was clean-shaven, and my hair was short. I'd cut my fingernails and toenails and had even trimmed my eyebrows, nose hair, and ear hair, for Christ's sake. Once I started, I couldn't stop. I wanted to wash all trace of my previous filth away and flush it down the drain.

I got dressed in my new outfit—shiny blue track pants, red check Miller western shirt and gleaming white Nike pumps, and for the ultimate finishing touch added my pimped-up sunnies. I checked myself out in the mirror and cracked a smile for the first time since Sally had died. She would have loved this outfit; it was exactly the oddball look she rocked. I grabbed some cash from my stash that I had weighted down in a waterproof bag at the bottom of the toilet cistern, then grabbed my push-bike and headed out the door of my motel room.

I rode the few miles to the police station, parked my bike in the hallway and made my way to the desk sergeant, noting with dread that it was the same asshole who had refused to take my missing person report. Thankfully, my marbles were more together than the last time I'd been in here, and I also had a different appearance. He still looked me up and down, but at least wasn't dismissive. Clearly, he wasn't much of a talker—anyone with half a brain should obviously interpret the meaning of his one raised eyebrow as, 'Yes? May I help you?'

Responding to the unasked question, I inquired, 'Is Detective Delaney in?'

This time the other eyebrow went up, which I gathered meant the sergeant had just asked another question. This man was the most economical wordsmith I'd ever encountered.

'My name is Simon Winter,' I answered.

Still, there was no verbal response from the impassive man behind the desk. With a flick of his head, he motioned me to the hardwood bench in the lobby, silently instructing me to wait. He picked up his phone, punched in a number and grunted something in a quiet voice down the phone, then again raised both eyebrows in my direction. His lip curled up in a sneer that silently communicated, 'You have *got* to be shitting me! *That* guy?' He put the phone back in its cradle and returned his attention to whatever mindless task had previously occupied him.

Half an hour later, Delaney finally appeared. He came out of the secure zone of the station's inner sanctum, out into the lobby and then stopped in his tracks, looking me up and down. 'Nice outfit, dickhead,' he said in a perfectly deadpan delivery. 'Did you build a time machine and go back to the eighties just to ransack a charity bin? Looks like the drugs knocked out your fashion radar.'

'Nice to see you too, Delaney. I've missed you,' I responded.

'At least you can fucking talk this time and you're not jumping up and down like you've got fire ants in your jockstrap. And you're not sweating and puking all over my police station. Looks like you cleaned up a bit. What's it been, a couple of weeks? I wondered where you'd got to. Thought you might have OD'd and died in a gutter somewhere.'

'No, decided against that option. I haven't touched it since Sally died. Locked myself away in a motel room for ten days and went cold turkey.'

'That's hard-core Winter, I'll give you that. It's no picnic doing that on your own.'

'Yeah, I've had better times. But I've got no one to blame but myself for what I had to go through. I deserved that withdrawal hell for getting Sally hooked on drugs.'

'Didn't end well for her, did it?' said Delaney. 'Or her family, for that matter. Her parents were real cut up about it. Something tells me you're not on their Christmas list anymore. They've taken out a restraining order against you. So don't contact them. Understand?'

This news came as a bit of a shock, but I guess it wasn't entirely surprising. I had only met Sally's parents twice, early in our relationship, and that hadn't gone well. They had smelt a rat. Sadly, they were right. Before I'd met Sally, in my last year of college, I had blown out my knee playing football and after a long recovery ended up addicted to oxycodone, the powerful opioid painkiller. Apparently, I have an addictive personality.

After college, I had another serious knee injury—Sally and I met in hospital while I was in recovery. She was a cute nurse on my floor, and I was a charming patient; there were instant sparks, especially when it was time for my sponge bath and I couldn't control my junk, which had a mind of its own.

Unfortunately for her, Sally had wanted to experience everything with me, and I was too selfish and self-absorbed to stop her. I'd been deeply in love with Sally and wanted to be with her all the time, doing anything and everything together in a destructive downward spiral. What started as bonding over alcohol soon escalated to pills, then cocaine, then crystal meth and finally onto the big daddy—heroin. If Sally hadn't met me, she wouldn't have gotten hooked on all that shit and would still be alive today. And I wouldn't be standing on the wrong side of a charge desk, staring like a dope at a silent police detective with a gloomy look on his face as I was processing all this and thinking about my dead junkie girlfriend.

'You still in there somewhere, buddy?' said Delaney, as he snapped his fingers right in front of my eyes. 'Looks like you cooked that noggin of yours pretty damn hot, Winter. Dropped yourself down the old I.Q. scale a few notches, I think.'

'Sorry, Frank. Still recovering. That shit does some damage. It'll take me some time to get back with it. Did Sally's parents ID her body?'

'Yep. The Medical Examiner cleaned her up first, took the syringes out of her eyeballs, for example. Sick bastard,' said Frank with an involuntary shudder and a slow shake of his head.

'Any progress on the case?' I asked hopefully.

'Nope. Nothing. Cold as an Alaskan winter. Nobody saw anything. The only person who could have helped her was unconscious, dead to the world and completely useless,' he replied, with a deliberate stare right at me. 'We processed the scene. Found a lot of evidence of *you* there, but not much else. The killer was careful. Brutal, but careful.'

'Hm… sorry to hear that. Kind of hoped you would have made some progress by now,' I said, in a disappointed tone.

'What can I say? There's only so much we can do. I'll keep working the case, but don't get your hopes up. A junkie taken from a park in the middle of the night is not exactly the case to generate any heat to get it solved. Sorry, Winter, but that's all I've got for you,' said Delaney with an air of resignation in his voice.

'Okay, thanks Frank, I appreciate you giving it to me straight. I know the score. Can you at least tell me where she's buried?'

'Yeah, she's over in Columbia Gardens Cemetery on Arlington Boulevard,' he replied. 'Good luck, Winter. I hope you can keep yourself clean. And find yourself a new fucking tailor.'

'Thanks Frank. Good to see those charm-school lessons are paying off. See you round,' I replied, and took off down the hallway. I grabbed my bike, exited the station and then got my bearings and headed over to the cemetery. The closer I got to the graveyard, the heavier felt my heart, like an expanding sack of rocks in my chest.

After some searching, I found Sally's grave, fresh with the beginnings of new green shoots coming through the soil. I laid down beside her on the grass, on my side and facing her headstone. I started my goodbye with a deep breath and immediately felt the tears form in my eyes and then spill out, running down my face. I placed a single sunflower on her grave, on a stem that was four feet tall. The head was a stunning bright yellow, almost glowing. Sally would have loved the deep hues. She was my sunshine, my light, and my colour. This flower captured all that; it was my gift and my apology.

'Oh, Sally, I'm so sorry!' I cried. 'I'm sorry I dragged you down into the cesspit of my life. I'm sorry for debasing your beautiful life with the filth of my existence. Look what I did to you! I put my needs before yours—that's not what love is. That's not what a good man does. I'm sorry, from the bottom of my wasted heart.'

By now my tears were a flood, streaming down my face. I sat up, cross-legged beside Sally, with my left hand reaching out and resting on the dirt where I imagined her heart would be, buried under six feet of earth and inside a thick wooden box.

'My soul exists in two states at once,' I continued. 'Full to bursting with love for you, but achingly empty without you in my future. The time we spent together was so precious, I'll cherish it forever. I miss you so much, babe. I don't know how I'll survive without you. I nearly didn't. I know I can't make it up to you, but I'll find the bastard who did this to you, I promise. I'm off the gear and I'll stay clean. I'll get my life back on track, work the case and keep going until I find him, even if I need to spend the rest of my life doing it, I promise. Goodbye, my beautiful angel. I love you.'

Leonard had an extremely strict routine with his mail. He would collect it after work each day from his post office box at the Washington Square Post Office and put it straight into his briefcase without looking at any of it. Then he would get home to his apartment, remaining in his suit to stay in work mode. He would open all the bills and official mail, deal immediately with any urgent matters and put others in his in-tray on his roll-top desk for action on the coming weekend. On the rare occasions that he had any personal mail, he would leave it unopened on the dinner table. He would then get changed out of his suit into his casual slacks, polo shirt, black cashmere sweater, and brown loafers. Next step was heating his dinner, then settling down at the table that Esmerelda had set for him. The last step in the routine was to open his personal mail and read it while enjoying his dinner, finishing with one of his favourite long, thin Cuban cigars—the famous Cohiba Lancero.

Tonight was a good night; a letter from Ryan was waiting for Leonard. He had enjoyed the suspense since collecting his mail, wondering what was in store for him, but now it was time to find out. After his initial shock at Ryan's request to imagine the murder of The Junkie, Leonard had enjoyed mapping out the strategy and developing the plan to feed Ryan's imagination. It had seemed to help his pen-pal, and Leonard had enjoyed the distraction from his own mundane existence.

Leonard opened the letter and slowly absorbed every word. Normally he was a man on a mission and practiced speed reader, but he liked to take his time with Ryan's letters. They were his only genuine connection with another human being.

This time Ryan talked about his smoking habit and that he was thinking about giving up. He had joined a Quit Smoking group, and everything had been going fine until this one guy opened his mouth and just killed the vibe of the whole group. He was a loud, arrogant asshole who had abused everyone, including the group leader and Ryan himself. Ryan talked about how poorly the guy treated his wife and kids, how he was worthless and sponging off his wife, and how the world would be better off without him.

Then Ryan shared the idea he had of what he imagined would be a perfect way to take him out, symbolic of his chronic smoking habit. Leonard smiled at the thought and imagined what an interesting end that might be for such a pig of a man. He pulled out his notebook and made some meticulous notes and diagrams to help feed Ryan's imaginings.

Leonard found his thoughts disturbing, but oddly compelling.

CHAPTER 19

'Bye, George. See you tomorrow,' I called as I left the diner. George was the cook and the owner of the diner and seemed to be an okay guy, judging from my first couple of days. I was working as a busboy, clearing tables, washing dishes, mopping floors and occasionally flipping burgers on the grill. I was working for minimum wage plus tips but doing an honest day's work for a fair day's pay. I wasn't stealing from anyone or hurting anyone. It will be an endless road, but I'm on the path to bringing my Chi back into balance, slowly making my way back up the Karma ladder. This was the first job opportunity that came up, plus it had the bonus of eating the leftover food off the plates.

Back on my bike, I ride, and I remember. I relive the murder scene repeatedly in my mind. Etched in my memory is every detail, seared into my brain with the intensity of my feeling for Sally and the shame of what I did to her, how my actions led to her hideous death.

The fog is slowly lifting from my mind; I'm regaining some of my previous mental function. Thankfully, it seems I haven't totally obliterated all my brain power by my severe drug abuse.

The cravings are brutal. The urge to give in to the rampaging horse is a monumental struggle that constantly drives me—pushing every part of me to give in and once again find the bliss of the needle. But I know down that path lies my death, and I now have a purpose driving me, so I can't give up. I need to find the sick bastard that did that to my Sally— I *must* avenge her death.

I rode across town and returned to Sally's crime scene. There was no sign of activity at the abandoned warehouse; nobody cared. Nobody had fixed the smashed window and there was still glass everywhere. Blood stained the floor where Sally had laid. I looked around, examining the scene again, looking carefully everywhere. I even found a stray syringe the careless cops had left behind under a workbench. The police didn't care about Sally—to them she was just another junkie, and the state of this murder scene showed it.

I looked around on the workbench and found an old rag, folded it over and jabbed the needle into it, then stuffed the syringe into my pocket.

I continued my examination of the crime scene and everything came flooding back to me in sharp relief, like a movie playing in front of my eyes. My recall was perfect, but unfortunately the original film was flawed. My mental and emotional state at the time was drug-addled and desperate, so what I saw was haphazard and intermittent; a collection of images lacking continuity and consistency. I was forced to work with what I had.

The rust-coloured stains on the floor showed where Sally's body had been, and the shiny marks around equipment and bars nearby showed the tying points of her binding ropes. I could picture the scene, with her profoundly damaged body laid out in front of me. I studied the current scene, took myself back and connected to that time that seemed like a lifetime ago, to another version of me. I shook my head in disgust at what I had been and knew I had now changed fundamentally—I had been born again (save the Halleluiah Brother, because I don't think the church is ready for me just yet). It was time for this alternative version of me to find out what had happened.

In my trancelike state between then and now, I thought back to the note. Sally hadn't written it. I realised now that the handwriting was nothing like hers. So, that was an important clue—we had the handwriting of the killer which we could use when we eventually found him. I also had the syringe which might turn up something. Then, standing there in the eerie silence of the abandoned building, I thought of the quiet night that I found Sally and remembered the sudden blast of sound. I remembered the harsh intrusion of the distinctive, loud motorcycle exhaust as the engine suddenly burst into life just outside the building and took off into the distance. Convinced the killer had been outside, watching as I discovered Sally's body and seeing my reaction, I thought *the discovery and the grief are part of his thrill!* He got off on seeing the impact of his kills, the feeling of power it gave him over not just his victims but those close to them, witnessing the emotional trauma delivered by his hand.

I was assembling some physical evidence and some insight into the killer's psyche.

I was on the hunt.

CHAPTER 20

Everything was in place. Ryan had been scoping The Smoker's place for the past week, as outlined by Leonard in his letter. He had all his supplies; he was all set. He knew the man's routine and that of his wife, who was working hard tonight packing shelves in the local supermarket while her lazy bastard of a husband hung around the house watching TV and smoking out on the back deck.

Ryan waited long after the children were in bed and fast asleep—he didn't want any collateral damage. He crept around the backyard and onto the deck, avoiding the light from the kitchen window that cast a faint glow on the decking boards. After a few minutes, The Smoker came out to light up yet another cigarette. He put the cancer stick in his mouth and reached into his pocket for his lighter. Ryan stealthily stepped up behind him, clamped his hand like a trap over his victim's mouth, then flicked out a switchblade in front of the man's eyes and pressed it hard against his throat.

'Not a sound, not one sound, or I'll slice you from ear to ear. Got it?' whispered Ryan in an ominous tone, right in the man's ear.

The Smoker slowly nodded. Ryan continued holding the knife to his victim's throat, then reached down into his pocket and pulled out an ominous looking muzzle and strapped it around the man's head. The muzzle had a hard, plastic tube mounted on the inside that forced The Smoker's teeth apart, leaving his mouth slightly open, but with a heavy cover tightened with Velcro fasteners over the top of the muzzle. With his prey silenced, Ryan ushered him across to the rocking chair on the deck and sat him down, knife still held firmly to throat. 'Remember, any struggle and you won't have a windpipe anymore,' said Ryan, enforcing his control.

With his victim safely seated, Ryan pulled a handful of large plastic zip-ties out of his pocket, handed one to The Smoker and instructed, 'Okay, nice and slow, strap your left wrist to the arm of the chair using your right hand.'

Understanding that he was in severe danger, The Smoker decided it was time to resist. He violently rocked his head and struggled in the chair but instantly felt how serious Ryan was when he felt the switchblade press into his neck and slice across his throat from right to left, the knife cutting through the skin over his Adam's apple. As he felt the blood streaming down his neck, he stopped struggling, hoping that somehow tonight wouldn't end with his death, but knowing that if he continued to fight that he would be dead for sure right now.

Ryan felt the man go slack, eased off the pressure on the knife and said, 'That's better. Now tie your wrist like I said.' This time, The Smoker cooperated and zip-tied his wrist to the arm of the heavy rocking chair.

'Okay, now place your right wrist on the other arm,' instructed Ryan, then grabbed another of the heavy zip-ties and expertly pinned his victim's arm to the chair, pulling the clasp tightly closed. 'Now the legs,' said Ryan, and repeated the process, pinning the man's four limbs to the heavy rocking chair. Ryan went back and checked on the first zip-tie that The Smoker had applied to himself, tightening it up hard.

The last step was to immobilise the head. Ryan joined two zip-ties together end to end for added length, then pulled The Smoker's head hard against the back of the chair. He weaved the long zip-tie around the man's neck and through the gaps in the chair back, ratcheting the zip-ties tight to hold the head firmly in place. The man had enough slack to breathe, but his head and neck were locked firmly in position, with no hope of movement.

The Smoker felt the tightness around his limbs and throat and now feared the worst. He had been hoping this would somehow end with just some punishment or a theft, perhaps. But he knew deep down this was the end and was losing all hope of survival. With his head locked in position facing forward, the slightest turn of his head caused the sharp edges of the zip-ties to cut into his neck, slicing new wounds in the already bloody skin. He turned his eyes sideways as far as possible to see what was going on, hating not knowing what his attacker was doing behind him. Then he saw a black shape come around from behind the chair and his attacker stopped in front then leaned in, gazing deep into his own terrified eyes.

Ryan smiled a wolfish grin and licked his lips, eyes dancing with delight. Then he raised his right hand and placed it on the pinned forehead and gave it a gentle push, setting the rocker back and forth. The man was at one with the chair, moving like he was a part of it, rocking back and forth in unison.

The rocking motion somehow soothed The Smoker's fear, for he had rocked so many nights away in his smoking chair, it had a calming effect on him. Still silenced by the strong, tight muzzle strapped around his head, the man could do nothing except watch and wait. Ryan reached into The Smoker's top pocket and pulled out the packet of cigarettes and well-worn lighter. Ryan extracted a cigarette from the pack, gave it a practiced tap-tap on the pack, and then lit it up. After a big drawback, he leaned right in close to The Smoker, pulled back the Velcro flap of the muzzle and breathed the full exhalation of smoke right into the man's mouth, then shut the muzzle flap again. The man in the rocking chair responded by breathing in a deep lungful of air long and hard through his nose, driving the glorious smoke down into his lungs. After a brief pause, a long and lingering breath escaped slowly out through the man's nostrils, the smoke swirling up in front of his eyes.

'You really are an addict, aren't you, man?' Ryan said with a smile.

'You really got off on that, didn't you? But you realise your habit is bad for you, right? Come on, you've seen all those ads on TV—"Smoking Kills". Well tonight, it sure does, dude.'

The Smoker's stomach dropped as he confirmed his worst fear; tonight would be his last night alive. He struggled again against the zip-ties binding him to the chair and grunted and groaned into the muzzle. But it was hopeless.

Ryan moved away and got to work. He strode off the deck to the yard and picked up an ominous black bag, then moved back onto the deck over to his victim's pride and joy—his enormous Texas smoker barbecue. Ryan lifted the lid and poured a bag of charcoal into the firebox along with some paper, followed by a very generous splashing of lighter fluid. He then pulled the still-smoking cigarette out of his mouth and casually tossed it onto the drenched charcoal, which instantly exploded in a mini-fireball four feet high out of the smoker box. Ryan waited and watched, making sure the large load of charcoal was well alight, then closed the firebox and the lid of the barbecue.

The Smoker continued to watch silently from his rocking chair, helpless and immovable. He really did not understand what was going on—was this psycho going to kill him or cook him a fucking steak?

Ryan reached down into his bag and extracted a steel funnel, some heavy gaffer tape and a pair of tin snips. He cut the chimney cap off the Texas Smoker, then upended the funnel and placed it on top of the chimney pipe, which was already belching out a healthy dose of smoke. He gaffer taped the funnel to the chimney, making an effective seal that pushed the smoke faster out of the narrow nozzle. He reached into his bag again and pulled out a length of large diameter rubber hose, then looked at The Smoker with a chilling smile. It did not look good for the man in the chair.

Ryan placed one end of the thick rubber hose over the nozzle of the inverted funnel and taped around it, fixing it firmly in place. He brought the other end of the hose up and studied it with a fascinated look on his face as the smoke puffed out. He moved over to The Smoker and laid the hose down on the deck at the man's feet, still puffing away.

Ryan reached down into his bag once more and extracted a big, mean-looking industrial stapler. The Smoker did not like where this was headed at all and struggled and thrashed against his bonds, oblivious to the searing pain it caused. He groaned and strained at the muzzle, trying to scream for help, but unable to make a sound audible beyond their private little circle of two.

Ryan moved close to The Smoker until their faces were only inches apart and stared deep into his eyes. The Smoker squeezed his eyes tightly shut and tears streamed out the sides as the horror of what was coming finally gripped him completely. His stomach dropped yet again and this time he lost control of his bladder, feeling the warm piss running down between his legs. His struggling eased as the hopelessness of his situation took over and he flopped back down into the seat, now wet with urine.

The helpless man opened his eyes to see impassive, unfeeling eyes staring back at him, deep into his soul. 'You brought this on yourself, it's your own fault,' said Ryan. 'All you had to do was give up smoking and not be such a fucking asshole. But you couldn't, could you? You were such a prick at that Quit Smoking meeting, you made my choice easy— it was no contest. Goddamn addict!' he snapped in disgust. Quick as a flash, he shot out his hand, pinched The Smoker's nose with his fingers and then clamped the big stapler tight over the nostrils and squeezed. Hard.

The Smoker howled in pain into the muzzle and thrashed around in a new struggle against his restraints, but they held him tightly immobilised. Ryan reached out again with the stapler and bang, bang, bang, drove three more big, needle-sharp staples through the nostrils, sealing them shut tight. The Smoker almost passed out through the pain and fear, but unfortunately for him, remained conscious.

Ryan bent down and picked up the thick rubber hose, then quickly peeled back the Velcro flap on the muzzle and jammed the hose through into his victim's mouth. More gaffer tape finished the job, completing the seal so nothing but smoke could drive its way into the lungs of The Smoker. Ryan stood back and admired his handiwork. His hapless victim was gasping for air and his chest was heaving, desperately fighting against the putrid fumes that were invading his body so completely. After just a few minutes of pointless struggle, it was all over. The addict was dead, his fate sealed by smoke, to which he was so addicted.

'Stick that in your pipe and smoke it,' said Ryan, with a satisfied smirk.

'Cool plan, Leonard, thanks for the help "imagining" this little display,' Ryan finished with a chuckle. He hoped Leonard wouldn't find out about this murder, just like he had missed the news about The Junkie.

As planned, Ryan left everything in place, staging the scene for the discovery. There was nothing there that could tie him to the crime. All the items he'd used were commonly available and purchased from several hardware stores in various parts of town. He was wearing gloves, so there would be no fingerprints. The cigarette he had smoked was long burnt in the firebox. He was clean.

Ryan retreated to the back of the garden to wait for The Smoker's wife to return home. Half an hour later, waiting in the still night amidst the silence of suburbia, Ryan's pulse quickened as he heard a car out front. He could feel his dick getting hard as the anticipation built up. After a couple more minutes, he heard the wife angrily call out, 'You better not be smoking out there, you bastard!' It was all Ryan could do not to burst out laughing at the irony of it all. His pulse racing, Ryan saw the woman at the screen door, angry face illuminated by the kitchen light as she looked from behind at the figure in the rocking chair with smoke wisps rising from his mouth.

'Goddamn it, that's the last straw, I've had enough of this shit!' she cried out and stormed through the screen door. She grabbed the back of the rocking chair and set it rocking wildly back and forth and then came around to confront her husband. Then the full force hit as she absorbed the horrific scene.

Her scream pierced the night air, the sound waves travelling down the yard to Ryan's eagerly awaiting ears. She went crazy, pulling the hose out of her husband's mouth and ripping the muzzle off him as she tried desperately to save him. But she soon calmed down as she realised there was no hope—her husband was long dead. His cheeks were sunken and his face was puckered and drawn like an old prune, dehydrated from the drying effects of the insidious smoke. Understanding the truth, she collapsed on the deck, sobbing her heart out at the cruelty of the act.

Ryan was in heaven, absorbing the glory of the scene he had created and the anguish it brought.

The upstairs light came on and jarred the poor woman back to awareness as she understood she had to protect her children from this horror. She got to her feet and rushed inside to tend to her children, phone already in hand, calling the police.

Excitement over, Ryan exited through the back of the property and walked to his motorbike, jumped aboard, gunned the engine to life and raced off down the street, out of the suburban nightmare.

CHAPTER 21

'Stop harassing me, Winter!' said Delaney, who was getting more and more frustrated with each of my visits.

'Whoa, take it easy, Delaney. Don't have a cow, man. Did you get out of the wrong side of the bed again this morning?' I asked. 'I'm only checking in to see what's happening with the case.'

'Like I told you last time, and the time before that, the case is a dead end. Nothing's happening. I'm sorry to have to say it again, but your girlfriend was a junkie! And it's just another junkie killing. Probably an argument with her dealer. After all, mainlining heroin is not exactly the safest leisure activity you can engage in, so it's no surprise it ended badly,' he replied.

'I'm just frustrated at the lack of progress, that's all. And I want to make sure you don't give up on her,' I said. 'She was important to me. I didn't look after her in life, so now I want to care for her in death.'

'Look,' said Delaney in a softer tone, 'I understand this is tough. But my hands are tied. I've got other priorities that I need to look after. Like some psycho smoking a poor guy to death by rigging him up to a barbecue. So, I don't have time to be chasing down dead ends on a cold case. If something comes up, I'll call you, I promise. But until then, please leave me alone and let me do my job!'

'Fine, fine, okay,' I said. 'I'll ease off on the social calls. Bye, Frank.'

It looked like solving Sally's murder would be up to me.

CHAPTER 22

'So, tell me, Leonard,' asked Ellen, 'Do you engage much with the outside world?'

A look of disdain appeared on Leonard's face as he replied, 'If by "engaging with the outside world", you mean interacting with morons and wasting my valuable time on the mindless drivel that occupies the common masses, the answer is no, I don't. I refuse to read newspapers or watch commercial TV or indulge in idle gossip with stupid people. I have neither the patience nor the stomach for it. I deal in facts, numbers, and science.'

'Is it fair to say then, that you have minimal awareness of what is going on around you, or interest in current affairs, or news?' continued Ellen.

'Ha!' replied Leonard. 'If your so-called news represents who is the latest sleazy congressman embroiled in a sexual scandal with a nubile young intern at the White House, then no, I am blissfully uninformed. I have no interest in consuming the propaganda spouted by the corporations and special interest groups who are brainwashing the populace with their own agendas.'

'Would you say you are a recluse?' inquired Ellen with an air of expectation, bordering on accusation.

Leonard flared at this question, as Ellen had expected. She let the silence fill the air as she waited calmly, gazing across at Leonard. 'Only through shock comes change,' she thought to herself, reflecting on the loaded question.

Leonard collected himself and responded calmly, 'No. I am not a recluse. I enjoy my own company and that of my intellectual peers at Mensa. I converse with those who can match my high level of intelligence. And please remember, Miss DeMarco, that I came to you for a resolution to my hallucinations, visions and sleep spasms, not for you to assault me with your psychobabble!'

'Let's move on then, shall we? We can come back to the "psychobabble" as you so generously put it, another time,' she said, as she cast a significant and obvious glance up to her college certifications mounted proudly on the wall.

Leonard didn't miss the point of the glance, sniffed with derision and said, 'We can both use the word "Doctor" in front of our name, Miss DeMarco, so don't bother trying to impress me with your degrees in pseudoscience.'

Now it was Ellen's turn to flare as she bristled at Leonard's superior tone, boorish attitude, and lofty opinions of himself. Ellen was taking a significant dislike to her prickly patient. 'No wonder he spends all his goddamn time alone,' she thought to herself.

She took a deep breath, collected herself and continued the dialogue. 'In the interests of being thorough and to rule out any physical disorders or abnormalities, I would like you to have an MRI scan of your brain.'

'It's about time you went down this path. Let's see what the real physical science and medical fraternity have to say about what's going on up here,' replied Leonard, as he tapped his forefinger against his temple.

'Very well, I'll book you in for a scan and we'll see what comes back, and then take it from there. In the meantime, I'll see you next week for our next session of *psychobabble*,' said Ellen in a voice dripping heavily with sarcasm.

'Looking forward to it,' replied Leonard and then muttered under his breath as he walked out the door, 'like taking a bath in boiling hydrochloric acid.'

CHAPTER 23

With nerves jangling and hands trembling, I walked shakily up to the main entry of the enormous Marine Corps Base in Quantico, Virginia. Attending the famous FBI Academy as a New Agent Trainee seemed a lifetime ago.

The accident happened in my very last week of training before graduation. I was tearing along Hogan's Alley on one last big training exercise, running full speed and desperate to impress my instructors. And what was it that brought down the impressive hero? The all-star college quarterback and soon-to-be FBI agent was in full battle cry when sabotaged by a loose fucking shoelace! If I'd paid more attention to my mother all those years ago about tying my shoelaces properly, I wouldn't be in this goddamn mess right now.

It turned out that my bung college knee wasn't quite up to the challenge of tripping on my shoelace at full speed—my leg wrenched sideways, and I blew my knee all over again. They dragged my sorry ass to hospital; I met Sally, couldn't face the long physical therapy rehabilitation again, and that was all she wrote. A brilliant mind and a promising law enforcement career ended up in the toilet, all because of a few inches of loose cotton and polyester; of all the dumb luck.

I found out later that my story quickly became something of a legend at Quantico—I became 'Simple Simon', who was so dumb that he couldn't tie his shoes. Ironic really, considering that I had one of the highest I.Q.'s of all the trainees who had been through this place.

I signed in at the main entrance to meet up with my old instructor,

Melissa Munro, who had graciously taken my call the day before and agreed to see me. She had no inkling what I had been up to since I left the academy more than a year ago without seeing it through to graduation, so had been curious to see me again.

Since the police had been no help, I wanted to enlist Melissa's help on Sally's case. I needed help from a law enforcement agency; I needed resources and access to data. Melissa had been good to me when I was here—I'd met her husband and little boy and knew she had a nice family. She'd cared about her students and had wanted us to do well.

As my security escort drove our electric buggy through the grounds, some wonderful memories of this place came back as I remembered fragments of who I used to be and the man that I was back then. Then I cringed as we rode past Hogan's Alley, the scene of my disastrous fall from grace, and all the pain came flooding in.

My guard escort dropped me off at the Quantico academy and I waited in the lobby for Melissa. She appeared from around the corner and I remembered how attractive she was, even though she was ten years older than me. Her long auburn hair flowed behind as she strode down the grey corridor and her curvy body that I had in the past admired so much, still looked amazing. But she looked sad, seemed to have lost the positivity and vitality that I had remembered so well.

Our eyes met. She stopped in her tracks, with a shocked look on her face. Her eyes opened wide and her jaw dropped as she stood there for what seemed like an age. Brutally reminded once again of my appearance, I realised that I still bore the look of a strung-out junkie. I had only been clean for a few weeks and my wasted body was still recovering. And my wardrobe didn't help; a second-hand tie-died T-shirt from the thrift shop wasn't exactly an inspired choice, not only for what it looked like, but because it exposed my horrible street tattoos, druggie track marks and emaciated frame. Not to mention my sunken cheeks and hollowed eye sockets. I might as well have had the words 'HEROIN ADDICT' tattooed on my forehead. Not exactly the great first impression I'd planned.

Suddenly uncomfortable with her reaction, I folded my arms and hung my head in shame, staring at the floor. I put myself at Melissa's mercy and just hoped she would approach without dismissing me completely, to give me a chance to explain.

'Simon? Is that really you? Jesus Christ! What did you do to yourself?' she asked from across the other side of the foyer, still unmoving.

'It's not what it looks like, Melissa,' I said in a pleading voice. 'Well, actually, I guess it is, but I'm clean now. I'm not using anymore. Please, let me explain.'

'Simon, I have to tell you, I'm not in a good place. I've had a traumatic time in the past year, and I've only just come back to the academy. I can't handle any more drama, and you don't exactly look like you'll bring anything good into my life.'

'I'm sorry Melissa, I didn't mean to shock you like that. Because I'm getting better and I'm feeling healthier, I forget that I still look like… this,' I said as I looked down at myself and put my hands out, gesturing back at my body. 'Please, just give me a few minutes so we can talk. You were always my favourite instructor here and I feel you're the only one I can turn to now.'

Melissa's stance softened and then she came over to me, still looking troubled. 'We can have a coffee, but I can tell you that will be it. I've got no time for anything right now except my son and my job.'

We walked in silence over to the cafeteria, with Melissa occasionally glancing sideways at me and sadly shaking her head, so shocked and disappointed at what I had become.

We sat down at a table, her with a frothy cappuccino and me with a double shot long black. One benefit of being off the horse was that I was getting my taste buds and my appetite back, and I was enjoying coffee again.

'Simon, what the hell happened to you?' she asked. 'You had such promise, you were the best and brightest student in your class! What *happened?*'

I stared down into my coffee, unable to face the accusation and disappointment from the woman who had meant so much to me when I was here, who I had admired and desperately wanted to impress. I shrugged my shoulders and replied, 'I was pathetic and weak. After I blew my knee again, I just couldn't face another round of physical therapy, so I just gave up. You didn't know it then, but I was addicted to painkillers when I was here, from back in my last year in college when my knee went the first time. From there, it was a downward spiral to booze, then pills and on to hard drugs. I ended up addicted to heroin, shooting up every day.'

'Jesus. That must have been terrible. But how did you let yourself sink that low? When you had so much going for you?'

'I guess I just didn't appreciate the life that I had and pissed it all away. And the worst part was, I took someone else along with me, someone who was incredibly special to me. A beautiful soul, who's no longer with us. It's all my fault, she's dead because of me. If I hadn't dragged her into that hellhole, she'd still be alive right now.'

'So, what was it that finally made you get clean?' she asked.

'Sally. My poor Sally,' I replied, suddenly overcome with grief all over again. Tears welled up in my eyes as I looked at Melissa, transfixed, hoping desperately that she could see past what I had done to myself and would help me. Melissa looked back at me, seeing the anguish written all over my face and staying silent, waiting for me to continue my painful story.

'Someone killed her,' I said. 'Some psycho took her from right next to me in the park. I was completely stoned out of my mind, passed out unconscious, and when I woke up, someone had taken her. The next night, the killer left me a note and sent me to find her. He'd tortured her and stabbed her multiple times with syringes, they were all poking out of her like a great big junkie pincushion. Oh Melissa, it was terrible!' I sobbed, this time losing it for real. My body heaved with sobs as all my pent-up emotions burst out of me and I just sat there, hunched over in my misery.

I felt a gentle hand softly patting me on the back, but it felt deliberately distant, almost like she didn't want to give me the wrong idea or get too close. 'I'm so sorry for your loss, Simon, it's a terrible story,' she said. 'Sally didn't deserve to die like that.'

'Thanks Melissa, your sympathy means a lot to me. I've felt so broken and worthless for so long and have had no family or friends around me. It was just me and Sally against the world, and since I lost her, it's just been… me. I've been so lonely.'

'I understand Simon, believe me. I understand,' said Melissa, her own voice full of sadness.

'What do you mean?' I asked, suddenly concerned for my mentor.

'I mean I know what it's like to lose the love of your life in tragic, traumatic circumstances,' she replied, eyes moist and gazing into the distance as if she was trying to disconnect herself from the story she was about to tell. 'It was only six months ago. I was home at night with my husband and my little boy. We were all asleep together in the bedroom and we woke up to find two armed men at the foot of our bed, dressed all in black, with hoods over their heads. We were in the middle of a home invasion! My husband reacted instinctively the second he woke up. He jumped straight out of bed without thinking and rushed them. One of them just pointed his gun right at him and shot him straight in the head. Just like that, he was dead,' she said, her voice trailing off softly into silence.

'Oh my God, Melissa, I'm so sorry,' I said. Now it was my turn to comfort her with a pat on the shoulder, my grief suddenly diminished after this revelation.

'I was in shock. It all happened so fast; I couldn't believe that my husband was dead on the floor. I looked down at my little boy and his tiny face frozen in horror, looking at his daddy just lying on the floor in his boxer shorts, with blood streaming from his head. My poor baby was so scared that he wet himself,' she continued, her voice a monotone, like she was dead inside. Like she had been living with a grief so intense it had become part of her, had her clutched in a vice-like grip. 'I reached over and picked up my boy, to comfort and protect him. I had seen what these men were capable of and now that my son and I had witnessed what these killers had done to my husband, I knew we would be next.'

Dumbfounded, I just couldn't believe what I was hearing, that a random act of such casual but deliberate violence had shattered Melissa's domestic bliss so completely. 'What happened? How did you make it out?' I asked.

'I had a gun hidden in the walk-through closet. I showed the men that my son had wet his pants because he was so scared and that I needed to take him to the bathroom. I played scared and helpless, crying and blubbering—they didn't figure me for a threat. I walked through the closet, put my son in the bathroom, told him to be quiet and shut the door. Then I quietly came back through the closet, grabbed my gun from the top shelf, flipped the safety off and stepped back into the bedroom. One of them was going through my jewellery box with his back to me and his gun was on the dresser beside him. The other guy was nowhere in sight. They were dumb amateurs.'

Melissa's story hit me like a bombshell. Just a few weeks earlier I had been one of those men, breaking into people's houses. Not when they were home. But if someone had surprised me when I was mid-burglary, who knows what I would have done in my drug-addled state? Not exactly a story I wanted to share right now.

'I crept up behind the guy and jammed my gun in hard, right behind his ear. I told him to call out for his buddy and then we moved back to the centre of the bedroom, facing the door. I had the muzzle of my Glock pressed hard against the side of his head. The moment his partner appeared in the doorway, I shot him in the face,' she said coldly.

Now it was my turn to let the silence hang while I waited for Melissa to continue.

'The remaining guy panicked, pulled away from me and went for his gun. I let him grab it and turn just enough so he was facing me and then blasted a hole in his chest. He fell back and let off a wild shot, which lodged into the wall above me. Then there was silence. Until I heard the whimpering. The sad, soft cries of my poor little boy, hiding in the bathroom, terrified of the gunshots, not knowing what was happening, if I was alive or dead.' A solitary tear ran down her cheek as she finished her story and her gaze came back to me.

'Melissa, my God. I'm so sorry, I had no idea. I wouldn't have come and told you my story if I'd known what you'd been through. I really am sorry; I can't imagine how difficult this must have been for you and your little boy. I mean, my situation is tough, no question about it. But knowing the history and life you shared with your husband and having your son witness his father's murder like that, I really can't even begin to understand what that must have been like for you.'

'Yes, it's been difficult. The investigation afterwards was a formality, thankfully. Nobody questioned that they didn't deserve what they had coming, and I made sure that the physical evidence at the scene corroborated my altered version of the story. I just knew right there in that moment that my son and I needed a quick resolution and swift revenge—neither of us would have coped with a long, drawn-out investigation and trial. I needed to dispose of them in that moment because of what they did to our family,' she replied in a voice of cold steel.

There was an inner strength to Melissa, much deeper than I had ever seen in her instructions in my classes. Moments of crisis reveal a person's strength and resolve. And I gained even more respect for Melissa after hearing what had happened to her and how she had responded. She was no helpless victim.

'It took six months before I was ready to come back to work. The Bureau has been supportive of my need to look after my son. He's still traumatised, going through counselling. The healing process is a constant struggle. But I could tell it was time to resume a normal life and for me to get back to work and for my son to integrate back into a normal childhood.'

'Again, Melissa, I'm sorry to have troubled you with my story. I wouldn't have bothered you if I'd known your situation.' I suddenly regretting contacting Melissa just because I needed something for a terrible situation entirely of my doing.

'That's okay, Simon. It's good to see you, even in such a poor state,' she replied in a soft, sad tone as she looked me up and down once again. 'You really were one of my favourite students, and I've wondered in the past what became of you after the infamous "shoelace incident" in Hogan's Alley. And although I'm sorry to hear of your personal situation and what happened to you and your poor Sally, I'm glad you shared your story with me. And I'm happy to hear you're getting yourself back together. But what did you come here for? What do you need?' she asked.

'I'm sorry, Melissa, I was being selfish. I wanted someone to help me. The police aren't getting anywhere with Sally's murder investigation. As far as they're concerned, she was just another junkie who got killed, nothing important. They've moved on to other things. And I made Sally a promise at her grave that I would find her killer. But I know I can't do it alone. I need help, access to police records, that kind of thing. But after hearing what you've been through, I understand you can't help me. I'll find another way.'

'I'm sorry, Simon, but like I said before, I just have no room in my life right now for anything other than my recovery and my son's welfare.

I just can't take anything else on now, especially anything that might bring danger into our lives,' Melissa replied.

'I understand, Melissa, I really do,' I said and reached out and squeezed her hands. I felt a sudden charge of energy as our hands touched and felt her warmth and vitality. Our eyes locked and then she let go of my hands, letting the moment pass unacknowledged. 'Thank you for listening Melissa, I really appreciate it. I don't have a phone, but if you want to get in touch with me, I'm staying at the Shady Palms Motel in Arlington—you can reach me there.'

'Okay, thanks Simon. I'll give you my number if you need to contact me in an emergency instead of having to reach me here at the base.' She gave me her card and scribbled her number on the back and handed it to me, then reached out and shook my hand. 'Goodbye Simon. It was good to see you again, even under these difficult circumstances. Do you want a lift back to the gatehouse?'

'No, I'm fine thanks Melissa, I could do with the exercise. And thank you again for seeing me, I really appreciate it. Bye.'

'Bye Simon, take care,' she said and turned away and walked back across the lobby. I waited and watched her go, then smiled as she turned back around and gave me a wave before she entered the elevator.

I exited the building and began the long walk back to the guardhouse, enjoying the sunshine as it reminded me of Melissa's warmth when we held hands together for that fleeting moment. It had been the first soft human touch I had felt since Sally's death. My life was so empty without her.

CHAPTER 24

'Jesus, what a blimp!' thought Ryan as he stared at the man standing in the queue in front of him. It was late, just after eleven, and Ryan had dropped into McDonald's for a quick snack. The man was enormous—he had to weigh close to five hundred pounds. Ryan watched as he ordered four Big Macs, three Cheeseburgers, five large Fries, twenty-four McNuggets, three Chocolate Sundaes and half a gallon of Coke. The guy serving gave the obese man a wink; no money changed hands. After he'd taken his order away, Ryan looked up at the pimply faced young man behind the counter and said, 'You know that guy?'

'Sure do. I'm the night manager here. He's my brother; I look after him. He comes in every night on his break from the late shift at the parking lot. He sure can put it away,' he said, with a warped sense of pride coming through in his voice.

'Yeah, I can see the resemblance,' snapped Ryan. 'Give me a Cheeseburger and six nuggets.'

Taken aback at the thinly veiled insult, the man replied in a voice dripping with sarcasm, 'Thank you for your custom, *Sir*. Have a nice day,' as he rang up the order.

Ryan sneered in response, accepted his order and made his way to a table with a good vantage point of The Blimp. The man's piggy eyes peered out of a face rendered obscene with rolls of fat. His age was hard to determine, but Ryan guessed he was only in his early twenties. He didn't look like he would make it beyond thirty if he kept going like this—he looked like his heart was ready to explode any minute.

Ryan slowly ate his way through his small order. He watched with a mixture of admiration, fascination and disgust as The Blimp chowed through the enormous spread laid out before him. He shovelled thousands upon thousands of calories along with lashings of fat and sugar into his abused body. A good forty-five minutes later, the man finally finished his feast. With drippings of grease down his shirt and remainders of chocolate sundae on his chin, he sat back with a sloppy grin, looking satisfied with himself. He leaned back in his seat and closed his eyes.

Disgusted beyond belief at this extreme display of gluttony, Ryan knew he was looking at a true food addict and that he needed to teach him a lesson. Of the permanent kind.

Ryan had just found his next victim. It had been three weeks since his last kill and he had been feeling the urge building up inside him, so felt a wave of relief that Providence had delivered this perfect specimen to him just when he needed it. Ryan got up from his table, exited the building and waited outside the door.

A few minutes later, The Blimp lumbered out of the McDonald's store, swinging his massive bulk from side to side as he waddled along. Ryan followed in silence, stalking his prey with ridiculous ease. The Blimp was breathing heavily, wheezing and puffing with every step, all effort and attention focused on successfully putting one foot in front of the other. The journey wasn't far, just across the carpark. Ryan was glad to see that his victim would not walk far and exert himself too much, with the associated risk that nature might rob him of his latest victim because of a burst artery or ruptured heart. Ryan's target stopped at a big old 1974 Lincoln Continental Mark IV, a whale of a car with a big bench seat in the front that was perfect to accommodate the spread of The Blimp's gigantic ass.

Ryan hurried to his Harley, climbed aboard and then waited until the old luxury car had sailed out of the parking lot before starting the engine of his bike. He easily followed at a distance in the non-existent traffic for the quick trip to an all-night carpark, with lights ablaze in the night's darkness. The Blimp parked his car out front, struggled out of the car and slowly waddled over to the booth.

Ryan rode past with a smile on his face. It was time to write to Leonard and plan the spectacular demise of The Blimp.

CHAPTER 25

'God, I fucking HATE addicts!' came the opening line.

Leonard smiled as he started on Ryan's latest letter. His friend was on one of his rants again. 'This one truly is disgusting Leonard; you wouldn't believe what I witnessed tonight.'

Ryan painted the scene for Leonard in all its gory detail. He really had a way of describing his experiences that gave Leonard a vicarious taste of what Ryan's life must be like, so different to his own boring existence. Ryan finished by asking Leonard hypothetically, 'Can you imagine how we might teach him a lesson, how we could make an example of him to show just how disgusting is his food addiction?'

Leonard put the letter down on the table and immediately started planning. He had enjoyed the last couple of theoretical exercises of imagining the acts for Ryan and relished the thought of working out how they could send a message to such a disgusting, hopeless addict as The Blimp. He pulled out his notepad and worked through the problem, laying out the challenges and covering them off. Things like how to disable the victim, how to transport the massive bulk, what message to send, where to carry out the act and how to access the site.

Leonard carefully mapped it all out in his mind, imagining the details that Ryan's inferior intellect could not grasp, to fulfil the vision of Ryan's imaginings. The next night, Leonard committed the complete plan to paper as he prepared his reply to Ryan. He started with the same opening line he had used in the last two letters; "Ryan, this is only for us to imagine—I trust you won't do anything with this information."

CHAPTER 26

'It all started in college, after I hurt my knee and then got hooked on Oxy,' I explained to the group. It was another Narcotics Anonymous meeting in Arlington, with a group of twelve people in attendance. My first meeting had been tough, saying those jarring words for the first time in public; 'Hi. My name is Simon and I'm a drug addict. A heroin junkie.' It was the most difficult thing I'd ever said.

Owning what I had become and incorporating it into my psyche, making it part of my identity, was very confronting. But the meetings were getting easier, and they were really helping me on my ongoing path to recovery. I continued relaying my story to the group, which through repetition became easier. And not going through it alone was an immense relief, after my intense cold turkey detox period all by myself. I finished my story, got the usual wholehearted support from the group and then headed home after some free Oreos and a hot coffee.

The walk home was a reflective one, with many thoughts circulating in my head. It had been eight weeks since Sally's death, and I'd been slowly getting my life back together. I was eating again, my brain was recovering its function, getting back some of its former brilliance—I now had an attention span slightly longer than that of a goldfish. I was working, making some money, doing a good job at the diner, getting back to reading books and following the news. I was gaining in physical and mental strength every day. I'd taken up jogging and doing some simple exercises in the park, including push-ups and chin-ups on the playground bars. I was slowly regaining some of my former strength and muscle as my energy returned. My skin had cleared up, and I was looking healthier. I was still way underweight, but I had already gained thirty pounds since I'd stopped shooting up.

Now it was time for some emotional work. I'd been attending meetings and had worked my way through the first seven steps of the Narcotics Anonymous twelve-step program, all of which centred around me, my personal responsibility and my relationship with a higher power, which for me I called The Universe rather than God. I'd been thinking a lot about Karma lately and knew if I dropped dead this minute, I would come back as pond scum, so I had some serious work to do if I was to climb the evolutionary ladder in my next life.

It was time for the eighth and ninth steps in the twelve-step program—make a list of the people you have harmed and then try to make amends. Wow, that was some list. It had been a real in-your-face, fuck-you kind of moment, looking at that list, long as my arm. The friends I had screwed over, the family I had stolen from, the strangers I had robbed, the fellow junkies and homeless people I had pilfered from, the home owners I had burgled, the tip jars I had pinched, the church donation boxes I had ransacked, the people I had abused when I was high or coming down, the list just went on and on.

The enormous list was too daunting, so I'd decided I had to just start with the big one—family.

As I stood on the front porch that held so many happy memories for me as a child, my breath was fast and heavy, my palms were sweating, and my head was spinning. I hoped my family would welcome me back into the fold but thought they would likely reject me. I just had to suck it up and try. I knew Mom was the only one home. I had waited out front of the house for two hours to see Dad go out and watched with fondness as I saw her farewell him with a kiss at the front door, just like I remembered.

I drew back my hand, rapped my knuckles lightly on the front door, and held my breath. I heard movement in the hallway and then saw the front door swing open. The face staring back at me was so familiar, and yet so different. Mom looked like she had aged ten years since my serious drug use began, with worry-lines etched deep into her forehead. The happy, shining eyes that I remembered had become sad and tired. She didn't say a word; I think the shock was too much for her. Then her eyes rolled back in her head and she just dropped to the floor, flopped down like a rag doll right in front of me without uttering a sound.

'Mom? Mom!' I cried out, staring down at her. I quickly rushed into the house, went around behind her head and stretched her out. I sat down beside her and cradled her head in my arms on my lap, stroking her hair and waiting for her to come around. After a few seconds, her eyelids fluttered, and she opened her eyes, looking up at me.

She reached her hand up, brushed my cheek and whispered, 'Simon? Is that really you? Or am I dreaming?'

As the tears flowed down my face, I replied, 'Hi, Mom. Yes, it's me. It's Simon. I'm back.'

'Oh, Simon, I'm so glad to see you!' she cried, 'I didn't even know whether you were alive or dead! I kept having visions of your body lying in a gutter somewhere, thinking someday I would get a call from the police to come and identify you in the morgue.'

She raised herself up and buried her face in my neck, first crying and then sobbing uncontrollably. My tears grew and grew until I too was sobbing, my face contorted in anguish and my body heaving with each breath.

'Mom, I'm so sorry! Oh my God, I'm so sorry for what I've done to you and put you through!' I cried out through my tears. 'I'm so selfish and horrible. I was only thinking about me and what I wanted and didn't think at all about the impact I was having on those close to me, the people who loved and cared for me. I'm sorry, from the depths of my soul, for what you've had to go through because of me.'

We sat there together on the floor in the hallway for what seemed like an eternity as we both cried ourselves dry, without talking. Finally, Mom pulled away from my neck, reached out both hands and cupped my cheeks like she used to when I was a little boy, drew herself in and rubbed the tip of her nose on mine in the traditional greeting of the New Zealand Maori people and said, 'Welcome home, Son.'

This simple gesture and welcoming words from my mother melted my heart. We had travelled south to "The Land of the Long White Cloud" on a family holiday when I was young. We had seen the traditional tribal greeting and adopted it as our own special welcome when one of us had been apart from the other for any longer than one night.

'Thank you, Mom. You don't know how much it means to me to hear you say that,' I said.

She raised an eyebrow in response and replied in a tone with a hard edge, 'I know exactly how much it means, Son. And I don't say it lightly. That *welcome home* comes with a big condition.'

'What do you mean?' I gulped, nervous to hear what was coming.

'Four simple words. Don't fuck it up.'

My head snapped back like someone had slapped me in the face. I had never, ever heard my mother swear before, and I hadn't seen this hard edge to her. This simple statement from her brought everything into sharp relief for me. I had made some huge mistakes, hurt her deeply and busted down some big fences that needed mending. I was on fragile ground—she had opened her heart to me, even though she knew it was at risk of being crushed again.

I had taken the first big step of coming home, and she had made the second big step of welcoming me back into her life, but from here it was all up to me.

Up to me to prove to her I was worthy of her trust, support and love.

CHAPTER 27

Ryan's pulse quickened and his breathing sped up as the adrenaline surged through his body. After a week of planning and observation, it was time for action.

Ryan had arrived at the McDonald's restaurant well after closing time and parked his Harley way over in a dark corner of the carpark, then walked back to the all-night parking garage. He spotted The Blimp in his booth and the classic old Lincoln parked nearby. Ryan made his way over to the car on the side away from the booth, inserted a thin steel bar between the window and the door sill and quickly levered up the door lock on the old car. He slid into the back seat and lay waiting for The Blimp's work shift to end.

Ryan checked his pockets and removed his important items. He had the Ketamine, a horse tranquilliser stolen from a veterinarian's surgery. He had the alarm code of the McDonald's restaurant, purchased for fifty bucks from a disgruntled employee who Ryan had observed in an argument with the slovenly night manager. And he had the keys for the door to the loading dock along with the keys for the forklift, which he had taken unnoticed from the locker room at the back of the restaurant just before it had closed for the night. He was wearing his trademark black gloves and had his trusty switchblade ready to go. The last piece was the black ski mask to cover his face from security cameras. He was well prepared, thanks to Leonard's "imaginings", he thought with a smile.

Ryan peered out over the edge of the doorsill and noticed the next shift arriving. The Blimp squeezed his way out of the booth and lumbered over to the grand old vehicle and climbed into the driver's seat, oblivious to what was lying in wait for him. Ryan knew he must hurry to avoid any delay in The Blimp's departure being noticed by the new attendant in the booth. Just as his victim prepared to insert the key into the ignition, Ryan jammed the syringe right into a prominent vein in the man's neck and drove the plunger home, then pressed his switch blade against the fat folds of his victim's neck to control the shocked response. Ryan whispered urgently in his ear, 'Relax, boy, relax, no need to stress, you'll feel much better in no time.'

The horse tranquilliser acted fast; The Blimp weighed in somewhere close to a small horse, so it had been easy for Leonard to work out the right dose, with a healthy margin to make sure he would be well and truly out of it in less than a minute. Ryan felt the stiff body go slack, and then the massive head lolled to one side.

Ryan jumped over into the front seat next to The Blimp, reached for the seat adjuster and slid the seat back as far as it could go. Then he moved the thick legs out of the way of the pedals, sat in close next to him and turned the key in the ignition. The big 460 cubic inch V8 purred into life, and Ryan slipped the selector into gear. He carefully drove out into the street and went the couple of blocks to McDonald's, keeping the big steering wheel steady and controlling the pedals with his left foot reaching over into the driver's footwell.

Ryan eased the car around the back of the McDonald's, near the loading dock. He checked on The Blimp, who was still unconscious, then jumped out of the car and walked across to the rear door of the restaurant. He checked the keys and the alarm code one last time, then unlocked the door, hustled over to the alarm panel and entered the code, safely disabling the alarm. He went through the kitchen, hit the button on the wall to fire up the deep fryer, and then moved across to the loading dock. He started up the small forklift and drove it out through the door of the loading dock and parked it near the car.

Ryan pulled the driver's door open wide and looked in at The Blimp, sleeping calmly and breathing deeply. 'You are one big dude, my man,' said Ryan with a soft whistle, as he contemplated the task ahead of him. He drove the forklift right up to the car, pushed the fork tines close together and raised them up level with the door sill. Then he reached low inside the car and dragged out both the man's legs, resting them on one of the forklift tines. Then he reached in and grabbed the right arm and heaved, rotating and pulling the limp body from the car. It was heavy work, and Ryan soon worked up a sweat from the exertion as he heaved the body, working it out of the car and on to the forklift.

Finally, The Blimp flopped fully out of the vehicle and lodged safely face down on the forklift tines. Ryan was thankful the forklift was narrow and manoeuvrable, ideal for working in small spaces and simple for staff to use with little experience. He carefully reversed the forklift away from the car and shut the door, then turned it around and drove up the loading dock ramp and into the back of the restaurant.

Ryan made his way into the kitchen, carefully navigating the narrow passageway. As he reached the stainless-steel bench, Ryan raised the forklift and laid The Blimp on his enormous stomach on the bench beside the cooker, then reversed and slid the tines out from under the body and moved the forklift back out of the way.

Ryan returned to the kitchen and checked the deep fryer which had now reached the intense heat of boiling oil. He climbed up onto the other side of the cooker, sitting on the bench with his knees up and feet braced against the deep fryer. As he approached this glorious ultimate act, his heart raced, and a manic smile broke out across his face.

Ryan reached across the top of the deep fryer, grabbed The Blimp under his armpits and heaved, sliding the body towards him. Slowly, the head and shoulders inched towards Ryan, dropping closer and closer to the surface of the boiling oil. Finally, with one more enormous pull, the weight of the man's upper body dropped his head into the deep fryer.

The impact was fierce and immediate. Ryan leapt back from the deep fryer, out of the line of fire. The oil instantly bubbled up in a maelstrom of spitting bubbles as it attacked the soft flesh and fat. The searing shock and pain pounded an adrenaline rush through the poor man's body that burst through the effects of the horse tranquilliser. The head violently jerked up from the boiling oil and a blood-curdling scream emanated from the throat of the thrashing victim. His face looked like a horror movie—the boiling oil had seared off the skin and flayed it back to flesh and bone. There were no lips, eyes, nose, ears, or hair; all that remained was just a meaty skull.

There was no consciousness in the jerking response, just a primal reaction of the most basic of bodily functions. The heart stopped from the shock; the brain ceased functioning, and the head flopped back into the deep fryer. He was stone-dead, with the massive frame hanging limply into the cooker. The only remaining signs of life were a few spasmodic jerks of the arms and legs, which soon ended.

The smell of burning flesh and the sound of sizzling oil continued as Ryan stared wide-eyed, dumbfounded at the hell he had just unleashed. Slowly, he reached out and hit the button to turn off the deep fryer.

'Fat killed by fat. Nice touch, Leonard,' said Ryan as he studied the mess in the deep fryer. 'Gotta hand it to ya buddy, that was a doozy!'

The sheer enormity of what he had just done suddenly hit Ryan. This kill was more visceral and in-your-face violent than the quiet, calculated manner of his earlier two murders. It left him with a unique feeling, almost a sense of awe at his growing repertoire of murders, as he realised that this third act won him the official title of "serial killer".

Ryan got down from the bench and went to the office area. He found the night manager's phone number on the wall and dialled it. The response was quick, and a worried voice answered, 'Hey! Who's this? Why are you calling from my restaurant phone line?'

'There's a Blimp on the menu,' said Ryan. 'You should come and check it out—there's plenty to go around for everyone. But don't bring the cops, otherwise it won't go too well for your brother; he's fried.'

Ryan hung up the phone, then opened the drive-through window and exited through the rear door, retreating outside to a secluded vantage point where he could still see and hear the kitchen through the open drive-through window. Just a few minutes later, the night manager tore into the parking lot and raced inside through the back door. Ryan edged out of his hiding place and moved closer to the window for a better view of the kitchen.

He saw the night manager enter the kitchen and stop dead in his tracks, seemingly unable to process the sheer horror of the scene laid out before him. He walked over to the still-smoking vat of oil and said, 'Colin? Is that you, Bro?' and poked the lifeless body. Even though Colin's face wasn't visible, it was hard to mistake the body. As Colin's brother finally processed the scene, he broke down and started freaking out, crying, babbling, banging his fists on benches and throwing things around the kitchen in a flurry. The effects of the man's misery and anguish surged through Ryan like an electric shock and he felt supercharged as this all-important last act played itself out.

Ryan ran across the empty parking lot, jumped on his Harley, gunned the engine to life and took off. Inside, the night manager barely registered the noise on the periphery of his consciousness as he frantically pulled out his phone and dialled 911.

Ryan continued his wild ride straight to the streetwalkers, picked up a random hooker and had sex with her on a dumpster in a grimy alley. The perfect end to a perfect night.

CHAPTER 28

I was skilled in pattern recognition, ritual identification, and personality profiling. My high I.Q. and the ultra-functional logic centre of my brain had kicked back in. I was thankful that my extended period of drug abuse didn't appear to have done any permanent damage to my brain, although my ability to concentrate for long periods of time had still not returned. I was doing lots of research online through news feeds and true crime websites. My gut told me whoever killed Sally had done it before or again, so I was scouring the murder stories searching for a pattern. Her murder scene was too deliberate, too staged. The killer *wanted* me to find the body like that; it was part of the thrill, like the signature of a serial killer.

I spent all my spare hours at the local library as I used the public computers searching for clues. Finally, one day I connected the dots between a series of three kills in the wider DC area, all with a common thread—addiction.

First there was my darling Sally, a drug addict. Then a smoking addict. And finally, a food addict. All the murders were deliberately and elaborately staged, with each of the victims killed in a manner related to their addiction. Plus, a loved one discovered each victim in a deliberate, orchestrated manner.

I had been trying for weeks, desperately searching for clues to Sally's murder, to find some thread that might lead to something bigger. And now I had it! It was time to pull that thread of knowledge and see where it would lead.

CHAPTER 29

Ryan was sitting patiently at the bar, scoping the crowd. The Live! Casino and Hotel in Maryland wasn't exactly pumping with action at one in the morning on a Tuesday. Ryan was looking for the hard-core gambling addicts, the ones who couldn't stay away. His observations soon focused on an old lady with blue hair who had been playing the slot machines for two hours straight, without a break. The bartender said she had been there for two hours before Ryan had arrived and she hadn't moved in that entire time. He said she was in just about every night and was a real sad story. Apparently, she used to have plenty of money but had gone through almost her entire life savings gambling it away.

The bartender referred to her as an "ornery old cow", who was apparently a real piece of work, always ordering the staff around and being nasty to the other customers. All she cared about was her favourite slot machines.

Ryan walked over to the old woman, gestured at the chair next to her and said, 'Excuse me, is this seat taken?' in the politest voice he could muster.

'Does it *look* taken, you retard?' she snapped in a venomous tone. 'Is there a sign on it? Don't interrupt me, I'm on a roll. Take some other seat, there are hundreds in here. I don't need you bringing your bad luck onto my machine, you loser.' She turned back to her machine, completely ignoring Ryan.

This toxic response immediately got Ryan's rage burning, but he was conscious of the extensive camera coverage on the casino floor, so just shrugged his shoulders, turned around and muttered under his breath, 'You'll get yours, you crotchety old bitch,' and walked away from his next target.

The Gambler.

CHAPTER 30

'Simon!' said Melissa brightly. 'It's nice to see you again. You look much healthier and brighter, like you're getting yourself back together. And you got a new wardrobe.'

'Hi Melissa,' I replied. 'Thanks for seeing me again. I wasn't sure you'd want to, after the last time. Yes, I'm feeling much better, thanks. I'm getting myself back on track, and yes, I took a trip to The Gap Factory Outlet to improve my appearance. I hope you approve?' I had made sure this time to wear a long-sleeved shirt to cover my horrible street tattoos.

Melissa shot me a radiant smile that lit up her face and she leaned in and gave me a friendly kiss hello on the cheek. It had been a few weeks since our first awkward meeting and she seemed in a much better place mentally and emotionally.

'I definitely approve,' she responded. 'Urban chic is so much more attractive than strung-out junkie.'

Stung by the direct comment, I recoiled, and the smile dropped off my face.

'Sorry!' she said with a laugh. 'Too soon?'

'Hm… yes, still a bit too fragile for jokes, I'm afraid. I'm still raw and feeling unsure of myself around people and what they think of me,' I replied.

'It's all good. I'm in a good mood today. My son is doing well and I'm slowly feeling better every day too. My therapy is really helping my recovery. Even though it was hard, I enjoyed meeting up with you a few weeks ago and sharing our stories. We've both been through a lot. It was good to see you.'

The smile returned to my face as I realised there was no malice in Melissa's "junkie" comment. 'I'm pleased to hear that, Melissa. I'm glad I reached out to you and we caught up. Even though it was tough, and I wasn't in a fit state then, it really was great to see you again.'

'So, what brings you back to Quantico, Simon? Have you made some progress on the case?' asked Melissa.

'Yes, I think I have. Sally's murder was so deliberate, so planned and made such a statement, that I'm convinced there must be others. I'm sure I've found two other murders that share a similar theme, and I don't think anyone has put it together yet.'

'So, what's your theory? What's the common theme?' she asked.

'Addiction,' I replied. 'I found three victims who were all addicts.'

CHAPTER 31

Ryan's letters were coming more frequently, with Leonard receiving one just about every week, and quite a pattern emerging. In one letter, Ryan would outline his frustrations with some addict he had come across and how he wanted to imagine something bad happening to them and asking for Leonard's help. And then in the next letter, Ryan would be calmer and would ask about Leonard and what was going on in his life and how things were going with him.

True to form, Ryan's latest letter followed the pattern. He went on about how he was just minding his own business when a gambling addict had insulted him, how she was a bitter and twisted old bitch who had wasted her life and blown her entire savings on slot machines because of her gambling addiction. Ryan wrote about being extremely frustrated and needing Leonard's help to imagine a plan that would teach her a lesson.

After reading through Ryan's background information on the old woman, Leonard got to work on the plan. He found his imagination was running more freely with each new mental challenge that Ryan set for him. Leonard did some research and found a service centre that did maintenance on the old-fashioned slot machines with a big pull handle. He then prepared instructions to rewire the internal motor drive to a repeating cycle and to set it at double the frequency to drive the handle harder and faster.

When his notes were complete, Leonard wrote his letter back to Ryan, added the sketches and sealed them in an envelope ready for sending the next morning.

CHAPTER 32

It was still early days, but it was going okay with my family, all things considered. Mom had brokered a ceasefire between me and Dad, who was still burning over what I had done to them both and wasn't as forgiving as Mom. I had stolen a lot from them in the months I was using drugs when we were still seeing each other, until my father had finally put his foot down and cut off all contact, refusing to let me in the house, knowing that I would just lie and cheat and steal, no matter what I said. 'Once a junkie, always a junkie,' were his last painful words to me.

But we had met up a few times now; I had explained the whole thing, including Sally's death and the impact it had on me, and my efforts at recovery. Dad could see I wasn't using now and was trying to clean myself up. My sister, three years younger than me, was away at college and we had spoken on the phone a few times after Mom had filled her in on what was happening.

With amends being made with my family, I decided to take the next step and reach out to Sally's family. I knew this would be tough, but I had to at least try. It was a major step on my path to recovery, and I wanted to connect with them, to see if there was anything I could do. Sally came from a God-fearing middle America family, with very traditional values on religion, morality, race, and sexual orientation. One reason Sally and I had hit it off so well was her desire to rebel and be her own person, free of the judgement of her parents.

I took a deep breath and knocked on the front door of the home of Sally's parents. An American flag standing proudly in the front yard fluttered in the breeze, and a menacing crucifix mounted over the front door dominated the front of the house. I gulped as I waited for a response, almost hoping that nobody would answer.

The door creaked open, and a look of pure hatred unlike anything I had ever seen in my life hit me right between the eyes.

'BASTARD!' came the shout, from the face of Sally's father, immediately purple with rage. 'Murderer! How dare you show your face here, you pig! You killed our only daughter and then you turn up on our doorstep all sad-eyed like you want forgiveness? You'll never get that from this house! I'll burn in hell before I forgive you for what you did to our sweet Sally!'

He spat the venomous words at me with accompanying drops of spittle as he stared deep into my eyes with lips curled in a twisted sneer of hate.

'I'm sorry, Sir, I'm so sorry. I didn't mean for Sally to get hurt, I'm sorry!' I cried out.

He pulled a small crucifix from his pocket, held it out as if performing an exorcism and fixed his fiery gaze on me. In a voice as hard as flint he snarled, 'You listen to me, you worthless piece of shit. I curse the parents who spawned you. I curse the day my darling Sally first cared for you in that hospital, and I curse the drugs you hooked her on. I curse the path you dragged her down and I curse the life you created for her. But most of all… I curse YOU!'

He fiercely thrust the crucifix at my face with every curse, culminating with the final hex as he shoved the cross an inch from my eyes and held it there quivering, like it had taken on a life of its own.

Shocked at the vitriol of his attack, I backed away and said, 'I'm sorry, all I wanted to do was apologise for what I did to Sally, to make amends. I swear I'll find her killer.'

'Find her killer?' he said, in a voice of derision and disdain. 'There's no need for that, Boy. He's standing right in front of me. He'll be looking back at you from the mirror every day for the rest of your life. God is the ultimate judge and his fury is unmatched by mere man! You will burn in hell for all eternity for what you have done.'

My stomach dropped, and my blood went ice-cold at this judgement as I looked at Sally's father, a broken man. On the surface I knew this wasn't all my fault, and his response wasn't exactly rational, but the visceral nature of his attack cut me to the core.

'Martha!' he shouted back into the house. 'Get my rifle and bring it here. Now!'

Then he looked back at me and said, 'Boy, if you know what's good for you, you'll get the hell out of here before Martha arrives with my gun, because I guarantee I *will* shoot you if you are still standing on my porch. Get your ass out of here and don't come back!'

I turned tail and jumped off the porch steps, ran down the path and out onto the footpath. With pounding head and burning gut, a horribly familiar need came flooding over me. Filled with remorse and self-loathing, I saw the truth in what Sally's father had said.

In a moment of despair, I gave into my urge to chase the dragon and headed straight to my old dealer. I bought a hit of junk and bummed some gear from him. Unlike my recovery time so far, I didn't have the strength to resist my ever-present urge this time.

I went back to the place in the park where I had seen Sally for the last time. I sat down, hid under my jacket, pulled out the spoon, water, lighter, rubber band, and syringe. I applied the tourniquet around my arm and started heating the solution. With a look of fascination and anticipation I saw the white smoke drift up towards me, placed the needle into the solution and drew back the plunger. I tapped a prominent vein in my arm to plump it up and punctured the skin with the razor-sharp needle point. I grasped the body of the syringe between my fingers and positioned my thumb on the plunger. My heart was racing, preparing my body for the imminent rush.

Suddenly, the simple sound of a child's laughter broke through my drug fever. I peered out from under my jacket and saw a woman walking along the river with a young boy and a dog. I thought of my mom and dad and everything I had put them through, and what it would do to them if I sank back down into this cesspit again. I thought of Melissa and everything she had been through with her son. And I thought of Sally and my pledge to her to stay clean and find her killer. The photo I had taken of myself naked in front of the mirror came back to me in a flash, image vivid in my mind.

I looked down with fresh eyes at what I was about to do, seeing the syringe hanging out of my arm with its full dose of poison about to enter my bloodstream, and jolted out of my drug-state. Repulsed, I pulled the syringe out of my arm and jammed it down into the dirt, then drove the plunger home, injecting the heroin into Mother Earth. I then whipped my jacket around to clear the air while filling my lungs with deep gulps of fresh oxygen.

The enormity of what I had almost done hit me in the chest like a battering ram, and suddenly my heart was pounding so hard it felt like it was jumping out of my chest. I *must* be strong! I know I can't just give in like that whenever I hit a setback—I'll face challenges with my past and my addiction throughout my whole life, and I need to have coping mechanisms in place to deal with that.

This is the price I must pay for what I did to Sally. It will be a burden I carry for the rest of my days.

CHAPTER 33

Ryan continued to be delighted at the letters from Leonard. His pen-pal was yet to let him down with his imaginings. Leonard's high intelligence and active imagination were proving an intoxicating combination to assist Ryan with his nocturnal activities, violent urges, and bloodlust. Preparing for The Gambler killing had been challenging, but Ryan knew it would be worth it and was looking forward to it with eager anticipation.

Ryan parked his Harley at the kill site and then caught the bus to the casino. He spotted The Gambler's car in the carpark and waited outside to avoid the cameras. He took up position close to the tired and faded old Chevrolet Impala, waiting patiently. Finally, Ryan spotted The Gambler coming out of the building, with her shiny, frizzy, bright blue hair glistening in the moonlight and her oversized yellow handbag glowing like a beacon. Ryan moved quickly across to the car and ducked down on the front passenger side, waiting quietly.

The woman clicked the remote central locking, climbed into the driver's seat, then inserted the key in the ignition. Ryan quickly climbed in the passenger side and before the woman could react, had the cruel ten-inch blade of his hunting knife pressing at her throat.

The old woman's eyes widened in shock and her mouth opened into a terrified, silent scream. Ryan said nothing, raised his forefinger to his lips, breathed a menacingly quiet, 'Shh,' then pressed his knife even harder against the thin, saggy turkey neck. The woman responded by closing her mouth and staying silent.

'Hello there. Another long night racking up losses on the slot machines, I assume?' said Ryan in a smoothly sinister tone. The woman nodded silently in response. 'Start the car and drive slowly out of the carpark, then turn left,' he instructed.

The Gambler followed orders, hands shaking on the steering wheel as they headed out onto the street, then the highway. She drove the car with unsteady hands and occasionally weaved right and left as they went.

'Take this exit,' said Ryan, then directed her down a side street off the main road and down a deserted back alley.

The woman opened her mouth as if to speak for the first time on the entire journey, but Ryan quickly gagged her, ensuring her silence for the brief trip from the car to the back door of the deserted old bar. Ryan had already broken in previously and made his preparations. The place was empty, had been vacant for months, with nobody around. He had set up temporary power from a large truck battery fitted with a power invertor and had staged the place with flashing lights and a big old slot machine right in the middle of the floor. The slot machine was lit up by a spotlight and had a low chair and a high bar stool in front of it.

'Well, you're about to play the most important slot machine of your life,' snarled Ryan, his voice no longer silky smooth, but rough and raspy as the anger rose in him like bile. The old woman knew there was no point protesting—she had accepted her fate and understood that her life would soon be over. She looked around at the dingy and deserted old bar and at the brightly lit old-fashioned slot machine in front of her, and she wondered what the payoff for this gamble might be.

Ryan removed the gag and sat the woman down on the low chair, facing the machine and said, 'Before you try your luck on this classic old slot machine, I'd like you to reflect on what your gambling addiction has done to your life. You seem like a bitter and twisted old woman. Were you always like that?'

The poor woman hung her head in shame, shaking it from side to side and said, 'No, I wasn't always like this. I used to have a husband and a family who loved me, a house of my own and savings in the bank. But now it's all gone!' she sobbed in reply. 'My husband divorced me, my kids won't talk to me and I lost my house. All I've got left are my slot machines. Sometimes I wish it would just all be over.'

'Well, maybe I can help you with that,' said Ryan with a smile. 'It's good to know that you can see what your gambling addiction has cost you, the price you've paid for your weakness. Now, just in case something happens to you, give me your ex-husband's name and number so I can get in touch with him if I need to.'

The Gambler looked up at Ryan quizzically, shrugged her shoulders and gave him the information, figuring she had nothing more left to lose. From her position down on the low chair, Ryan leaned The Gambler over and placed her head ear-down on the seat of the high wooden bar stool. He grabbed some rope and tied her head lying sideways onto the bar stool. The hard wood and rough ropes made the woman grimace and cry out in pain. Ryan bound her legs to the chair and her left arm to her body, then stepped back to admire his handiwork with a satisfied nod.

Ryan could feel the tension and excitement rising in him like a flood. As the adrenaline pulsed through his system, he thrust his hands in the air and roared, 'Okay Gambler, now you really are a one-arm bandit—let's see what you got!'

The woman whimpered in response and refused to move, but Ryan whipped out his hunting knife and brutally dug it in deep against her throat, forcing her to act. His helpless victim gingerly reached out and up with her right hand, grabbed the handle and pulled it down towards her. As the handle clicked past its trigger, suddenly it leapt forward and downward, flying out of her hand. The big, bright, hard red ball on the top of the handle smashed down on the side of her face, sandwiching her head in a crushing impact against the hard seat of the bar stool.

'Jackpot!' shouted Ryan with delight.

The poor woman spasmed and cried out in pain. The handle

immediately flew back up again to its home in the machine's side. Then Ryan's hot-wired repeater kicked in and the handle hurtled down once, bashing into The Gambler's open wound. This time she whimpered like a wounded puppy as Ryan gloried in the scene he'd created.

Again, and again, the handle repeated its gruesome task until there was nothing left of the poor woman's head but a gory mess of blood and bone. Finally, Ryan killed the power to the deadly slot machine and smiled, feeling very satisfied with how his plan had worked out. He went out the back door and down the alley to the payphone on the side street, pulled out the number he had gotten from his victim and dialled it. The sleepy voice of a tired old man answered, and Ryan said, 'Mister Watson? I've just seen your ex-wife and I think she's in trouble. There's a bar on Patrick Henry Drive out back of Home Depot. Hurry! And no cops, they'll just make it worse.'

Suddenly awake, the response came, 'I'll be right there.' Ryan hung up and waited.

At first, the distant sound of police sirens was of no concern to Ryan; they blared often. But as they got closer and closer, Ryan switched to high alert. He raced over to the vacant lot where he had stashed his motorbike and jumped on. Suddenly, the stupidity of bringing such a noisy beast to a kill scene became apparent, but he knew he couldn't leave it there. 'Leonard would not approve of this part of the plan,' he thought suddenly. As he caught his first glimpse of the police lights, he knew he had to get away—The Gambler's husband had unexpectedly called the cops instead of turning up on his own.

Ryan slowly wheeled the heavy Harley along the flat section of the vacant lot over to the rear exit, then built up speed as the gradient fell away from him—he rolled nearly all the way down to the bottom of the long hill and then just before he hit the trough, cranked the engine and it barked into life. Ryan jammed the throttle full on and roared his way through the gears. 'FUCK! Fucking cops! Jesus Christ! The perfect stage and he killed it for me. Bastard!' shouted Ryan, his fear of capture now receding and getting taken over by his fury at being robbed of his special thrill that came with the discovery of his victims by a loved one.

Purple with rage, Ryan rode on and on until he came upon a late-night bar with a country and western themed "Howlin' Dawg" neon sign flashing out the front. Blood still boiling, Ryan knew he needed some release. He slid off the Harley and strode into the bar with a murderous look in his eyes, stormed over to the bar and glared at the tired old barmaid, who recoiled at the dark look he gave her.

'Give me a whiskey and a beer. Now!' snapped Ryan. She obliged and handed over a double shot and a pint of beer in a big, heavy glass with a handle. She glanced over and nodded at the bouncer who had eyeballed Ryan at the door as soon as he came in. Ryan immediately chugged half his beer.

The doorman was a big dude, six-foot five-inches and 250 pounds, but unfortunately for him he was all beef and no game. He never stood a chance with Ryan and the mood he was in. Half a head taller than Ryan, the looming bouncer drawled, 'Hey Mister. You best mind your manners in here.'

Ryan looked up at the bouncer and shouted, 'Mind THIS, you fucking asshole!' and smashed his half-empty glass of beer right into the side of the poor guy's face, spraying an explosion of glass, beer, and blood across the room. Ryan looked down at the glass handle still in his hand, then at the bouncer on the floor. He slowly turned to the barmaid, who's eyes were wide and mouth agape in shock at what had happened so quickly on what was an otherwise dull night. Ryan grabbed his double shot of whiskey, downed it in one gulp and slammed it violently back down on the bar. The barmaid flinched instinctively, terrified of what might come next from this psycho who had just stormed into the bar.

'Thanks for the beer, *bitch*,' snarled Ryan as he turned on his heel and marched out of the bar. The whole interaction had lasted less than three minutes. Ryan jumped back on his Harley and headed for home, feeling better but not satisfied with how the night had gone.

<h1 style="text-align:center">CHAPTER 34</h1>

Leonard's regular walk home from Court House Metro Station to his apartment was typically an uneventful affair. Usually he spent it walking with his head down, staring at the pavement and doing his best not to engage with his fellow commuters. Tonight, unfortunately, was different. It was later than usual, owing to a big Mensa meeting that went on longer than it should have, and the streets were uncommonly quiet, with little activity.

Leonard was halfway home when he heard a sharp, 'Hey, buddy! Over here!' and looked up to see a suspicious-looking character in black sweatpants and a black hoodie beckoning to him. Leonard ignored him, put his head down once more and increased his walking speed, determined to avoid any contact and return to the haven of his apartment.

'Hey! I'm talking to you buddy! Slow down, goddammit!' the man snapped. Leonard increased his speed once more, this time looking across at the man who was now walking towards Leonard at speed, trying to head him off on an intersecting path. Leonard quickly calculated the angles and speed and judged that unless the man broke into a run, Leonard would make his corner and get home safe. Leonard increased his pace up to his top walking speed.

Being naïve in such things, Leonard hadn't considered the man might have an accomplice. Too late, Leonard looked up ahead of him and in a moment of shock and realisation, saw a similarly clad man standing directly in front of him, blocking the footpath.

'Hey man, what's the problem? My friend here just wants to talk to you. Don't you know it's rude to ignore people and run away from them like that?' he said in a smarmy, sarcastic tone.

Leonard tried to walk around the figure, but the man sidestepped and headed him off. Leonard changed direction, but the man sidestepped again, and this time stopped Leonard in his tracks. The first man arrived on the scene and flanked Leonard on the roadside of the pavement, boxing him in against the mouth of a dark alley.

'Okay, buddy. Just take it easy, and nobody will get hurt,' the first man said as he pulled a nasty looking handgun out of his pocket. 'Step back into the alley and keep your mouth shut.'

Leonard did as instructed and silently stepped back off the street. 'Okay, hand over your bag and empty your pockets,' said the man with the gun as he waved it at Leonard.

'Okay, okay. Just stop waving that gun at me. You're making me nervous,' wailed Leonard in a quivering voice as he opened his briefcase and handed it over, along with the scarce contents of his pockets.

'What the hell is this?' snapped the second man as he studied what Leonard had handed over. 'What are you, some kind of retard? Where's the laptop? The tablet? The smartphone? Credit cards? What are you trying to pull here? Where's the rest of your shit?' the man demanded, obviously angry.

'Look, I don't own a laptop or tablet. I only have a desktop computer and I don't have a smartphone. I think they make people dumber because they stop thinking for themselves. And I don't believe in credit cards because they put people in debt,' replied Leonard. Even in this frightening situation, Leonard still sounded smug and superior.

'Are you trying to tell me that all you have on you is a lousy fifty bucks, a transport card, a library card, an old book, and a fucking purple *lunchbox*?' the man snapped, in a voice rising in intensity with every item mentioned, so that by the end he shouted out the last word.

'I'm sorry!' cried Leonard. 'That's all I've got. If I had anything else, I would give it to you, I swear!'

'Jesus Christ! You are useless! We've had better scores off first-graders, you useless prick,' snarled the second man. 'Have some respect for hard-working muggers like us, just trying to make a living. Here's something to remember us by, so next time you come prepared with some more valuable stuff than this crap!' And with that, he drew back his fist and punched Leonard hard, right in the solar plexus. He doubled over in pain with the wind knocked right out of him, sagged down on to his knees and then toppled over on to the ground, whimpering and crying.

'Shut up, you girl!' snapped the man with the gun. 'Don't be such a wimp.' And off they went, leaving Leonard curled up in the foetal position on the ground in the alley, gasping for breath.

It was in times like these that Leonard wished for more brawn instead of more than his share of brain.

CHAPTER 35

The Gambler killing created a sensation. The prominent police scene made a splash, and the media picked up the story and ran with it on an otherwise slow day, so it gained serious traction in the news cycle.

I saw the headlines and knew immediately that the Addict Killer had struck again. I contacted Melissa straight away and told her there had been another addict murdered. Now that it looked like my theory was right, she agreed to help me; we would approach Frank Delaney together.

Melissa had instructed at police academy training before the FBI, so knew a lot of the local cops, including Delaney. She put in a friendly word for me, and thankfully I looked a *lot* better than the last time I saw Frank. I was almost unrecognisable now with tanned skin, clean-shaven face, tidy hair, bright eyes, and straight back, along with the fifty pounds I had regained since I last saw him. I also had on my now-usual long-sleeved shirt covering up my horrendous tattoos.

We met with Frank and I ran him through my theory on the Addict Killer. I laid out all my research notes and ran through my logic and reasoning. A series of three killings might not have been enough, but this fourth one pushed it over the edge. After much deliberation, Frank nodded and said, 'I think you've got a point, kid. Sorry I didn't listen to you before, and sorry about your girlfriend.'

'That's fine, Frank, I totally understand. I probably wouldn't have listened to a strung-out junkie like me either,' I said with a wry smile.

'So, what's your story, Winter? How did you come up with all this when the city's finest didn't put it together?' asked Frank.

Melissa interjected before I could reply. 'Simon was my brightest student. He spent nearly five months in training at Quantico, but unfortunately imploded just before graduation. So, he's basically an agent without the badge.'

'So what happened? Why didn't you graduate?' asked Delaney.

I responded, 'The short story is I was playing college football and was the unfortunate quarterback who got sacked by a couple of three hundred-pound gorillas and my knee exploded. I got shipped off to hospital and ended up hooked on opioid pain meds. Fast forward to Quantico and then I blew my knee again, but this time graduated from oxy to heroin, which kind of messed up my graduation from the academy. And that's all she wrote.'

Melissa said, 'Frank, we'd both like to help on this case. Simon knows it intimately and you know I've got the profiling experience that could really help here. If I organise clearance from HQ, can we join your team? As you know, we've got the National Center for the Analysis of Violent Crime over at the academy at Quantico, including the Behavioral Analysis Unit, who could help us out on this. We're in the neighbourhood, so we might as well help your local boys.'

Frank pondered for a moment, then nodded and said, 'Fine by me, I'll just have to clear it with the Chief.' Frank stepped out of the office and Melissa rang Quantico. She had her clearance by the time Frank came back into the office with a smile and a thumbs-up.

'Let's go check out the latest work of your Addict Killer,' said Frank. 'But Winter, you're on notice here, Boy. You have no authority and no jurisdiction; you're just an observer with no official capacity. So, keep your head down and your mouth shut, or you'll be off this case in a heartbeat. Got it?'

'Got it, Delaney. Understood,' I replied with a nod.

We took off in Frank's unmarked cruiser and drove over to the murder scene of The Gambler. The press were everywhere; the grisly nature of the murder scene and the helpless old lady victim was an irresistible combination, so the ghouls were circling. We made our way through the police cordon and entered the old bar. There was no body at the scene; it was already lying on a slab over at the morgue, ready for the autopsy.

The gruesome murder scene triggered an eerie sense of deja vu, although I must admit I was much more aware during this crime scene investigation than I had been for Sally's.

The building was a derelict bar, the last customers long gone. The floor and room surfaces were grimy with dust and the room had long fallen into disrepair. The current central feature in the middle of the room was a large slot machine, one of the old-fashioned mechanical kind with a long pull handle adorned with a big bright red knob on top. A rusty red-brown stain of dried blood ran over the knob and the entire length of the handle. Intense blood spatter was visible all over the slot machine and the floor, and the wooden bar stool had a pool of congealed blood on the seat, dripping down the legs to the floor where it had overflowed.

Frank had photos of the body before they'd removed it. He spread them out on the bar for us, so we could get a sense of what it looked like. It was horrific. The poor woman looked to be in her seventies, with the classic blue rinse that seemed so inexplicably popular with women of her vintage. But blood now matted and stained the blue hair. Someone had bashed her with the proverbial blunt instrument, which judging by the scene was the rock-hard big red ball on the end of the long handle. There was some serious leverage on that thing.

After viewing the photos of the body, we continued scanning the room, looking for anything that stood out. Of obvious importance was the lighting and the slot machine, which the killer appeared to have brought, as it didn't seem to fit the original bar decor. The murderer had gone to a lot of trouble to set the scene; it looked like he had tried to recreate his own little casino scene for the victim.

'Shall we power up this thing and see what happens?' said Delaney as he went around behind the machine and flicked the switch on the power board connecting the lights and the slot machine. Instantly a maniacal banging and crashing came from the slot machine as the handle jerked into life and smashed down into the bar stool, then sprang back up into position and then smashed back down again. The lights above the slot machine had glared into life, flashing the scene with light and colour. Frank quickly flicked the switch off again, not wanting to demolish the arm of the slot machine or damage the scene any further.

The scene stunned all three of us; this was some seriously messed-up shit. Someone sure had gone to an awful lot of effort to make a point about this gambling addict. A fatal point.

The old lady's number had come up last night.

CHAPTER 36

'Well, Leonard, these MRI results are interesting and informative,' said Ellen. 'They show that you have no corpus callosum, which is the bundle of nerves connecting the right and left hemispheres of the brain. It looks like you had surgery to remove it many years ago. You have what is known as *Split Brain Syndrome*.'

'Ah… what? Say again?' replied Leonard, totally confused by this surprising revelation.

'There is no connection between your right-brain and left-brain. There is nothing linking them together. Has there been anything significant in your medical history?'

'Well, I remember being in hospital for surgery on my head, but it was nothing serious,' said Leonard in a puzzled tone. 'My mother told me it was nothing bad, just that the doctors had to take out a tumour. She said nothing about major brain surgery and never took me back to the hospital for any follow-ups. It happened after my father died, so we had no money, no medical insurance, my mother was working minimum wage as a waitress and she was a fully fledged alcoholic by this time, so not exactly the most attentive with medical care. I just figured it was nothing important, like she said.'

'Hm… okay, this could explain a few things. Do you know which hospital it was?' asked Ellen, lost in thought.

Leonard shook his head in response, 'No. I don't have a clue. My mother never mentioned it and I never asked. I was too busy surviving and looking after myself.'

'Okay,' said Ellen. 'We've got some homework to do. You see what information you can find at home and I'll see what I can find out from your medical records. Let's compare notes at our next session.'

CHAPTER 37

Ryan was restless and antsy. The Gambler killing had gone perfectly according to plan, and he'd gained some satisfaction from it, but the cops had interrupted the big reveal to the victim's husband, robbing him of a key part of the thrill. He was on the prowl again, scoping out a suitable prospect for his next victim. He'd been out the last few nights searching without success and his dark need was pushing its way to the surface, driving him on and on to find his next victim.

He'd moved Downtown for his search and was starting out with a meal in a diner when he saw a sleazy guy with slicked back hair, a gold front tooth and a wedding ring on his finger, chatting up a waitress. Ryan's radar was up, and he figured him for a suitable target, so decided to stalk him. Ryan quickly finished his meal and followed his target out of the diner and shadowed him to his workplace.

The man was a night manager at the Grand Hyatt in DC. Ryan followed him inside and snuck into the housekeeping area, keeping a watchful eye. He observed the man hitting on the housekeeping staff and overheard him talking to one of his buddies. The man talked about needing sex all the time, multiple times a day. His friend called him a scumbag for cheating on his wife, to which the man shrugged and said, 'Hey, what can I say? I'm a sex addict, it's not my fault if I need it all the time. And don't worry, there are lots of women out there who want a piece of this,' pointing down at his groin. 'There's been no complaints yet, my friend. It would be a crime not to satisfy these women. And don't worry, there's plenty left in the tank to keep my wife Bonnie satisfied.'

This verbal exchange signed the man's death warrant. Ryan felt a surge of excitement at finding his next victim.

The Cheater.

CHAPTER 38

After working late one night going over the case, Melissa invited me back to her place for dinner. I noticed the place was like a fortress, with solid reinforced front and back doors, dead bolted windows fitted with toughened glass and a high-tech alarmed security system. Melissa was super careful after her previous home invasion experience. Who could blame her?

I met her little boy, Bobby, who was only five years old. The family home was full of pictures; a warm, inviting and comfortable place. Memories of Melissa's dead husband were strong in the house. Bobby was quiet and sad; I figured he missed his dad. We sat on the couch together, playing with Lego, building cars and trucks. I thought back to my childhood when life was simple and fun before I screwed it up so completely.

I had fun with Bobby, and we bonded quickly. I saw his innocence, unaffected by the filth I had experienced. It seemed so long ago now.

I feel a genuine connection and growing affection for Melissa, but we're both damaged goods. I'm still mourning Sally, and Melissa is still grieving for her husband. Something is stirring in our relationship, but it's as fragile as a butterfly's wings and needs time to develop.

We said goodbye at the front door. I stayed there while Melissa flicked the alarm on and then shut the front door and headed upstairs to bed. I turned from the door, walked down off the porch and jumped on my bicycle for the ride home.

CHAPTER 39

Ryan's latest letter involved a request for Leonard's creative imagination to come up with a suitable punishment for a sex addict who was constantly cheating on his wife. Ryan justified it by writing that a close friend of his was suffering because of her sex fiend husband.

Leonard was increasingly concerned that Ryan might do more than just *imagine* what to do with all the addicts he kept talking about in his letters, so he decided that this time in his return letter, he would question Ryan about his motives and actions. But still, Leonard couldn't help himself, because he so enjoyed the thrill and the challenge of thinking of ways to punish these people for their pathetic, weak addictions. So he put his mind to work anyway, imagining an appropriate treatment for The Cheater.

His plan involved the purchase of three Transcutaneous Electrical Nerve Stimulation (TENS) machines, one each from a different drugstore, along with a bronze anal plug from a sex shop. With sketches and notes complete, Leonard completed his letter to Ryan and put it in his bag, ready for posting the next morning.

CHAPTER 40

Melissa and I worked late again, and it turned into another home-cooked dinner and more fun for me hanging out with Bobby. I was getting a glimpse of what a domestic life could be like, how good it could feel to be in a nice house full of warmth and enjoyment, instead of the harsh reality of life on the streets. I knew I would never go back out there, to being homeless, and couldn't believe I had done it for so long. I resolved never to relapse, not now that I knew how glorious life could be with the right person in the right circumstances.

However, I also realise how unprepared I am for life as a husband and a father. I'd had my share of fun with girls, had my time at college, but my wealthy parents, my privileged upbringing, and constant access to money when I was growing up had turned me into a selfish jerk, concerned about nobody but myself. The way I sucked Sally into my vortex of hell was a perfect example of my complete disregard for anyone but me.

It suddenly dawned on me that I've never even cooked anyone a meal before! I'd been pampered at home and had eaten at the dorm in college, with everything catered and paid for. And what did I do for that? How did I repay my parents? By disgracing them, shitting all over everything they had done for me, stealing from them to feed my habit and lying to them. I burned with the shame of it all.

After Bobby was in bed, I suddenly poured my heart out to Melissa about everything I'd done, how selfish I'd been, how I'd hurt Sally, the people I had disappointed and let down, even her as my favourite lecturer, who always tried her best to help me. I broke down, crying like a baby, tears running down my face as I let it all out, everything. I had never shared my shame like this with anyone; I don't know if I'd been too scared and ashamed to admit it, or if I really didn't care, just didn't give a shit because I was so self-absorbed.

But I sure as hell care now. The shock of Sally's death and my role in it completely changed my perspective. I understand and appreciate how precious life is and how lucky I am to be alive. I'm firm in my resolve to make amends for the hell I've put my friends and family through, and I will live a better life, be a decent human being and do my job of bringing scumbags to justice.

'Wow,' I said. 'I'm sorry Melissa, I didn't mean to lay all that on you. But once I started, I just couldn't stop. I'm sorry, that was too much for you to hear.'

We were sitting close next to each other. I realised she had slipped her hand into mine and hadn't let go through my whole admission. My cheeks were still wet with tears and I felt drained and empty inside.

'That's okay,' she responded with a gentle smile, 'You obviously needed to get that off your chest. I'm glad I was here to listen to what you needed to say. It's given me a much better sense of who you are and what you're about. And it's okay. What matters is not what happens to you, but how you deal with it. And I think you're doing just fine.'

She stretched her arms out around my shoulders and pulled me in and gave me the warmest, most heart-felt and comforting hug I had ever experienced in my entire life. It was bliss; I had never felt so safe.

Time stood still until we parted from our embrace and she held the space between us, looking into my eyes as we stayed close. Finally, she puckered her lips slightly, leaned in and gave me a gentle kiss full on the mouth. It was deliciously affectionate, but not overtly sexual, with just a hint of possibility. I could feel a wide, happy smile spread uncontrollably across my face.

I made to leave, and Melissa came with me to the front door. We said goodbye outside, this time with a kiss. Melissa stepped back inside, reached across and turned the alarm on and then shut the door with a smile. For a few seconds I gazed at the closed front door, barely able to control my spirit of happiness, at the same time feeling so unworthy, but so grateful.

Finally, I turned and left the beautiful energy and warmth of Melissa's house to make my return to the cold emptiness of my dingy motel room.

CHAPTER 41

Ryan was nervous. He'd carefully prepared the scene, but this was a unique environment for one of his kills. Ryan had so far operated in deserted, out-of-the-way places, but now he was in a room at the Grand Hyatt, a swanky and public place. He'd been careful—booked the room under a false name, paid in cash and checked in late at night, wearing a realistic flesh latex mask of an old man.

Ryan picked up the phone, dialled housekeeping and asked to speak to the night manager. 'Hello? Can I help you, Sir?' came the silky smooth voice on the other end of the phone, instantly getting Ryan's hackles up.

'Yes, please,' replied Ryan. 'I've got a maintenance problem up here that I need you to come and look at. I need you, someone experienced, not one of your junior staff.'

'Of course, Sir, I'll be right up,' came the reply, and the phone died.

Ryan readied himself at the door and after a few minutes responded to the knock, opening the door and seeing the sleazy, gold-toothed playboy standing in the hall. 'Come in,' said Ryan as he stepped aside and opened the door to let the man in and then closed it behind him.

As his victim walked past, Ryan swung his right arm around the man's neck and brought his left arm up onto the man's left shoulder. Then Ryan locked his right hand onto his left bicep and placed the palm of his left hand on the back of the man's head, applying a perfect sleeper choke hold in less than two seconds. Ryan then applied pressure to The Cheater's neck with his right forearm as he simultaneously pressed the head forward with his left hand. This immediately restricted the blood flow to his victim's brain, and he slumped unconscious in less than twenty seconds.

Ryan dumped The Cheater on the bed, gagged him and tied his arms and legs tight to the bed with thick cord. The man regained consciousness and immediately started thrashing around, trying to scream through the gag, but could make no sound of significance. Ryan felt confident the walls were thick, and the door was solid and sealed, so there was no chance of minor noises arousing suspicion.

The Cheater's eyes opened wide in horror as he finally calmed down and looked up to see Ryan hefting his trusty hunting knife with an evil leer on his face. Slowly and deliberately, Ryan paced towards the man, knife in hand; slowly twisting and turning it so it caught the light, glinting and reflecting from the fearsome, shiny blade.

Ryan leant down over his victim and slowly and carefully started slicing the clothes off with his hunting knife and said, 'Don't worry dude, I'm no fag. I won't make you my bitch, but you will pay for your sex addiction and what it's doing to your wife, Bonnie.'

The man found a fresh burst of energy and struggled and thrashed around again on the bed. Ryan immediately pressed the knife against the man's groin, looked up at him, smiled and said, 'Careful buddy, you wouldn't want me to cut something off down here, would you?' The Cheater immediately settled down and Ryan continued his excision of the clothes, leaving only the jockey shorts.

Ryan ran the knife over the man's stomach while he writhed in helpless despair, then slid the knife down into his jockey shorts and cut them free, leaving him naked on the bed, bound and gagged. Ryan looked down at his work in progress and smiled at the haunted eyes staring back at him.

Ryan went to his black bag and pulled out the three TENS machines and the brass anal plug. Then he went back over to the bed, focussed on his victim and said, 'I won't lie to you. This will hurt. Like a *motherfucker.*'

The Cheater's eyes opened even wider in response. Ryan continued, 'You know, you've got nobody but yourself to blame. If you'd just kept your dick in your pants, you wouldn't be in this mess right now.'

Ryan held the anal plug up to the light and studied it, then said, 'I ain't never done nothing like this to no dude before. This is seriously weird for me. But then again, I'm sure that's nothin' to how weird it's about to get for you. Here goes!'

Ryan put his hand under the man's ass and raised it off the bed, spread the cheeks and jammed the anal plug in position, eliciting a groan of pain from the stricken man on the bed. Ryan then clipped the wire terminals of the first TENS machine to two nodules on the electrically conductive anal plug and then got to work on the next phase of his bizarre plan. From the second TENS machine, he taped one electrode to each of the exposed testicles and then from the third machine he secured one electrode each to the base and the head of the penis.

The Cheater by this time was beside himself, thrashing around like a man possessed and screaming into his mouth gag. Ryan was as calm as ever and stepped back to admire what he thought of as his work of sadistic human art.

Ryan studied each of the TENS machines and said, 'You know, this machine is like a car with a stock V-six, but I've done some wiring modifications to turn this into a supercharged, turbocharged V-eight. I hope you're ready to rock-and-roll this bitch, coz this shit's about to get real! And remember, you brought this on yourself. For your wife's sake, your addiction is a sickness that we need to remove. And this seems like the perfect way to do it!'

Ryan quickly amped up all three TENS machines to their maximum power, driving the full force of the stimulating voltage simultaneously into The Cheater's anus, testicles, and penis.

The man's body convulsed madly as the intense electric current ran amok through his most sensitive parts. Designed for stimulation of large muscle groups such as the quadriceps and then significantly amplified by Ryan's wiring modifications, the net effect of all this power on such delicate parts of the male anatomy was staggering.

Ryan gave his helpless victim thirty seconds of electric torture to his genitalia and then suddenly cut the power. The body on the bed instantly went limp with relief and sagged down onto the mattress, already exhausted. Ryan went over to The Cheater and looked deep into his eyes, revelling in the pain, misery, and fear that stared back at him through milky eyes already shot through with little bursting blood vessels. Ryan shook his head, raised his right forefinger and wagged it from side to side as if he were a kindergarten teacher admonishing a naughty student and said, 'Tsk, tsk, tsk. Should have kept it in your pants, Cheater.'

As Ryan retreated from the bed, the victim's eyes opened wide with terror as he realised his torture was about to continue. He struggled and protested, but Ryan had done an excellent job restraining him to the bed, so his efforts were to no avail. Ryan reached out again to the TENS machines and looked over at the man on the bed. He was now crying and whimpering in anticipation of the flood of pain that he knew was coming. A broad smile came over Ryan's face as he cranked each of the three dials up to maximum again, this time slowly and deliberately.

The Cheater's body arched up off the bed like a man being shocked with a defibrillator. Higher and higher off the bed he went, as the current through his most delicate bits steadily grew in intensity. This time, Ryan left all three machines on maximum power without a break. The man's body continued its spasmodic convulsions, with the intervals between them getting longer and longer while his body slowly gave up the struggle. Before long, The Cheater lay limp and lifeless on the bed, destroyed by the electric overload of his nerve and muscle stimulation.

Ryan turned off the machines and then checked for a pulse, but there was nothing. He announced with a smile, 'Killed by Genital Electric.'

Feeling very satisfied with his work, Ryan pulled the man's phone out of his jacket pocket and unlocked it with the dead thumb. He found Bonnie's number and texted, 'Hi honey, I need you here at work—it's an emergency, come to room 105 as quick as you can. Don't call anyone, just come now. I'm okay, but I need you here. Come quick.'

A few minutes later, The Cheater's phone buzzed with a texted response, 'WTF?? I was in bed asleep, you shit. This better be good. I'm on my way.'

Ryan opened the door of the hotel room, put a thin piece of cardboard over the door latch and closed it, so the door looked shut, but could be pushed open. Then he put on a black ski mask, hid in the closet and left the closet door open a crack, just enough to see the body lying naked in a mess on the bed. And waited.

He soon heard movement in the hallway and a knock at the door. 'Hey!' came a fierce whisper from outside. 'Open the door, goddammit. Shit. Crazy bastard.' And then the woman pushed enough on the door to feel it open and slowly pushed it all the way. Ryan watched, transfixed, as he saw the woman take in the scene. He could feel himself getting hard as he watched her break down, run to the bed and shake him, then screamed, 'Noooooo!!'

Ryan had never been *this* close to any of his kill discoveries, and it brought a new level of excitement for him. He felt the danger of discovery drive another surge of adrenaline through his veins and felt an enormous rush as he lay lurking in his hiding place.

The chaos continued in the hotel room, as Bonnie cried and wailed over her husband's limp body, with the gruesome electrodes strapped all over his groin area.

That was Ryan's cue—among all the noise, he quietly opened the closet door, unnoticed by the distraught woman, and snuck out the door of the hotel room. Clad all in black and with his head covered by the black ski mask, the imposing Ryan resembled a large Ninja. He sauntered down the hallway in full view of the hotel security cameras as he raised the middle finger of his right hand. Then he entered the stairwell, walked down to the street and into the back alley where he had left his bike.

The loud noise of a big motorbike from the laneway outside distracted Bonnie for a moment, but she quickly turned back to her strung-out and very dead husband, crying and shaking her head at the insanity of it all.

Ryan raced off into the night and made a beeline for his favourite S&M club, which was heavy with activity. In less than fifteen minutes he had picked up a girl in a black leather bondage outfit and they had fierce sex on his Harley in the alley behind the club.

The night had gone perfectly according to Leonard's audacious plan. Ryan's excitement, boldness, and desire for more kills was thriving with each violent act.

CHAPTER 42

The very picture of health and vitality, Sally's gorgeous clear eyes gazed deep into mine, full of love and affection. My heart felt ready to burst from the feelings that welled up from deep within my body. I looked down at my hands and arms in wonder; my skin was clear with no track marks—I was blemish-free with no sign of hideous tattoos.

I looked back at Sally in wonder, struck by how young, beautiful and pure she was, just like the day I first saw her when she bounced into my hospital room full of enthusiasm and energy. She leaned in closer and closer, her face right in front of mine. She parted her lips and drew in so close I could feel her soft breath on my lips. The anticipation of the soft kiss that I knew was coming made me ache as I longingly moved in to meet her moist mouth.

Suddenly the sound of our old favourite Billy Joel song made its way into my mind, '*I said I love you and that's forever, And this I promise from the heart, I could not love you any better, I love you just the way you are.*'

But sadly, old Billy was way too loud for such a romantic moment, and the kiss vanished; Sally suddenly withdrew and disappeared like a fleeing ghost from my consciousness. My confused mind couldn't make head nor tail of what was going on. The battle of the foggy transition between sleeping and waking addled my confused brain. Finally I jerked awake to the sound of the new musical ringtone I had programmed on my FBI-issued mobile phone I had just received as part of my involvement on the case.

Left with a feeling of emptiness at this rude disturbance of such a beautiful moment, it was like I had lost Sally all over again. I finally shook myself awake properly and grabbed the phone off the dresser, noting the time as I answered the call. It was four-thirty in the goddamn morning!

'Winter!' barked Delaney's voice from the earpiece. 'Your freakazoid buddy has been at it again. And this time he's taken it to a whole new level. Get over to the Grand Hyatt in DC. Make it quick!' The phone went dead. I hadn't even said a word. Frank sure had some work to do on his phone manner.

I dragged myself out of bed, staggered to the bathroom and stared bleary-eyed at my reflection. I looked a hell of a lot better than I had when I was using, but I still looked like shit. The tattoos and track marks missing from my dream had sadly returned to haunt me. I washed my face, threw on some clothes, left the house and jumped on my bike.

As I pedalled through the darkness, the road ahead was illuminated by the streetlights and my trusty bike lamp. The activity picked up around Metro Center Station on G St NW and then as I rounded the turn onto Eleventh Street NW, a cacophony of noise and a blazing of red, white, and blue lights assaulted my senses. The place was a Zoo! Definitely not the image the Grand Hyatt likes to advertise in its swanky brochures to its well-heeled customers.

There were cops everywhere. The police had set up a perimeter around the main entry, there were media vans all over the place, reporters breathlessly talking to camera and hotel staff buzzing around like flies trying to defuse the situation. It was chaos!

Suddenly regretting riding my bike instead of catching a cab or an Uber, I ran the gauntlet of police and media, rolled to a stop in front of a scowling uniformed cop, swung my leg over the bike seat and removed my pink bike helmet. The man's right eyebrow raised quizzically, somehow leaving the left one remaining in a fierce scowl as he snarled, 'Move along, buddy! I don't know what the hell you think you're doing here riding your damn bike around like a faggot with that pansy-ass helmet of yours, but there's nothing here for you to see. Go on, get out of here, away from my police line.'

'Winter! Jesus Christ, Winter, you're an embarrassment! Get yourself a goddamn car, will you? And get rid of that ridiculous helmet—you look like a fucking schoolgirl in that getup!' came a voice from behind the police tape.

Despite the insults, I was relieved to hear Delaney's voice. I gave him a sheepish look, then turned to the beat cop and shrugged my shoulders. The officer shook his head in disbelief and raised the tape for me to duck under. I walked through, wheeling my bike next to me with the pink helmet hanging off the handlebars, and leaned it against one of the police cruisers.

'Is Melissa here?' I asked Delaney.

'Yep, she just arrived. Looking a damn sight better than you, I might add,' he growled in response. 'She's over here, we'll go up together and I'll brief you on the way.'

A warm feeling of affection came over me as I saw Melissa in the wash of light from the hotel lobby, and she gave me a wave and a smile. She looked beautiful, very natural with no make-up, I guess because of the rushed exit from the house.

'Hi Melissa,' I said with a smile of my own. 'Who did you find to look after Bobby at this time of the morning?'

'Hi Simon. My neighbour was kind enough to come in and look after him, even though it was such a rude shock waking her at this ungodly hour,' she replied, with a shake of her head. 'Unexpected phone calls in the middle of the night is one thing I don't miss about being active in the field anymore.'

'Okay, let's go up and I'll show you the craziness before the lab geeks take it apart,' said Delaney as we entered the prestigious lobby of the Grand Hyatt, walked over to the elevator and hit the button for the first guestroom floor. After a quick vertical trip, we got out of the elevator to more police tape and the last stragglers of guests that were being evacuated from the immediate area around the crime scene. We walked down the hallway and I glanced up at the discreetly placed security cameras. Delaney noticed my look, nodded and said, 'The techs are on it now; we should have something to look at soon. Let's have a look inside first, although be warned–it's not a pretty sight in there.'

Delaney nodded at the cop manning the door and we walked through into the hellish scene. The body on the bed was naked, violently contorted into a rigid, locked set of muscles of rock-hard intensity. His groin was a mess of wires and patches, hooked up to three sinister looking machines with electrode terminals and dials on the front. Clearly, the victim had suffered immeasurable pain in his last moments.

The man's genitalia were swollen, puffed and bruised, with discolouring already showing in the nasty red inflammation of the penis and testicles, embellished with a faint bluish tinge. Buried under his balls were another two wires, which then went in the back entrance. Not a pleasant way to go. At all.

'Well Delaney, I agree this is some fucked-up shit, but what makes you so sure it's our guy?' I asked.

'Dude was a sex addict, according to his wife. Put two and two together and figured it was our sick puppy,' he replied.

'Fits the profile of what we've seen so far,' I agreed with a nod. 'What do you think, Melissa?'

'Yep. Similar M.O. to the other crimes and what appears a related motivation consistent with your theory about the Addict Killer,' she replied.

'Okay, let's have a look and see what we can find,' said Frank and then addressed the room in a louder voice, 'Guys, can you clear the room for a few minutes, please?'

The night quiet settled in as the room emptied. The first thing I noticed as I looked around the room was the closet door slightly ajar. I went over to investigate and asked Delaney, 'Did any of your guys open this closet?'

'Nope. Was like that when we came on scene. Why?'

'Just something about when I found Sally. When I look back on that night, I felt like I was being watched. And shortly after, I heard a big motorbike take off, like someone had been there.'

'Interesting,' said Delaney as he pulled out his notebook. 'Yep, here it is. And here, and here. All the witnesses who discovered the bodies were all loved ones, and they all reported hearing a loud motorbike leaving the scene, even this poor bastard's wife. Looks like you're onto something, Winter. Do you think the killer could have been in the room when the woman discovered the body?'

'Yes, I think so. He would have been able to see the bed from here. I think it's part of his kill thrill—seeing a loved one break down and lose it when they see his work in all its glory.'

'We'll check out the camera footage; if he was in here, we'll see him leave down the hallway,' said Delaney. 'We might get lucky with a good shot of him.'

We had a look in the closet and there was evidence that someone had been in there, with hangers and shelving disturbed. 'Make sure the techs get in there and check that out thoroughly,' I said to Delaney, who responded with a nod.

The next step was particularly uncomfortable. We moved across to the body and got the full picture of what the killer did to this miserable wretch. Accompanied by an involuntary shudder, Delaney explained, 'The geeks have checked out this machine and say it's souped up with double the normal dosage and elevated current capacity, all of which adds up to something like five times the regular maximum treatment on these things. Plus, on maximum power they're designed to stimulate large muscle groups like the quadriceps, not a cock and balls or even a goddamn butt plug, for God's sake. I can't believe what that animal did to this poor guy, no matter how many women he was nailing behind his wife's back.'

We spent another fifteen minutes going over the entire crime scene, analysing the key points and the staging of the scene to help flesh out our profile of the killer. Finally, Delaney called the gang back into the room and we headed down to the security area for a look at the video recording of the security cameras.

We discovered the killer was no fool. This guy was careful—he planned his entry and exit down to the last detail. At first shocked to see him check in at the front desk as an old man, we then zoomed in on his smooth, young hands and noticed a visible crease at the neckline. We soon realised he was wearing a lifelike latex mask. Then on his exit from the kill room, he was clad in a black ski mask. The man knew there would be cameras and had prepared for them. Not to mention the annoying touch of flipping us the bird on his way out. The detailed strategy, careful preparation, and methodical planning seemed at odds with the theatrically violent nature of the kills.

As the first light of dawn broke over the swarm of humanity outside, a multitude of news reporters from different outlets all put their own spin on this hot, breaking story from the heart of the Nation's Capital. The media announced the actions of a serial murderer.

Maybe a cop had leaked the direction of the investigation or someone in the media had made the connections just like Simon had done.

The biggest story in DC and the entire country was the Addict Killer.

CHAPTER 43

'But surely you must have some records, you imbecile!' snapped Leonard to the poor woman on the other end of the phone. 'I was a boy, not a ghost.'

'I'm sorry, Sir, but we don't have any record of anyone of your name admitted here back then,' came the response.

'Fine, I'll keep looking elsewhere,' grunted Leonard, frustrated after being given the run-around by four hospitals. He tried his fifth and last chance among the facilities that could have performed his complex brain surgery.

'Hello, Children's National, how may I direct your call?' came the friendly voice of the receptionist.

'Medical Records, please,' sighed Leonard, all hope gone from his voice as he prepared for another unbearable dose of Greensleeves on the interminable hold queue.

'Hello, how may I help you?' came a cheery voice after only two rings.

Caught off-guard by the immediate response, Leonard collected himself and said, 'My name is Leonard Price. I think I might have had brain surgery there about ten or twelve years ago. My mother died, I have no other family, no medical records and had no follow-up with other doctors, so I don't know where the surgery took place. But it really is most important that I find out what happened and when.'

'Just let me have a look on the computer Sir, stay on the line,' the woman replied and then a moment later continued, 'It looks like we might have something here Sir, but obviously I can't say anything over the phone. Please come down to the hospital with some identification. Ask for Judith in medical records and then we can have a talk face to face.'

Less than an hour later, Leonard walked into the hospital, apprehensive about what he might discover, but also hopeful that he might get some answers. He made his way down to the basement and the medical records department and rang the tiny bell on the unoccupied reception desk.

A tubby middle-aged woman with a jovial smile came up from behind the desk and said, 'Hello Sir, can I help you?'

'I hope so,' replied Leonard. 'Are you Judith, by any chance? My name is Leonard Price.'

'Ah, Leonard, that was quick! You're an eager beaver, aren't you?' chuckled Judith, setting her extraordinary double chin wobbling and resonating around her neck. Leonard responded to the woman's friendly jocularity with an impassive, blank stare and total silence.

Judith shrugged her shoulders and asked, 'Can I see your ID please, Sir?'

Leonard reached into his briefcase and produced his passport, birth certificate, tax record, and utility bill and said, 'Is this sufficient?'

Now it was Judith's turn for the blank stare, unused to such efficiency and uncertain whether this man was taunting her with sarcasm or was just highly organised. She said, 'Just the passport is fine, thank you Sir, let me take a copy of that for our records.'

Judith disappeared in back with Leonard's passport and then returned a few minutes later, clutching a wad of paper in her thick, stubby fingers. 'Here you are, Sir—your passport and a printed summary of your file from our computer archive. Have a nice day.'

'Thank you for your help Judith. You have been most efficient,' responded Leonard with a curt nod as he took the printout and his passport from Judith's extended hand, turned on his heel and walked through the door without another word or further acknowledgement. Judith shook her head as she watched Leonard stride out the door and muttered, 'Pleasure doing business with you, Mr. Jerk,' and got back to work.

Leonard made his way to the hospital cafeteria, where he subjected his palette to a stale donut and a cup of rancid coffee. Grimacing with distaste from the miserable fare, he laid out the paperwork in front of him on the plastic tabletop and started scanning. Keywords leapt off the page as he read on through his file; words like *large brain tumour*, *corpus callosum*, *severed connection between left and right hemisphere* and *Split Brain Syndrome*.

The revelation of the absence of such a significant portion of his brain function shook Leonard to his core. Dazed and confused, he collected his things and left the hospital, mind racing with a jumble of thoughts and uncomfortable emotions. It felt like a giant joke from beyond the grave—yet another dereliction of duty from his neglectful and spiteful mother.

The trip home helped Leonard calm down and take stock of the situation. He made himself a cucumber sandwich and a soda, then sat down at his computer and got to work on his research. Leonard touched the scar on his head and realised it had much greater significance than his mother had told him; it was the surgical scar where the neurologist had performed a craniotomy. They had cut into his scalp, removed a large section of bone and pulled back a section of the dura, the tough membrane that encases and protects the brain. The surgeon had then removed the brain tumour and in the process had to conduct a Corpus Callosotomy, cutting the corpus callosum and severing all connection between the left and right hemispheres of his brain.

Continuing his research, the comments from doctors, medical researchers, and people with Split Brain Syndrome jumped off Leonard's screen and resonated deeply within him. There were comments like *generally has difficulties with social interaction, trouble forming meaningful relationships with other people, each hemisphere of the brain functions independently, alien-hand syndrome, memory lapses* and *acute hemispheric disconnection symptoms. Also, inability to play the piano because both hands must work together to play the music* and *difficulty with fine motor skills requiring both hands.*

The pieces of the puzzle that was his life clicked into place as Leonard delved deeper and deeper. He had always prided himself on his extreme left-brain dominance; his logical, mathematical and analytical mind, undistracted by such trivial pursuits as art, music, and creativity. He now realised that this total absence of right-brain activity was because of a physical defect in his brain and suddenly felt a sense of loss at what might have been. A feeling of yet another betrayal at the hands of his long dead mother washed over Leonard as he tried to fathom why the hell she wouldn't have shared this vital piece of information with him, her only son.

CHAPTER 44

This was seriously intimidating.

A pair of fully black, dead-looking eyes containing absolutely no trace of white were staring at me. The guy facing me had obviously been on the street for a long time; he was covered in tattoos and piercings. He'd even taken things to a whole new level by getting the whites of his eyes tattooed completely black and they now stared blankly at me like a real-life horror movie.

I was in a needle exchange centre, investigating the syringe I'd found at Sally's crime scene. The place was crawling with junkies; human shells, the walking dead, hunting, searching, desperate for their next fix.

I had hit a dead end. The attendant I spoke to about the syringe said there were literally millions of that type around the country. Anybody could have gotten it from anywhere. There was no control on issuing the needles, and that was the whole point. If they tracked people, nobody would come in. Only by the guarantee of anonymity were the druggies willing to exchange their dangerous old needles for new, clean ones.

I sidestepped around the black-eyed freak and made my way out of the shelter, shuddering and shaking my head in disbelief. Had I really sunk that low? Had I been one of those desperate, down-and-out losers? As I looked inside myself and back to what I had done and who I had been, I had to admit to myself that yes; I had been as strung-out as those sad, empty husks wandering the halls.

CHAPTER 45

After a fitful night's sleep teeming with vivid hallucinatory images, Leonard woke up exhausted. He dragged himself out of bed and endured a torturous commute and day at the office that was almost an out-of-body experience. It seemed like he just wasn't Leonard anymore. He didn't know how to *feel*, who he should *be*. He imagined he could sense the defect in his cranium, that black void deep inside his brain that he desperately wanted to fill by connecting with something or someone.

Leonard's distraction continued on his way home from work. Instead of his usual head-down walk of isolation, Leonard looked around, as if searching for something, looking for a connection, an unknowable something that he hadn't known was missing. He felt the aching void spread from his brain, down his neck and fan out across his shoulders and chest like a dark cloud, threatening to envelop him completely. He staggered, then stumbled and pitched forward, about to lose consciousness completely when suddenly a pair of powerful hands grabbed his arm and held him steady. Leonard's knees buckled under him and the hands directed him to a plastic chair nearby.

'Take it easy buddy, you're gonna be fine,' said a deep voice close to Leonard's ear. 'You just sit tight, man. Lean on your knees and put your head forward while I get you a drink of water.'

A large pair of shoes reappeared in Leonard's clearing vision a few seconds later, along with an open bottle of spring water. Leonard gratefully reached out for the water, took a few sips and then sat up, breathing carefully and deliberately. The black fog receded from his chest, back up his throat and returned into the dark, empty cave of the centre of his brain. Leonard looked up and saw an enormous black man with a tuft of grey hair on his head standing next to him, blocking out the sun. 'Feeling better?' the man inquired.

'Yes, much better, thank you. I appreciate your help,' responded Leonard.

The man thrust out his giant bear-hand and said, 'I'm Jonah, what's your name?'

'I'm Leonard. Pleased to meet you, Jonah. Thank you again for your help. You saved me from a nasty episode,' said Leonard as he shook the outstretched hand. As he became more aware of his surroundings, Leonard realised he was sitting on a plastic chair, not a park bench and asked, 'Where did this chair come from?'

'Oh, that's mine. I always bring it with me to my newsstand. These old bones get tired standing all day. Lucky for you I always have my chair with me. Comes in handy for saving passing strangers,' he said with an enormous smile of white teeth that lit up his face.

Leonard looked around and absorbed more of what was around him, the busy people walking past in a rush, the DC buildings, the shops, and the man's newsstand, plastered with the day's headlines. Leonard's heart skipped a beat, and he sucked in a deep breath, whistling through his teeth as he saw the screaming headline glaring in giant letters across the tabloid page.

ADDICT KILLER.

The words pounded Leonard right between the eyes. He could feel the force of the words as they pushed their way through the cornea and then onto the retina, down the optic nerve and into his brain for processing. It had to be Ryan! He had broken their deal and gone back on his word; he had carried out Leonard's plans, transforming the so-called "imaginings" into a sickening reality.

Numb and sick to his stomach, Leonard bought the newspaper,

thanked the newsman and somehow made his way home in a trance. The shock was almost too much for Leonard—two earth-shattering revelations in two days had pushed him to the brink. He collapsed on the bed, closed his eyes and focused on his breathing, forcing his pounding, pulsing brain to settle.

Finally, Leonard collected himself, got up off the bed and made his way into the kitchen. While not a drinker, he figured the situation demanded it. He reached up to the top cupboard in the kitchen and grabbed the only alcohol in his apartment, an unopened bottle of local Virginia Whiskey, and poured himself a stiff drink. He settled at the kitchen table and then devoured the article and every other detail he could find in the newspaper, then continued searching on his computer. He uncovered the story laid out in all its gory detail with every murder exactly as Leonard himself had planned it. First, The Junkie, then The Smoker, followed by The Blimp, The Gambler and finally The Cheater. Five gruesome deaths, all caused by his planning.

The realisation hit Leonard like a runaway train. He was an accessory to multiple murders.

Ryan had turned Leonard into a serial killer.

CHAPTER 46

'So, I guess this qualifies as our first date, doesn't it?' I said with a smile as Melissa climbed into my new-to-me but still old lime green Chevy Cavalier.

'Well, it is the first time we've gotten together for a reason other than the Addict Killer, but we can call it a date only if we say nothing about the case tonight. Let's see how we go, shall we?' replied Melissa.

We went to a great Italian restaurant down in Springfield and enjoyed some scrumptious pasta, delicious wine, and delightful conversation. Setting ourselves the challenge of not talking about the case was great for consciously talking about things other than the filth of what we were investigating. We talked for hours about Bobby and how he was doing, how my recovery was going, my Narcotics Anonymous meetings, how Melissa still missed her husband, and I missed Sally, my life before drug addiction, all manner of things. It was the most normal I had felt in a *really* long time, and it felt great.

We talked until the staff kicked us out and then I drove slowly all the way back to Melissa's, because I just didn't want the night to end. Finally, we arrived at her house and I walked her up the path to the front door.

'Goodnight Melissa, sleep well,' I said, jumping in first to neutralise any awkwardness about her asking me in. I knew that neither of us were ready to spend the night together and wanted to make that clear.

With a smile and a sigh of relief, Melissa responded, 'Goodnight Simon, and thank you for a *lovely* evening. I think we *can* call that our first date. The first of many, I hope.'

She looked up at me, inviting me with her eyes to kiss her goodnight, and I obliged. I leaned down, right in close to her until my lips were almost on hers, but not quite, and let her come the last step to move into me. This time, her lips parted, and her tongue searched into my mouth and across my lips in a burst of sweet sensation. I responded with a pressure of my own and my tongue explored hers, entwining together in a passionate kiss. I put my arms around her and drew her close. I could feel the whole length of her body against me, with her full breasts deliciously firm against my stomach.

Finally, we parted, both feeling like schoolkids on a date, the sexual tension high, but knowing that now was not the right time to take our passion any further.

'Well, cowboy, that was some goodnight kiss!' exclaimed Melissa in a breathless, husky tone. 'It's late, I'd better get inside to relieve the sitter and check on Bobby.'

'That sure was some kiss, Missy. You get on inside now, and I'll see you tomorrow,' I said in my best cowboy western drawl, and gave her a pat on the behind as she turned to the door and went inside.

Oh, man, I was really falling for this girl.

As I turned from the porch and looked out into the darkness beyond the bright light, a sudden dark feeling of dread came over me that something terrible was building. A shiver ran down my spine and I tried to shake off the feeling, but it still lingered as I walked down the path to my car.

Ryan felt superhuman. He was famous! The news breaking about the Addict Killer was such a rush. It was the icing on the cake of death he had carefully mixed and baked to perfection.

Seeing all the gruesome details come out in all their glory had allowed him to relive the killings all over again. The TV was blaring in the bar and he could see the newsreaders all talking about him, laying it all out for people in lounge rooms across the country watching in morbid fascination.

Ryan looked smugly around the bar at all the usual losers absorbed in their drinks, talking about "that psycho on the news". Ryan loved that he was right here among them, and they were clueless! They would absolutely shit themselves if they knew they were drinking with a serial killer right now. Ryan lapped it up, and it spurred him on, inspired him to add fuel to the fire and make another bold statement. It was time to work on his next theatre of violence.

Once again, Ryan put it out to the Universe, and it came back in spades. Immediately after the news, the latest episode of "Hoarders" started playing on the TV in the bar. Ryan suddenly recognised a street in DC; he knew the house! He'd been past it plenty of times. Instantly Ryan knew his next move. His excitement mounted even further as he felt the familiar urges return. It was time. Time for another display. The Addict Killer was on the move.

Ryan left the bar, jumped on his Harley and headed straight for The Hoarder's house. He couldn't believe his luck! Just a few moments ago he had been wishing for another victim and then one had flashed up on the TV right in front of him! Ryan knew he couldn't pass up this opportunity.

He eased the Harley to a stop a few homes down the street from the house that had featured so prominently on the TV. A bright full moon assisted the streetlamps and highlighted the dilapidated mess of a house; all peeling paint, junk in the front yard, busted windows and screen door hanging off the hinges. Walking up the path, Ryan snorted as he saw the newspapers covering the windows, the overgrown yard and the grime covering the place. A big black tomcat looked disdainfully at Ryan as he carefully stepped up onto the front porch, as if to say, 'Who the hell do you think you are, shit-for-brains? Get off my goddamn porch—this is MY house!' Ryan sneered at the cat and kicked out with his left boot to get the feline out of his way. The cat turned around, pointed its puckered asshole directly at Ryan and walked off slowly with a typically superior cat attitude.

'Fucking cats,' snarled Ryan as he peered in through a gap in the newspaper covering the window and got an excellent view of the front room by the light spill from the kitchen. The sight inside filled Ryan with disgust; there was rubbish everywhere! Crap was piled up from floor to ceiling, and he counted at least five cats just in that one room. He could see cat turds scattered all over the room—the place was a cesspit of filth.

Suddenly, a shadow appeared inside and Ryan huddled down further at his vantage point on the porch. A middle-aged man in a frayed old tartan flannel dressing gown walked down the hall and into the kitchen, holding a cat in each hand. He was naked under the dressing gown and his junk was poking out through the gap in front. The man put the cats on a kitchen bench littered with filthy dishes and piles of newspapers and knick-knacks. He poured a glass of milk, offered some to each of the cats, who drank their fill, then the man finished the remains.

Ryan shuddered in disgust. He was the one. Ryan knew he had found the next victim for the Addict Killer—the press would love this one, they would eat it up and his legend would grow.

The Hoarder would soon be in a whole different hell. A six feet long wooden box buried under six feet of dirt.

CHAPTER 48

'What!?' exploded Leonard in a rage as he opened Ryan's letter. 'The nerve of this guy! He's *actually* asking me to help him again, even after it's all come out! Well, not this time Ryan, I'm putting a stop to this.'

Leonard immediately took out his pen and started writing. 'Ryan, I know you're stupid, but even for you, this takes stupidity to a whole new level. You'd like me to *imagine* another punishment for you? Did you think I wouldn't find out? That I wouldn't know it was you who was killing those poor people? There are so many words for people of sub-standard intelligence—cretin, retard, imbecile, idiot, moron and more. But I think we need a whole new word to describe your stupidity. How about Retardiot? Seems appropriate. I can't believe you have the *audacity* to ask me for help again after the way you drew me into your insane scheme! You've made me an accessory to multiple murders and turned me into a serial killer, you bastard! There is no way I am ever "imagining" anything for you ever again. This is the last time I will ever write to you. You're on your own from now on. Keep me out of your mad plans. Goodbye.'

While Leonard was genuinely angry with Ryan and recognised the need for what he had written, it was with a touch of sadness and regret that Leonard posted his last letter to Ryan. Leonard understood that Ryan was the only friend he'd ever had. Now he would be on his own again, desperately alone.

'Ellen, I really don't know what to make of all this, I feel lost. What does it all mean?' pleaded Leonard from the psychiatrist's couch.

'Well, Leonard, this is certainly a great deal of information to process. You've just discovered something incredibly significant about yourself, along with a physical explanation for the mental and emotional challenges you've faced for most of your life,' replied Ellen.

'But how do I not remember the surgery? How can I not know what happened to me? Why didn't my mother tell me any of this?' wailed Leonard, the pitch of his voice rising with every question as the frustration and anger built up inside him.

'Calm down Leonard, it's only natural that you feel conflicted about this and will have questions. We just need to work through them together.'

'Okay, okay, I'm calm. Let's talk. Give me your best shot, I'm all ears,' said Leonard in the sarcastic tone that he used so often it had become part of his normal speech pattern.

Ellen paused and sighed quietly at the prickly nature of her patient, gathered herself and continued, 'Well, you were young when you had your surgery, only just finished Elementary School. Your mother, who was the only adult of influence in your life, lied to you about the surgery and didn't provide you with any medical follow-ups. You had no friends to talk to and no other family. Plus, the trauma to your brain because of the surgery severely affected your social interactions, your motor skills, your memory, your very identity. The surgery transformed you. One day you were little boy Leonard, the next day you were… different. And to top it off, you changed from Elementary School to High School, your mother was a raging alcoholic and an extremely unreliable sole parent who died just a few years after your surgery. Then, you were pushed from pillar to post around several foster homes, and it was all you could do to just focus on survival. To be frank, I'm amazed that you could navigate your way through all that and function as a human being at all.'

'Hm… yes, I guess you have a point. When you lay it all out like that, it makes some kind of warped sense. So, what do I do with this information now that I have it?' asked Leonard.

'Follow the research, absorb the data and process the findings. That's what you do, and you do it well,' responded Ellen. 'And don't limit yourself just to the medical findings of other people, apply it to yourself. Look into yourself, how you deal with situations. Having the awareness of what's missing is the first step to creating your complete self. Reach out to others, people who also have Split Brain Syndrome. Communicate with them, talk to them, share your experiences. I'm sure you will find commonality in the challenges you face integrating with so-called "normal" society, whatever *that* means.'

'You're actually making sense today, Ellen. Less psychobabble, more physical science. I like it,' said Leonard, without a hint of irony in his voice.

'You're too kind, Leonard, as always,' said Ellen with a smirk. Somehow, something had happened that was making her warm to Leonard. Perhaps it was the knowledge there was a physical contributor to Leonard being such a superior asshole.

CHAPTER 50

'Well, fuck you, Leonard,' said Ryan as he held the letter out in front of him and stabbed his middle finger up in the air with a vigorous thrust.

Ryan put Leonard's final letter down on the table in his studio. He was angry, steaming at Leonard's insulting response and pissed off that his strategic planner had taken himself out of the game. Ryan was on his own, but that was fine. After all, he'd been the one to pull the trigger on the murders. He was the one who had the balls to kill the addicts, who so deserved their fate.

Ryan decided on impulse to do his next deed immediately. He would do it freestyle, with no planning. He flew out of his studio in a rage and rode through the darkness straight over to The Hoarder's house. Again, he parked his bike a few houses down the street and walked the last few steps to the kill zone. He walked stealthily around the back of the house, made his way up to the back door and looked through a gap in the newspaper lining the glass. The kitchen was lit up, with cats roaming around on the hunt for food to eat or places to shit.

Ryan checked himself and realised how unprepared he was this time. He reached into his pockets and noted that all he had was his switchblade and knuckledusters. He had no other supplies with him. Thankfully, he was at least wearing his trusty black gloves.

It would be full-on, seat-of-the-pants stuff this time. The exhilaration of the unknown fired him up even more; he had never killed without a plan, he would just make it up as he went along, going with the flow and being in the moment.

He took the switchblade out of his pocket, pressed the trigger and watched, fascinated as always, at the evil-looking blade that flicked out of the handle. He held the knife up to his eyes and drank in the moonlight reflected off the shiny steel blade. Then he jammed the tip of the hard steel in between the soft timber of the rotten back door and the frame and jimmied the lock with a quick flick of his wrist.

As he opened the back door and crept into the kitchen, he could hear a TV down the hallway. One of the seven cats in the room looked up at him, curled its lips back and bared its teeth, then looked away. All the other cats ignored him completely. 'No wonder normal people prefer dogs over cats,' whispered Ryan, as he made his way across the kitchen floor.

The smell in the place was unbelievable, a foul assault on the senses. 'The so-called *intervention* on that crappy Hoarders TV show obviously didn't work,' thought Ryan grimly. The stench got worse as he walked through the house, further away from the fresh outside air that had crept in the back door into the kitchen. Ryan's nostrils flared, and his eyes started watering as the combined odour of stale cat piss and shit, rancid food and rotting rubbish united into an almighty stink.

The signs of hoarding he had seen outside were nothing compared to the inside, with collections of all kinds of assorted junk imaginable in every room. From boxes of new, unopened appliances to various items that looked like they'd come from junk piles or yard sales, to stacks of newspapers and magazines, and then to plain old bags of garbage. As he picked his way through the chaos, the walls were closing in on Ryan and he felt like the mess would engulf him.

Down the hallway he went, following the noise of the TV to the bedroom. Ryan peered around the edge of the door frame and instantly burst out laughing hysterically at the scene that welcomed him. The Hoarder was on a single bed in the corner, naked, laying on his back and holding a life-sized, fully realistic, inflatable sex doll straddled on top of him, pumping it up and down as he screwed the rubber vagina. Surrounding the bed was more crap, including stacks of rubbish six feet high that looked like they would topple over at any moment.

Shocked and confused at the invasion, the man leapt off the bed, his cock still in the doll, grabbed a book from beside the bed and threw it across the room. Ryan started laughing even harder at the sight of this middle-aged, pot-bellied, balding, naked man standing among a pile of crap with a blonde sex doll impaled on his erection. The Hoarder looked down at himself and in some attempt at dignity, removed the doll from his junk, grabbed his dressing gown and tied it around him.

'What the FUCK are you doing in my house?' screamed The Hoarder. 'Get out! I'm calling the cops right now!'

'Settle down, Pops. You're not going anywhere and you're not making any fucking phone calls,' said Ryan in a calm, menacing tone as he waved his switchblade back and forth in front of him.

The Hoarder looked back at Ryan, transfixed, as his eyes followed the knife's path back and forth, head moving from side to side. He sagged back down onto the bed and said, 'What do you want? You won't rob me, will you? Steal my stuff?'

'HA! You must be joking. Your stuff? Who the hell would want any of this crap? That's exactly your problem right there, man. You're a hoarder, an addict. You're addicted to stuff, but it's all shit, it's worthless! What I *want* is to teach you a lesson. A lesson about addiction. Lay back on the bed. And turn off that goddamn shit on the TV.'

The Hoarder stayed still, so Ryan stepped closer, sensing the man was about to make a move. On high alert, Ryan continued forth and then noticed the telltale signs of the sudden tightening of the leg muscles and stiffening of the shoulders as the man prepared to launch himself off the bed. Ryan was ready and neatly manoeuvred away from the man's flailing fist and then stepped in with a crushing left hook to the man's right eye. The combined momentum of the charging body meeting the hardened brass of knuckledusters crushed the man's cheekbone and fractured his eye socket, splashing a crimson spray of blood all over his face and back onto Ryan.

The Hoarder went down like the proverbial sack of potatoes, unconscious before he hit the floor. Ryan knelt, dragged the body across the floor and then heaved it back up on the bed. He removed the dressing gown, exposing the man in full nakedness. Then he retrieved the sex doll from across the room and laid her face down on The Hoarder's groin, mouth on cock. He cut some electrical cord from appliances scattered around the bedroom and quickly tied him to the bed. Then he turned off the TV and waited calmly in the silence.

A few minutes passed and then the bound man slowly started coming around. He groaned as he left the bliss of unconsciousness and into his awareness blasted the pain of his demolished face. His right eye was a bloody mess, so he could only see out of his good left eye. Suddenly he noticed the bindings on his hands and feet and started thrashing around on the bed.

'Tsk, tsk, tsk,' admonished Ryan as he waved the knife and pressed the blade hard down on the man's distended, bloated gut. 'You'll disturb blondie, she's hard at work down there.'

The Hoarder's left eye opened wide, and he yelled, 'You fucking psycho! What do you want from me? Why are you doing this to me?'

Fear had given way to panic as The Hoarder realised this would not end well.

'Why won't you listen, dickhead? Like I said before, you've got a serious problem, an addiction that needs treatment. That Hoarders episode sure didn't do you any good, did it? Your poor daughter on there, trying to get you help. You fighting with the production people, abusing the cameramen, upsetting your poor daughter. This filth you have created is a stain on humanity that needs to be removed.'

Ryan paused, looked around the room and said, 'Sorry about this.

Normally, I'm more organised. Usually I have a plan for my victims, but because my so-called *partner* grew a goddamn conscience, I'm freestyling tonight. I need to send a message about addiction to all your fellow hoarders out there, about how having all this stuff really is not good for you.'

As he scanned the room, Ryan spotted a kit of magic tricks, still in a box in the corner. He pointed and said, 'Hey, what's that? Where and when did you get that stuff and why?'

The Hoarder looked at Ryan, dumbfounded about why on Earth he was being asked these questions and replied, 'I dunno. I bought it from a yard sale, maybe about four years ago. I can't say why I bought it; I just knew I had to have it.'

'You don't look like no magician to me. You bought it and just left it sitting in the corner of your bedroom for the next four years? Seems like a bit of a waste, don't you think? Let's open it and have a look,' said Ryan as he walked over to the corner of the room, grabbed the box and tore it open.

'*Ooh*, now I get it, I can see why you bought this stuff, it just looks so *useful*, I can't *possibly* imagine my life without these two magic wands and four juggling balls!' said Ryan in a jeeringly sarcastic tone, full of insult.

Ryan moved over to The Hoarder, holding the two hard plastic magic wands, leaned down and then violently jammed them hard up into the nostrils of The Hoarder. Ryan felt the wands smash through the cartilage and then jam against the nasal bone, filling the nasal cavity.

The Hoarder cried out in pain and began whimpering like a small child. Tears streamed out of his good eye and a fresh wad of blood burst forth from his pulverised right cheek and eye socket at this fresh surge of force.

With his nasal airway blocked and panic now turning to terror, The Hoarder was breathing hard through his mouth, blowing out every breath and sucking for air. Ryan waited, checked the breath timing and then on the next big gasp, he grabbed the man's chin, forced it wide open and jammed all four of the rubber juggling balls deep into his mouth.

The wretched man was writhing on the bed, throat gagging and chest heaving as the diaphragm and lungs struggled against the airway blockages. The lizard brain kicked in, doing its best to drive the body to survive, but it was no use to The Hoarder. There was simply no way for air to make it in to keep him alive. The remaining oxygen in the body faded fast because of all the activity; the writhing and struggling slowly eased and consciousness faded away. Soon, death came to The Hoarder.

Ryan felt something of an anti-climax. While he had enjoyed the quick thrill of the kill, he felt it was missing the lead-up, the planning and strategizing that was so much a part of the process for him when Leonard did the planning. Ryan decided he needed more effects and some scene staging. So, he chose the nearest tall stack of trash and pushed the pile over onto The Hoarder, partially covering the upper part of the body. Then he continued on and on, piling more and more junk on top of his victim. Finally, he surveyed the scene with a nod and a smile—over the upper half of the body he had amassed a pile of junk reaching almost to the ceiling, cascading over the side of the bed and down to the floor, encasing half the body in a sarcophagus of crap.

The Hoarder's naked groin and legs were sticking out from under the pile, with a rubber sex doll face down between his legs, complete with the voluptuous curves of a generous ass in full view. Satisfied with the scene, Ryan smiled at his creation, then turned and went down to the kitchen. As he walked past a stack of blank envelopes piled in the corner, Ryan had an idea to get back at the so-called partner who had completely deserted him at the first sign of trouble.

'What did you call me, Leonard? Retardiot? Let's see how you like this, you prick,' said Ryan as he grabbed a pen and wrote Leonard's name and post office box address on the envelope, then crumpled it up and dropped it just outside the back door as if it had fallen out of his pocket.

Still on his own and freestyling, Ryan looked around the kitchen, trying to work out his next step when he struck gold. On The Hoarder's fridge was the phone number of the man's daughter and the producer of the Hoarders TV show! Given Ryan's sudden fame and The Hoarder's past TV appearance, Ryan wanted to make a bigger statement with this kill. He picked up the house phone and carefully held it away from his ear and mouth so as not to catch some horrible disease, then called both the daughter and the TV producer, telling them they should come right away. He also instructed the producer to bring a camera. He then returned to the bedroom, opened the curtains and removed a section of newspaper lining from the window.

Ryan then left the bedroom, unlocked the front door and then went out the back to wait outside the bedroom window, building with expectation and anticipation. In perfectly synchronous timing, the TV producer turned up first and then a minute later the man's daughter arrived.

'Hey Mimi, what the hell are you doing here?' asked The Hoarder's daughter.

'Hi Brandy, I got a random call from some guy, who said I had to get down here right away,' responded the TV producer.

'That's weird. Me too,' replied Brandy.

'What now? Should we go in?' asked Mimi.

'I guess so,' said Brandy and rapped her knuckles on the faded front door. After waiting a moment with no response, she reached out, turned the door handle, opened the door wide and looked in. 'Jesus Christ! Nothing's changed in here, obviously. So much for the help from your show, Mimi.'

'I'm sorry, what can I say? Some we can help, but others are too far gone,' replied Mimi. As Brandy turned and walked inside, Mimi checked that her lapel video camera was recording okay, then followed her in.

As they walked into the chaos and stench of the front living room,

Brandy said, 'Eww! Yuk! It is *so* disgusting in here. I can't believe I used to live in this shit hole! Dad? Dad! Where are you?' she called out.

With no answers coming, Brandy walked down the hallway to the bedroom with Mimi following right up close behind her, then she paused for a breath and turned and investigated the bedroom.

'Fuck! Dad! Are you serious? What the hell is it *this time*?' shouted Brandy. Mimi caught the full glory of the scene as she entered the room; Brandy's reaction, the bottom half of a body protruding from beneath a pile of hoarder's trash on the bed, a big-ass sex doll face down on the man's groin. Mimi scanned the room, capturing both audio and video.

'Brandy? Are you okay? Is that your Dad? How do you feel about all this?' asked Mimi.

'Honestly, right now Mimi, all I can feel is relief. Relief that this is all over and I can get on with my life,' she replied, full of sadness at what her father had become and how his life had ended.

Tonight was just full of anti-climaxes for Ryan. There was no grief from the daughter for him to get his rocks off. He watched the whole thing with a quiet detachment, unexcited. But he knew that with the TV producer there, the attention would come, and that would have to do. He snuck away out of the yard before the cops turned up, walked to his machine and then took off down the street in a hail of noise.

CHAPTER 51

'The Three Amigos, back together again on another early morning before dawn,' I said as I arrived at the murder scene and met up with Melissa and Delaney. 'What fun.'

'I think shooting up all that heroin has given you a warped idea of what fun is, Winter. It ain't no picnic in there, I can tell you. Looks like our boy again, the AK. I see you got yourself some wheels, finally,' he said with a nod at my Cavalier.

'Yes, I graduated to a grown-up set of wheels, finally,' I replied. 'Hi Melissa,' I said with a smile as a flush of warmth came over me.

'Hi Simon, good to see you again,' said Melissa with a warm smile of her own.

Delaney was no fool and spotted the interaction immediately, giving us both a sharp look. 'No distractions, you two. Keep your eyes and ears and attention focused on this case, not on each other. Clear?'

'Yes, boss. Clear,' I said with a mock salute back to him.

'Jesus, Winter, I'm missing the good old days when you weren't such a wiseass,' he replied. 'Let's give you two a look-see.'

We traipsed inside through the mess, filth and stink as we chased the cats out of the house and cleared a path through the clutter. We inspected right through the bedroom and the rest of the house, analysing and absorbing everything we could, including the sex doll on the bed with the victim. Once finished, we sent in the techs in the white coats to undertake the laborious task of carefully sifting through all the junk piled on top of the victim, noting any important evidence along the way.

I decided to look around outside. If this really was our guy, part of his kill routine was to observe the aftermath. We knew he had called the victim's daughter, which was consistent with the previous crimes, indicating he would have lain in wait somewhere outside. I grabbed a torch and Melissa and I went to check out the back of the house. We stopped at the back door and I shone the light down and around on the deck just outside the door. A flash of white caught the light, and I knelt for a look. It was an envelope with a name and postal address on it!

'Can you hold an evidence bag out for me, please Melissa?' I said and picked up the envelope with my tweezers and dropped it in the bag. We would study that carefully.

We continued our inspection around back, careful not to disturb any footprints, and noted signs of activity around the back window of the bedroom outside where the victim had died.

Back inside, the techs were just about finished. They'd found nothing of note that looked worthy of bagging for evidence but were now getting closer to the body. We joined in as observers, making sure we disturbed nothing vital. As they removed the last edition of the all-important series of 2004 Cosmopolitan magazines, we finally got our first good look at the body. What a mess! The right side of the man's face was swollen and smashed, he had a magician's wand jammed up each nostril and what looked like rubber balls rammed in his mouth. It looked like he'd been severely beaten and then suffocated by magic.

Except this trick didn't end with the assistant springing back to life to everyone's surprise and delight.

'I think I saw an empty box before that had magician tricks in it. There it is, over in the corner. Can you guys grab that and bag it, please?' I said to the techs.

Melissa continued the examination of the body and said, 'The M.O. seems to be a fit with the addict angle and the phone call and the killer hanging around outside to see the aftermath, plus the witnesses heard a motorbike leave the scene. But the nature of the kill seems different. It's more random, less planning, less thought to the staging. It seems almost compulsive and not well thought-out.'

'I agree, Melissa, it seems different. Not so well planned,' I replied. 'Unlike the other crime scenes, the killer didn't appear to bring any props or anything with him, there was no effort to the staging. He just used whatever he could find lying around, almost like he was making it up as he went along. Do you think this might be a copycat killing?'

Delaney said, 'Let's let these guys finish processing the body and get all this stuff back to the lab. We'll reconvene at the station this morning to go over this some more. You two lovebirds can go get yourself some breakfast.'

'Thanks, Boss. Sounds like a plan. The International House of Pancakes is calling to me,' I said, with a cheerful smile at Melissa.

Delaney shook his head and lumbered off to his squad car.

CHAPTER 52

The media storm broke about ten in the morning. We'd been at the station for a few hours running the evidence when a beat cop yelled to turn on the news. And there it was. The Hoarder murder scene in all its gory detail was plastered over the TV screen. Complete with the rubbish pile and sex doll going down on The Hoarder. It was a goddamn circus!

'Jesus Christ!' exploded Delaney. 'Where the FUCK did that come from?'

'Mimi must have been wearing a hidden camera!' I exclaimed.

'Find her. And get her back in here. Right now! And charge her with obstruction of justice. Goddamn media think they can run the world!' shouted Delaney as he slammed his office door in fury.

Melissa and I watched the whole recording play out on the TV, amazed at the gall of the producer to put that out to the world illegally, without even telling us about it or showing it to us. She would have made a pretty penny, selling something as dramatic as that to the media outlets on a story so white-hot as the Addict Killer.

Just as the video neared the end, Melissa and I both heard it—the big motorbike tearing off down the street. 'We have to get the original of that video!' said Melissa. 'We can analyse that sound and we might even get a glimpse of the killer watching in through the window.'

The boys in blue first went to Mimi's house and then her workplace with no luck, but quickly found her holed up at her parent's place. She wandered sheepishly into the station, escorted by two uniformed cops, who immediately put her in an interview room.

'Mimi, what the hell were you thinking? You know what you did is illegal and has caused a major disruption to our investigation. Why didn't you tell us about the video?' asked Delaney.

'I'm sorry, I'm sorry. I was desperate for money; I can't pay my bills and my student loans are killing me. I saw an opportunity to make a quick buck selling the video, and I took it. I'm so sorry, I didn't think it would go *this* crazy!'

'Seriously? The biggest case in the country featuring a serial murderer who sets up a sex doll giving his victim a blow job and you think *that* story won't take off? Every press outlet in the country is running it, and the public is eating it up! It's a goddamn feeding frenzy out there. And my ass is swinging in the breeze because I'm the poor sap that has to catch this psycho!' yelled Delaney. 'They'll charge you with obstruction of justice and you *will* suffer the consequences. Hand over the original video to us and we just might not throw the book at you.'

'Yes, yes, of course, you can have the video. It's right here, I've got it with me,' replied Mimi in a panic and handed over a portable hard drive.

'Fine. I'll give it to the techs so they can start processing it. You come with me to the charge counter,' said Delaney, and disappeared in a huff out of the interview room. Melissa and I went back out to the main Stationhouse and returned to working the evidence.

While the video was being processed, the key piece of evidence we were working on was the envelope that was addressed to a Leonard Price with a post office box number. We ran the post box down with the US Postal Service and got a hit, with a clean name that matched the envelope, along with a residential address.

Melissa and I got straight into her car and checked out the address. It was an actual building, with an actual apartment and the name Leonard Price on the buzzer. We tried it but there was no answer, which since it was a workday was hardly surprising. We talked to the building manager and asked about Leonard, and he said Leonard was at work, because he had seen him leave that morning. But he added that Leonard got home at precisely 5:40 p.m. every evening like clockwork, because he was a 'real stickler for time, kind of a squirrelly dude'. After our successful scoping mission, we agreed to return that evening to meet Leonard in person.

Back at the Stationhouse, one of the techs set up the original video. We settled down and watched it again, this time in a quiet room where we could pay proper attention to all the details. 'Look! There, at the window,' exclaimed Melissa. 'Is that an outline of a head? Freeze the image and zoom in, let's see if we can get a look at AK.'

We had reached a point in the video where Mimi had been looking around the room, making sure she got everything in shot, and her field of view had passed across the bedroom window. There was someone outside peering in through a gap in the newspaper stuck to the window. But the light inside was too bright and outside too dark. All we could see was a dark outline, with no identification possible.

We continued through the video and saw the shape outside disappear soon after Brandy and Mimi discovered the body, then a minute later heard the barking exhaust of a loud motorbike. We needed someone who knew about bikes, so we called the captain of the police motorbike unit and asked him to come down and have a listen. He came in just a few minutes later, listened intently to the recording and picked it as an old Harley. He couldn't give any more detail than that, and so directed us to his head mechanic, who he said was a "real bike nut".

The head motorbike mechanic really knew his stuff; we played him the recording, and he immediately identified it as a late 1970s Harley Davidson running the "famous twelve hundred C.C. shovelhead engine" (whatever that meant). When I asked him if someone put a gun to his head and forced him to guess a specific model, he said he would probably pick the FXS Low Rider, the first of Harley's "factory customs".

Today's investigations had really given us some solid evidence to work on. The killer's decision to invite a video camera to the scene was a genuine error in judgement. The more we looked at this, the more we realised that while there was a similar theme, this latest murder was quite different to the previous five scenes.

As the afternoon faded, it was time for us to meet our hot lead, Leonard. Melissa and I arrived at his apartment at 5:30 p.m. and asked the building manager to identify Leonard for us when he came in. Sure enough, right on schedule at 5:40 p.m., a man walked in the front door of the apartment building and our contact gave us a nod. We followed Leonard at a slight distance all the way to his front door. As he was getting his keys out of his bag, we walked right up behind him and Melissa said, 'Excuse me, Mister Price. I'm Special Agent Melissa Munro from the FBI and this is my deputy, Simon Winter.'

Melissa flashed her badge at Leonard, who peered at it intently without saying a word, then looked up at her and with a sideways nod of his head in my direction said in a sarcastic tone, 'Where's his badge?'

Melissa replied, 'Like I said, Mister Winter is my deputy assisting me with the investigation. He doesn't have a badge.'

'Fine. What can I do for you?' asked Leonard, then added, 'And by the way, it's *Doctor* Price.'

'Perhaps if we could come in, then we could discuss it more comfortably rather than out in the hall, Sir,' replied Melissa in a tone of a statement rather than a question.

Leonard considered his options for a few seconds and then shrugged his shoulders and said, 'Suit yourself,' then turned around, opened the door and led us inside.

The apartment was sparse. Neat and tidy. The furnishings were drab and plain, with not a splash of colour in the place. There was no artwork or photos on any of the walls. The only visible decoration in the apartment was an Albert Einstein quote:

Pure mathematics is, in its way, the poetry of logical ideas.

The apartment was depressingly beige and thoroughly uninteresting.

Leonard was tall, but moved lightly, precisely and deliberately, like he was trying not to make an impact on the world around him and just blend into the background. He looked bookish and nerdy, carried a gunmetal briefcase and had a pocket protector complete with a small calculator and a black pen, a blue pen, and a red pen peering out of his shirt pocket. He slowly and deliberately sat down on a simple timber chair at the small kitchen table. His knees were out straight in front of him and he placed each of his hands palms down on top of his knees, perfectly aligned with each other and fingers neatly arranged in precise lines.

'Please, have a seat,' said Leonard in a quiet, clipped and controlled monotone. No question Leonard was an interesting cat, but certainly not looking like the Addict Killer based on these first few minutes of interaction.

A weird silence hung in the air for a full minute as all three of us sat there, looking across the table at each other. Leonard appeared calm, staring across at us without blinking, waiting for us to speak. It was like a game of cat-and-mouse, where whoever speaks first loses. In the end, it was Melissa who broke the silence.

'Leonard. May I call you Leonard?' she asked. Leonard gave a slight, almost imperceptible nod as his only response, so Melissa continued. 'The FBI is working closely with the DC police helping them out on a case. I assume you've seen the recent news about the Addict Killer?' Another tiny nod was Leonard's only response. I felt like we were under a microscope, like there was some supercomputer inside Leonard's head that was busily collecting data, processing, analysing, projecting. But the interface was giving nothing away.

Melissa continued, 'Then you would be aware of the most recent victim, which the media have dubbed The Hoarder?' This time, there was a noncommittal shrug of the shoulders in response.

Melissa decided she needed to ask a question that would prompt a verbal reaction, so she said, 'Where were you last night, Leonard?'

To this question there was finally a hint of a response from Leonard, a slight narrowing of the eyes and movement of the shoulders. He considered his response for a second and then replied, 'And may I ask what possible relevance my whereabouts last night has to do with anything concerning the FBI, the DC police, or the Addict Killer investigation?'

'The *relevance* of your whereabouts, Leonard, is that we found your name and postal address at the crime scene last night, written on a crumpled envelope and dropped outside the house,' replied Melissa in a sharp tone.

'Was there a stamp on this envelope?' asked Leonard immediately.

Taken aback by this entirely unexpected question, Melissa looked puzzled and said, 'Well, actually, no, there was no stamp on the envelope. Why do you ask?'

'Why on Earth would I have an envelope with my name and address on it unless someone had sent it to me? In which case it would have had a stamp on it. And if I were clever enough to have killed half a dozen people right under your noses without getting caught, do you think I would be stupid enough to leave my information at the crime scene?'

'Well, how do you explain the envelope being there?' asked Melissa.

'Well, I do believe that's *your* job to find out, Ms. Munro. I really can't fathom what it was doing there, other than to suggest that perhaps it's the actual killer trying to distract you with pointless, time-consuming activity that keeps your attention away from him or her. Maybe the killer knows me, maybe it's someone from my workplace. Hundreds of people know my name and that my post office box is in the building where I work, so someone could easily have followed me there, observed me collecting my mail and got my box number. I'm surrounded by cretins and am not particularly well-liked by my co-workers, so any one of them could have decided it would be amusing to put some "heat", I believe is the correct slang expression, on to me.'

'Well, that's an interesting theory, Leonard. You came up with that quickly,' said Melissa.

A slight curling of the lip and a raised right eyebrow accompanied Leonard's response, dripping with sarcasm, 'Ms. Munro, you seem to suggest that the speed of my well-reasoned response is somehow caused by me having developed a plausible theory in advance to explain your circumstantial evidence. However, the fact is that I have a genius I.Q., am a leading member of Mensa and received a Ph.D. in Applied Mathematics & Statistics from Johns Hopkins in record time. My intellect is vastly superior to the morons with whom you would be accustomed to dealing, so I can understand that my powers of observation, reasoning, and deduction might lead you to assume some guilt on my part. But the fact is, I was home fast asleep in bed last night and I had nothing whatsoever to do with your so-called Hoarder killing.'

Man, this guy was sharp. Not to mention a real asshole. I could see Melissa was fuming at Leonard's superior attitude and didn't have an immediate comeback, so I stepped in to break it up a bit and said, 'Since you claim you have nothing at all to do with these killings, I assume you would be happy to provide us with a sample of your handwriting?'

'Not that I have any obligation to do so, but in the interests of us all moving on with our lives, certainly,' he replied. He pulled out a notepad, picked up a pen in his right hand, wrote a brief sentence, folded the paper and handed it over.

'Thank you for that, Leonard. One last question; do you ride a motorbike?' I asked.

'A motorbike? Certainly not! I drive a Toyota Prius. I've never ridden a motorbike in my life. They are interminable machines, loud and exceedingly dangerous. I'm an insurance actuary. I spend my days analysing the probabilities of injury and death. So, there is no way you would ever catch me on a motorcycle. Check with the Department of Motor Vehicles, you'll see I only own one vehicle.'

'Thank you for your assistance, Leonard. We'll be in touch if we have any more questions,' I said. We got up and walked towards the front door of the apartment.

'I can't say it was a pleasure. Good luck with your investigation,' said Leonard as he ushered us out and closed the door firmly behind us.

As we walked away down the corridor, Melissa and I looked at each other and shrugged our shoulders in unison. 'Man, that guy is such an asshole!' she said.

'I agree. But it seems highly unlikely he's the Addict Killer.'

CHAPTER 53

Ryan was already stalking again, but this time it was personal. It had taken some time to go through all Leonard's letters, but Ryan had finally found the name of Leonard's therapist and the street where her rooms were, which Leonard had written in one of his letters when he was whining like a girly little bitch about all his "problems".

The Hoarder killing hadn't satisfied Ryan's bloodlust. He now understood that a big part of the thrill was the strategy, the build-up, the staging, and the satisfying resolution of a grand plan. Without Leonard's brilliance to help him, Ryan was just another dumb, brutal killer operating on impulse. Ryan wanted more than that, wanted admiration for the sense of theatre that he brought to his kills. Waking that night to the media storm that had hit after The Hoarder killing had been a thrill, but Ryan wanted more. He wanted to punish Leonard for leaving him, and for insulting him so deeply. Ryan had a hole deep inside that he needed to fill with violence.

Leonard hadn't included the street number of the psychiatrist's office in his letter, so Ryan had to search up and down the street for a half-hour until he found it. It was well into the night, but the light inside was still on; like someone was working very late. Ryan approached the window and peered in. He saw a woman who looked to be in her late thirties, not unattractive, sitting at a desk with a bunch of papers next to her, tapping away intently on a keyboard. Ryan hadn't a clue what Ellen looked like, but it seemed likely that it was she. After a few minutes, the woman reached down into the bottom drawer of the desk and pulled out a half-empty bottle of whiskey and poured herself a generous half glass, straight up, and necked it in two quick gulps. 'Interesting,' muttered Ryan to himself.

After about thirty minutes and three more half-glasses of straight whiskey that almost polished off the bottle, the woman got up from her desk, wobbled on her feet, then put on her jacket. She killed the lights and left out the front door, locking it behind her, then crossed the road and stumbled down the street. Curious, Ryan followed her quietly on foot. After just a few minutes' walk, the woman turned into a bar. 'Even more interesting,' muttered Ryan.

He quickly followed her in, wanting to see the greeting from the staff to see if she was a regular. 'Hi, Ellen!' came the cheery call from the barmaid. 'How lucky are we? Four nights in a row! Great to see you babe, how are you?'

'Hi, Jude,' came Ellen's tired reply. 'I'm beat. It's Friday, the end of another tough week. Set me up with a nightcap, will you? The usual. Times three.'

Things were clicking into place as Ryan observed the woman's entry. Yes—this was Ellen, Leonard's therapist. And if she was such a regular in this bar so close to her work and was slugging down straight whiskey like lemonade, then she had some serious drinking credentials. 'Hm,' thought Ryan, 'out of all the addicts, I haven't even bagged the biggest one of all, The Drunk. It could be time to change that, and I can really fuck Leonard over in the process.'

Ryan took a seat at the bar and observed his target, watching silently. In the space of twenty minutes, she downed three double whiskeys and was clearly feeling the effects. It was time to make his move.

Ryan called the barmaid over and bought a whiskey double for Ellen. She took it over and said, 'Hey Ellen, it looks like you have a young admirer over there. He's kind of cute, don't you think? He bought you a drink, sweetie.'

Ellen looked up from where she'd been gazing down at the bar, grabbed the drink and drained it in one hit. She looked at Ryan with glazed eyes and said, 'Well, thank you, kind Sir. To what do I owe that honour?'

'You looked like you could do with another drink, and I felt like I could do with some company. Not much of a stretch, really,' responded Ryan.

'Come on over here boy, come talk to me. I might even let you buy me another drink.'

Ryan sauntered over to Ellen and sat down next to her at the bar. She leaned back, shook her head and squinted her eyes to get clarity through the booze. With a puzzled look on her face she said, 'Do I know you? You look *really* familiar.'

'No, we've never met. I know I'd remember meeting someone as gorgeous as you, honey,' replied Ryan, heavy on the charm.

'Whatever. No matter,' said Ellen with a shrug and a pause, then fixed him with a stare and continued, 'And thank you for the compliment, by the way, I'm not too drunk to miss that one. So, what's your name, sugar?'

'I'm Ryan. Pleased to meet you,' he replied.

'Likewise. I'm Ellen,' she said, and thrust out an unsteady hand, which Ryan gently picked up and brought to his lips and planted a soft kiss on her fingers. Ellen raised her eyebrows in surprise and said, 'Smooth, laddie. Very smooth.'

Ryan gave her his most charming smile and let out a dry, gentle chuckle and kept hold of her hand. 'They seem to know you well in here. Are you a regular?' he asked.

'Oh, I come and go, now and then. My office is just down the block,' she replied.

'I like a woman who enjoys a good drink. Looks like you can put it away pretty good.'

Now it was Ellen's turn to laugh. 'Plenty of practice, my friend. Plenty of practice. I've looked at the bottom of many an empty bottle of whiskey and I'm not ashamed to admit it. I'm what they call a high-functioning alcoholic. And right now, I'm too bombed to care what anybody thinks of that.'

'Has it always been like that for you? Or is this a talent you've gained recently?' asked Ryan.

'I've only been perfecting my drinking craft for around the last ten years. Before that, I was sober as a judge.'

'What happened?' prodded Ryan.

'In another life I had a loving husband and a beautiful young daughter. But one of my patients, a very disturbed young girl, killed them both. She took away that life and left me… like this,' said Ellen as she raised her empty glass. 'Okay, that's enough of that. Let's you and I get drunk, pretty boy.'

'Sounds like a plan,' replied Ryan, and ordered four doubles.

The drinks and chatting continued until closing, by which time they were both well and truly plastered. As the barmaid called last drinks, Ryan leaned in close to Ellen, reached out and drew her into him, kissing her firmly on the mouth. He found Ellen to be a willing partner. After a long, passionate kiss, Ryan said, 'Let's get out of here. My art studio's not far.'

'Art studio? Fancy! So, you're going to show me your *etchings*, I'll bet. You got it buddy, let's go,' drawled Ellen as she pointed her finger to the door. They staggered out of the bar, holding each other up as they went out onto the footpath.

'My Harley's just up here, a short walk up the block,' said Ryan, 'You can jump on the back and hold on to me if you're game.'

'Fine by me,' said Ellen. 'Sometimes I feel like I'm just counting down the days until the end, anyway. Who cares if we lose it?'

'My kind of girl. Let's go,' said Ryan, exceedingly happy with how this was all working out.

After their short walk, Ryan helped Ellen on to the back of his bike and then swung his leg over the seat, hit the starter and gunned the engine into life with a fearful racket. He loved the noise and the vibrations of his big bike and the throbbing power between his legs. Ellen put her arms around him and hugged him tight.

They tore off down the street, laying rubber as they went. The wind whipped them in the face and hair, with no helmets to constrain them. Ryan handled the bike expertly, even in his drunk state. They flew at speed down the quiet, dark streets all the way to his studio, with Ellen initially clutching on for dear life and then slowly releasing until by the end she literally had her hands out full stretch to either side, only hanging on to Ryan with the pressure of her thighs. She hadn't felt so free in an awfully long time. She'd gone home drunk with plenty of guys before, but this felt different. Clearly, Ryan was a bad-boy, and she felt a sense of danger with him, like anything could happen at any moment.

Ryan retrieved his keys from their hiding place behind the studio, unlocked the big door and then rode all the way inside and parked his bike in the lounge room, over an oil pan. Still on the bike, Ellen looked around, fascinated at all the artwork and supplies, with easels and paint everywhere. 'So, you really are an artist?' she said. 'I thought you were just bullshitting to impress me.'

'Yep. Sure am,' replied Ryan.

'Does that mean you can paint me naked?' cooed Ellen.

Ryan got off the bike, turned to Ellen, put his powerful hands under her body and lifted her easily off the seat, then kissed her longingly and said, 'I can, and I will. But later.'

He carried her over to the enormous, comfy couch and laid her down, full stretch. He kissed her forehead, then her eyelids, then her nose, her cheeks, lips, and chin, then moved down to her neck. He worked his way down her body, undressing her as he went and kissing her sensitive, naked flesh along the way, until he finished at her toes. He looked back up at her naked body reclining languorously on the couch, absorbed in the moment and ready for him, with an arching back and rising pelvis.

'Come on pretty boy, time to get naked. Let me look at you,' she said.

Ryan stood up to his full height and stripped off completely in just a few seconds. His firm erection stood to attention and Ellen reached out and grabbed it and pulled him to her mouth. Slowly she worked on him, taking him deeper and deeper into her mouth until Ryan was groaning in ecstasy and Ellen was panting with anticipation. She let go of his throbbing erection and pushed him down to her, spreading her legs and rising to meet him as she pulled him in to her warm, wet depths.

Ryan moved slowly at first, letting the tension build and waiting until he knew Ellen's desire was peaking, and then he increased the intensity, driving harder and deeper with every thrust. Faster and faster they went as their moans of pleasure built in intensity until they peaked together in one incredible rush of climax and pleasure.

They were both spent, completely exhausted in the delicious afterglow of sex, with Ryan lying fully on top of her and yet somehow not crushing her. Finally, Ryan pulled out and lay down beside Ellen, holding her in his arms in a closeness that it seemed he had never felt. He pulled a blanket off the back of the couch and laid it over the top of them. Already, this was lasting longer than he ever had before with a woman. He had never spent the night with anyone; it had always been strictly, "wham, bam, thank you ma'am" and then up and gone. He had never even slept the night in his studio before.

But tonight, it felt different. He felt content to just stay there on the couch with this woman in his arms and sleep.

CHAPTER 54

'How's the handwriting analysis coming along? Are you all set for the comparison?' I asked the geek in the white lab coat.

'I've examined the note from The Junkie killing and can confirm a left-handed person wrote it, in quite a careless and erratic style, indicating a somewhat manic personality. I've compared that to the writing on the envelope found at The Hoarder's crime scene and consider that the same person wrote it with close to one hundred percent certainty. It was a match. Do you have the other sample?' he asked.

The callous, detached tone of the lab tech as he mentioned "The Junkie killing" had shocked me and brought back the feelings of hurt, anger, and disappointment in myself that always came when I thought of Sally. I paused, centred myself, and focused on the task at hand.

I pulled out the evidence bag containing Leonard's note and shook my head once again as I looked at the message: *Te futueo et caballum tuum*, which I had immediately identified as Latin, but I had to admit I was a tad rusty; I had to look up the meaning and then cursed Leonard when I found the translation was *Screw you and the horse you rode in on*.

The handwriting expert carefully extracted the note from the evidence bag and placed it under his magnifier lamp and got to work. After a few minutes, he turned away from his lab bench and said, 'A right-handed person wrote this note. Immaculate, controlled. Nothing like the first two samples. There is no doubt in my mind that different people wrote those notes.'

'Are you absolutely sure? No doubt at all?' I asked.

'None whatsoever. I regard that as a conclusive finding,' replied the analyst.

'Okay, thanks. I appreciate you fitting that in so quickly. That's all for now,' I said and headed out the door.

'Hey Melissa, how are you going with the DMV? Any luck?' I asked.

'Leonard's story checks out,' she replied. 'The only vehicle he has listed in his name is a Toyota Prius. No motorbike. I've checked the DC area for registrations of Harley Davidson FXS Low Riders. There's quite a few of them, but none registered to anyone named Leonard. It would take us ages to check through them all. How did you go with the handwriting analysis?'

'That's a bust. No match. Leonard's writing was totally different to the note left at Sally's crime scene. But the envelope with Leonard's name on it *is* a match to Sally's note, so we've at least confirmed that the same person wrote them both.'

'Well, I guess the physical evidence matches what we saw of Leonard compared to the profile we've built up of AK from the crime scenes,' said Melissa. 'Leonard doesn't fit the profile, not at all like the picture we've established of the killer. He seems too ordered and timid to carry out those violent, graphic killings. It just doesn't look like Leonard is our guy.'

CHAPTER 55

Leonard's first stirrings to wakefulness filled him with confusion; the bright morning light glared through his closed eyelids, but he didn't get the morning light in the bedroom of his apartment. And the surface he was lying on felt different; rough and lumpy, not like his own bed at all. Sounds were unfamiliar; smells were different. His body felt strange; there was something, or someone, lying next to him!

Suddenly he was fully awake, aware of his surroundings. His eyes flew open, and he took in the scene. What the hell was going on?! He had gone to sleep in his own bed and woken up somewhere completely different, in what looked like an old warehouse. The assault on his senses grew, as he looked down beside him to see a woman lying next to him, completely naked!

'Argh!! What the HELL is going on here?' shouted Leonard as he leapt up off the couch.

The woman stirred and woke up at the noise and said, 'Jesus Christ, Ryan! Calm down, will you!'

Leonard's brain went into overload and he just about had an aneurism, as an even more astounding revelation pounded into his consciousness.

'Ellen? Is that you? What the hell are you doing here? With me? And why did you just call me *Ryan*?' shouted Leonard. 'And while we're at it, why are you *naked*?'

'Leonard? Is that you?' asked Ellen incredulously, suddenly fully awake. 'Well, now isn't that a surprise!' she said with a thoughtful smile.

'Can you please explain to me *exactly* what on Earth is going on here!' exclaimed Leonard, getting close to the point of hysteria.

Ellen replied, 'Okay, okay Leonard, let's just calm down and talk this through rationally. How about we both put some clothes on? Because I'm sure having a therapy session with the two of us in our birthday suits breaks a whole lot of the American Psychiatric Association's rules of engagement for doctors and their patients.'

Leonard looked down at himself and realised this was the first time that a woman other than his mother had ever seen him naked, and he immediately got severely self-conscious. He looked around and saw a pair of jockey shorts, black jeans, black T-shirt and black leather jacket on the floor. He picked up the clothes and dressed, while Ellen did the same.

'Sorry Leonard, but I'm busting to go to the toilet and am suffering from a bit of a hangover, so I just need to freshen up. Just give me a few minutes,' said Ellen as she disappeared into the bathroom.

Relieved in some sense that Ellen had disappeared for a moment because it allowed him to think, to process and absorb his surroundings, Leonard looked around the studio and cringed at the mess and the chaos. He stared at the striking paintings, full of powerful imagery, bold colours, and dramatic brush strokes. He felt no connection to these works of art, no emotional response at all. He might as well have been looking at a newspaper.

Ellen returned from the bathroom, thankfully now fully clothed. Leonard looked down at himself, dressed in clothes that didn't feel like him. In a familiar nervous gesture, he ran his right forefinger up to the bridge of his nose as if to push his glasses higher up and then remembered that they weren't on his face; realising they must be back at his apartment.

Now freshened up after the excesses of the night before, Ellen looked at Leonard and shook her head in amazement. 'I have to say, Leonard, this *is* a surprise. I've read about these kinds of cases before, but never seen one or treated one, let alone slept with one!'

Leonard was mute in response, just stared confusedly back at Ellen. She continued, 'Leonard, do you understand what's going on yet? Who you are?'

'The evidence is all pointing in one direction, but I'm not sure I like where it's headed,' he responded.

'Tell me what you're thinking, Leonard,' said Ellen. 'Let me help you, we'll work through this together.'

'The memory lapses, the sleeping problems, the exhaustion, the communication with Ryan, the brain surgery, the lack of a corpus callosum, Split Brain Syndrome and now this, is all leading me to the rather preposterous and incomprehensible conclusion that I am in fact, both Ryan and Leonard,' he said in a calm, detached monotone.

'Now in the morning light and with a sober mind, I can confirm that is exactly the correct conclusion,' said Ellen. 'I was extremely drunk last night when I saw you. Well, technically, when I saw Ryan. I seem to recall a familiarity, but in a dark bar after a multitude of whiskeys, with a different ensemble. And without glasses and a different hairstyle, character, speech pattern, and mannerisms, I simply didn't register that it was actually you, Leonard.'

'I have so many questions, I don't even know where to begin,' said Leonard. 'So, let's start with what happened last night. How did you and Ryan meet?'

'I was at the bar, already drunk. Ryan bought me a drink. We got chatting, continued drinking lots more, one thing led to another, then we came back here, had sex on the couch and then fell asleep. That's about it, in a nutshell.'

'You had sex with a patient? Isn't that against all the rules?'

'Well, I didn't know you were a patient then, did I? And no offence, Leonard, but if I'd known it was you, I sure as hell wouldn't have slept with you! My drinking has got me in trouble before, but this is just a whole new level.'

'So, I'm really Ryan? How is that even *possible*? How can I not know this? Why can't I remember any of it? Where is he when I'm me, and where am I when I'm him? God, this is so confusing, I really can't wrap my mind around any of this,' said Leonard, who was completely and utterly bamboozled by the whole situation.

'Okay Leonard, we've got all day to run through this. I'm not going anywhere, and neither are you. We'll get through it. How about you freshen up and have a shower? While you do that, I'll go get us some breakfast and coffee, then we can fuel ourselves up and focus on this properly,' said Ellen.

'You will come back, won't you? You're not just going to go out and disappear?' said Leonard with more than a hint of a fear of abandonment in his voice.

'No way, Leonard, I'm not running out on you. We're in this together—all day and all night. But we've got a lot to talk about and we need to prepare ourselves. You go relax, have a long, hot shower and by the time you're finished I'll be back with supplies.'

'Okay. But make sure you come back!' responded Leonard and looked sadly at Ellen as she disappeared out the door of the studio. Then he turned around and went into the bathroom, used the toilet, brushed his teeth and had what felt like the longest, hottest shower of his life, like he was trying to peel the layers off himself to reveal what lay beneath. When he finally finished, his skin was red raw from the heat and he finally felt clean. Unfortunately, the only thing he had to wear were Ryan's clothes, which were still dirty from the night before.

As Leonard dressed himself, he looked in the mirror at the reflection staring back at him and found something nagging at the periphery of his consciousness, like a bad feeling washing over him, a realisation of something horrible dawning upon him. And then it oozed into his consciousness like a dark, foul stench. He, Leonard Price, was a murderer! A serial killer! As the waves of knowing his true inner self came crashing down on him, a bout of dizziness and a blast of nausea suddenly hit him. The bile rose in his throat and he gagged, then his gut heaved, and he hurled the contents of his stomach into the toilet bowl, tasting the sour alcohol from the night before. He remained on all fours in front of the toilet bowl, stomach heaving, tears squeezing out of his eyes, snot running from his nose and sobs racking his body as the enormity of what he had done hit him with maximum impact.

'Leonard? Are you okay?' came Ellen's voice from the other side of the bathroom door. 'I'm coming in.' As Ellen came through the door and saw Leonard hunkered down over the toilet bowl, she wondered if there was more going on here than she understood right now. 'I guess breakfast can wait awhile, then?' she said, trying to lighten the mood which fell on deaf ears. 'Let's get you cleaned up.'

Leonard got shakily to his feet and staggered to the bathroom sink. He washed his face in cold water and brushed his teeth with a double dose of Colgate to wash away the aftertaste of vomit.

'Here, I got you some nice hot coffee, it should make you feel better,' said Ellen as she offered the strong black cup of joe to Leonard. He looked at it dubiously, then took it and had a sip, gave a nod of satisfaction, then sat back on the couch and continued to drink his coffee, staring off into infinity and saying nothing. Ellen sensed she needed to let Leonard get through this initial period, gather his thoughts and settle himself before talking. She occupied herself with a generous breakfast of a large bagel with cream cheese and a warm blueberry Danish, washed down with a long black coffee.

Once her breakfast was complete, Leonard finally looked at Ellen and broke the silence. 'So, as difficult and distasteful is the concept, is it really true that I am two personalities occupying the same mind and body? That I truly am both Leonard *and* Ryan?'

'Yes Leonard, that is exactly the case. Having seen both of you in just the last few hours, I can attest to the fact that you are indeed distinct personalities living in the same body, and neither of you has any awareness of the other personality.'

Not prone to profanity, Leonard uttered what was for him the rather unusual turn of phrase, 'This is, as I believe they say in the vernacular, somewhat of a "head-fuck".' He rested his elbows on his knees, put his head in his hands and slowly massaged his temples.

Ellen laughed and replied, 'Couldn't have said it better myself, Leonard. I mean, I know the theory and I've seen the evidence, and even I am finding this hard to grapple with, so I can't imagine what it must be like for you trying to process all this.'

'Okay, Doc. Give me the technical explanation and then we'll take it from there,' said Leonard.

'As we know, you have Split Brain Syndrome, where there is no communication between the right and left hemispheres of your brain. Rather than the often-quoted split personality, multiple personality, or dissociative identity disorder, you appear to have a condition theorised by neuroscientists called *Dual Consciousness*. Some people believe there could be a separate consciousness within each of the left and right hemispheres of the brain once the corpus callosum is severed, as it was in your case during your childhood brain surgery.'

'Hm… so, following that logic, I have been both Leonard and Ryan ever since my surgery?'

'I guess so. But it may have taken your alter-ego some time to develop, since you were the dominant consciousness from birth. Ryan might have taken some time to appear. It would have been strange for him, he would have just come from nowhere, with no history or previous life experience to hold on to.'

'Okay. Something that is bothering me is where does my consciousness go when I'm Ryan? My memory lapses that I'm aware of seem to be short, so I feel like I'm "me" for most of the time. So when does Ryan surface?'

'I believe your dual consciousness has a diurnal and nocturnal pattern. You inhabit the day, and Ryan inhabits the night. You yourself say that you sleep an extraordinary amount, ten or even twelve hours per night, and yet you're still exhausted during the day. After seeing Ryan active, bright-eyed and bushy-tailed in the middle of the night last night, I believe he is a creature of the night. In his mind, I'm convinced he thinks he sleeps all day, but the truth is that's when he is, in fact, you.'

Leonard nodded at this theory, recognising the sense it made. He moved on again, his mind covering all the bases as he went. 'Back to my childhood, my mother must have known what was going on, which is why she set up the elaborate subterfuge of Ryan, my so-called "pen-pal".'

'Yes, perhaps your mother first met Ryan one night when he awoke from your sleep. She would have talked to that uncertain little boy and realised it wasn't her son, that it wasn't you. I don't understand why she wouldn't tell you about it though. Perhaps her plan was to play the pen-pal game for a while until you were old enough to understand. But then she died before she could tell you the truth, and the secret died with her.'

'I have to give her some credit for this elaborate ploy. I didn't think she had the brainpower to even come up with such an idea, let alone execute it without me finding out about it. I guess it's not that complicated when you really think it through. I write a letter during the day and post it to Ryan's post office box. Ryan reads it at night, then writes a response during the night and posts it back to *my* post office box, which is a fresh box in a different post office. I never could understand why we had to schlep all the way into DC to collect my mail from the post office, when I could have just collected it from our mailbox out front of our apartment. But Mom called it our "special adventure" and said that Ryan could always keep in touch with me as long as I never changed my post office box.'

'Makes sense, I guess,' said Ellen. 'But what about the letters and the envelopes? Didn't you ever find any lying around your place?'

'I guess my mother must have kept the letters I wrote to Ryan. She must have collected them and then showed them to him at night when he woke up, then hid them or threw them in the garbage.'

'But what about after she died? What happened then?'

'Well, it's funny, but Ryan stopped writing to me as soon as my mother died, and I moved out of my apartment. We didn't communicate for a full seven years. And then, a few months after I moved back into the apartment after college, suddenly I received a letter from him, out of the blue. Maybe he already had this studio by then, and he kept all the letters and envelopes here instead of at my apartment.'

'Yes, I guess that explains it,' said Ellen with a nod, admiring Leonard's theorising and reasoning capabilities, like he was working on a solution to a mind-bending puzzle.

'Why do you think Ryan disappeared and then re-emerged again after such a long time?' asked Leonard.

'I suspect it was the familiar surroundings. Perhaps Ryan knew your mother was gone. She may well have been the only other person he ever met. So, with her gone and then the familiarity of the apartment gone too, he would have had nothing to cling onto, no semblance of a life, or sense of his own self. And then when you returned from college and moved back into the apartment, perhaps the familiar surroundings brought him back to life.'

'I finally understand now why my mother told me that Ryan and I could never meet. I never could understand it at the time; I so wanted to have a real friend, but clearly that would never work. What can you tell me about Ryan?' asked Leonard.

'Well, you and he are polar opposites, Leonard. I don't think I've ever met two people who could be more different, which makes it even more astounding to me that you both inhabit the same body. You are extremely left-brain in your personality. Highly intelligent, orderly, logical, analytical, socially awkward, timid, shy, devoid of any sense of humour, lacking in confidence and right-handed. As you know, I only met Ryan last night for the first time, so have only a few hours of observation on which to base my assessment of his character, and I must admit that alcohol impaired my judgement. But based on what I saw, I consider Ryan to be of relatively low intelligence, extremely right-brain in his personality, highly creative, supremely confident bordering on arrogant, dangerous, chaotic, impulsive and left-handed. Like I said, complete opposites.'

Leonard shook his head, still trying to come to grips with the fact that such an utterly distinct personality was inhabiting the same body as himself. He said, 'I remember my mother saying that I had to look after Ryan, because I was so much smarter than him, that he wasn't too clever and needed help from his only friend, Leonard the pen-pal.'

'Well, I think we've covered the key points of the story, Leonard. It all seems to make some sense. Is there anything else you particularly want to cover?'

Leonard was quiet for a moment, then looked up at Ellen with sad eyes and said, 'Well, the elephant in the room is just the relatively minor point that Ryan is a serial killer. Which therefore means by extension that I too am a serial killer.'

CHAPTER 56

'Um, excuse me?' said Ellen, not convinced she had heard Leonard correctly. 'Did you say *serial killer*?'

Leonard nodded and said, 'Yes, you know the "Addict Killer" that's been in the news? That's Ryan. Which means, of course, that it's also me. Oh God, I think I'm going to be sick again.' Leonard clutched his stomach, leapt up from the couch and ran to the bathroom where he gagged over the sink, suddenly thankful he didn't have a wad of cream cheese bagel sitting in his stomach.

Ellen followed Leonard into the bathroom and rubbed him on the back. He looked up at her reflection in the mirror through teary eyes and said, 'How could I have done those terrible things? How could I be such a *monster*?'

Ellen continued consoling him and said, 'But that's just it, Leonard; that's the crux of the whole thing. Ryan is *not you*. You are literally two different consciousnesses. It's not you that's a killer. And I'm really having a hard time believing that Ryan is even a killer. How do you know for sure? Are you certain it was him? And if so, how are you so sure?'

'Because I planned all those murders! Everything was my idea, down to the last detail. How could I be so stupid? I thought it was just a game, thought we were playing around, *imagining* what we could do to teach those pathetic addicts a lesson. I saw the news reports about the cases and all the details matched just like I planned them and described to Ryan in our letters. I figuratively loaded the gun and then Ryan pulled the trigger.'

'It all just seems so impossible! I'm having a great deal of trouble processing all this and believing that Ryan is capable of what you say he's done. I think we need a change of scene. Let's get out of here. It's Ryan's lair. We should go to your apartment; you'll feel more comfortable there.'

'You're right, that's a good idea, let's go,' said Leonard. They collected their things and made their way to the studio door. As they went, Leonard noticed the enormous old Harley and looked across at Ellen with a quizzical look.

Ellen smiled, nodded her head and said, 'Yes, absolutely, wild man! You rode that beast back here last night, blind drunk, with no helmet and me riding on the back. You are one serious biker on that thing, let me tell you.'

'Curiouser and curiouser, said Alice in Wonderland,' muttered Leonard, which was a very non-Ryan like thing to say.

They exited onto a backstreet, turned and walked up to the nearest main road, which Leonard immediately recognised as just around the corner from his apartment, a short walk away. 'Makes sense that Ryan's studio should be so close to my apartment, since he always slept in my bed and then walked back and forth to the studio, leaving his bike parked there,' said Leonard.

After just a few minutes' walk, they arrived at Leonard's apartment and entered the foyer. A look of surprise came over the building manager's face as he said with a raised eyebrow, 'Good afternoon, Mister Price. You're looking quite different today. And hello Miss, nice to meet you.' This really was most peculiar, seeing his most straitlaced resident turning up in an all-black outfit with a woman in tow, for the first time.

Leonard completely ignored the man, the comment, and the silent judgement and they continued to his apartment. He opened the door and Ellen immediately noted the natural habitat of the left-brain Leonard. An ordered, precise and structured environment with not a thing out of place. Compared to the creative, chaotic studio of the right-brain Ryan, this was so much more evidence of the extreme divergence of the dual consciousness. To her amazement, Ellen was collating a treasure trove of psychological phenomena. These dual personalities would make her famous! She would go down in history as the person who conclusively proved what until now had been mere conjecture.

Leonard went straight to his bathroom, stripped off Ryan's clothes and jumped in the shower again, trying to wash off all traces of Ryan and his own barfing episode earlier in the day. When he finished in the shower, he slicked down his hair, dressed in some casual slacks, cream loafers and a pastel turquoise polo shirt, then picked up his glasses from the bedside table and placed them carefully on the bridge of his nose.

Feeling much more himself, Leonard walked into the living room in full Leonard-mode. Ellen looked up at him and said, 'Well, well, well, Leonard, you sure are back in the house, aren't you? It's no wonder I didn't recognise you as Ryan, you two look so different. It seems you're feeling much more yourself and at home now.'

'Yes, I feel much better, thank you. This was a good idea, coming here to my place,' responded Leonard. 'I see you found the only alcohol in my apartment.'

'Took me long enough. I searched high and low for this bad-boy,' replied Ellen. 'I can't believe this is the only booze you've got in this place.'

'Bit early for straight whiskey, isn't it?' asked Leonard, with a derisive sniff.

Ellen unapologetically shrugged her shoulders and said, 'It's the afternoon. And it's been a hell of a day already, Leonard. Like I told Ryan last night, I'm a high-functioning alcoholic. This stuff helps get me through the day. Trust me, I'm better with this than without it.'

'Were you bombed during our sessions?' asked Leonard.

'I wouldn't say drunk, but I admit I take the edge off for many of my patients. Ordinarily I wouldn't share this kind of thing with a patient, but since we've broken just about every rule in the book by sleeping together, I figure another divulgence can't hurt my career much more,' she replied and drained the glass all the way to the bottom.

Leonard shook his head at this latest revelation from his psychiatrist and sat down on the kitchen chair opposite her.

'Seeing you change your clothes like that, I'm just wondering how on Earth an observant guy like you failed to notice Ryan's clothes lying around your apartment?' asked Ellen. 'Surely you must have noticed some trace of Ryan's presence?'

'I've been thinking the same thing since we got here,' replied Leonard. 'The only thing I can come up with is that Ryan always put his clothes away in the closet and his dirty laundry straight in the wash basket. I have a lady who comes every day and does my laundry and all the cooking and cleaning. She must have just washed everything and put it back in the closet. I had a look and noticed a pile of black clothes in the back corner of the closet that I never wear, and just always ignored. It's been there for as long as I can remember, and I just took no notice of it.'

'How about pyjamas? Ryan would have needed to wear the same thing to bed as you every time, otherwise you'd wake up wearing something different in bed.'

Leonard shrugged his shoulders and replied, 'I sleep naked. I guess Ryan does too.'

'What about dirty dishes? Or food disappearing?' she asked, continuing the line of questioning, trying to find holes and gaps in the story.

Leonard shrugged again and said, 'Nope. Nothing like that. Maybe he ate out all the time? Didn't want to prepare anything?'

'What about money?' asked Ellen.

'Nothing that I noticed. There were never any transactions showing in my bank accounts, nothing on my phone, no cash missing from my wallet. I assume he had his own source of income somehow, and just kept everything at his studio. I really can't say I ever noticed any sign of Ryan in my life, nothing that would arouse my suspicion that there was a total stranger living not only in my apartment, but in my body.'

'There's something I'd like to check on, Leonard. Do you have one of Ryan's letters here you can show me?' asked Ellen. Leonard nodded, went to his drawer and retrieved one, then handed it over to Ellen.

'Now you write something for me, Leonard,' she continued. Leonard followed the instruction and handed his note to Ellen, who laid both handwriting samples next to each other on the table, quickly studied them and then said, 'Anyone could see that the handwriting on these letters is different. You can even tell by the slant of the words you're right-handed and Ryan is left-handed. Your writing is precise and structured, whereas Ryan's is messy and all over the place. Clearly written by a different consciousness.'

Leonard nodded in agreement and said, 'Well, obviously I would have recognised if Ryan's handwriting was the same as mine. I simply can't believe the same body wrote these letters.'

Ellen paused, poured herself another stiff whiskey, took a large sip and said, 'Okay Leonard, it's time to get serious, back to that elephant in the room you mentioned. This slight matter of you being a serial killer.'

'Trust me, I'm serious. As a heart attack. Ryan is a murderer. And you need to take care. As much as I hate to say this, I honestly believe you should call the police, for your own protection.'

Ellen took another swig and said, 'I really don't want to call the police, Leonard. I want to sort this out, and I want to help you. Do you trust me? I have a plan.' There were several factors at play in Ellen's dangerous decision. They included Dutch courage from alcohol, an inability to believe the timid Leonard could hurt anyone, professional curiosity, a low regard for her own personal safety and a compelling desire to uncover something truly new and exciting in psychology.

They spent the rest of the evening talking and making plans, then

Ellen made dinner, which they both enjoyed. Ellen slowly discovered that under Leonard's prickly exterior was a desperately lonely man, hungry for human connection but unable to find it. They spent a moment recording a video on Ellen's camera phone of Leonard talking to Ryan, explaining the situation. Then they set up Leonard's video camera in the bedroom, focused on the bed and ready to record every detail of what was to come.

Their ultimate act of preparation was to tie Leonard to the bed before he fell asleep. Neither of them knew how Ryan would react to all this, so agreed that it was best to take precautions. Leonard dressed in some old pyjamas he found in the closet and then laid on top of the bed while Ellen tied him up with some rope they found in a cupboard in the laundry. Ellen waited in the bedroom, recording the whole thing on her phone camera and watched as Leonard drifted off to sleep and then suddenly his entire body twisted in a violent spasm that Ellen identified as a hypnagogic jerk. The pained expression on Leonard's face slowly faded, and he settled into a deep sleep.

Ellen went into the living room and settled on the couch to wait. She eyed the three quarters of a bottle of whiskey remaining on the table and told herself she would have just one more drink. Which turned into one more. And then another. And another, until the bottle was empty.

Slowly, Ellen drifted off to inebriated sleep.

Ryan woke up and felt the bindings on his hands and feet. He lifted his head off the pillow and looked down at his body on the bed, dressed in strange pyjamas and trussed to the bed like one of his victims. Then he noticed the video camera pointed at the bed with the red light on showing it was recording. 'Jesus. No wonder I never let chicks sleep over!' he said. The last thing he remembered was falling asleep on the couch at his studio after having sex with Ellen.

He looked around the bedroom, but except for the video camera, nothing was out of place, nothing to see. He called out, 'Hey! Is anyone there?'

A few minutes later, Ellen stumbled into the bedroom, still drunk and half-asleep.

'I have to say Ellen, this is really not the direction I saw our relationship going,' said Ryan. 'What the hell is going on here and why am I tied to my bed? And while you're at it, explain to me how I fell asleep on the couch at my studio and woke up in bed in my apartment!'

Ellen shook her head quickly, trying to clear the worst of the effects of the alcohol. She squinted at Ryan and forced herself to focus on the figure on the bed.

'Jesus, how bombed are you, Ellen? Is this some kinky sex thing you've cooked up? Coz I have to say, I'm into it, Baby, whatever you've got planned, except we need to lose these crummy old pyjamas, they're a mood killer,' said Ryan with a smile, turning on the charm.

Ellen replied, 'Just give me a second, okay?' She went to the bathroom, used the toilet, washed her face in cold water to clear her head, then went to the kitchen and made herself a strong coffee. She straightened herself up and returned to the bedroom, nowhere near sober but at least with a somewhat clearer head. She sat down on a chair beside the bed and said, 'I think this will have more impact and make more sense if I let Leonard tell you what's going on.'

'Leonard? What the hell has that snivelling little traitor got to do with me being tied up on the bed?' snarled Ryan.

'You'll see,' replied Ellen as she turned the phone around and pressed play on the video.

'Hello Ryan. It's me, Leonard. But, actually, it's also *you*. We are the same person. The thing is, I, or more correctly, "we" had brain surgery just over ten years ago. They removed our corpus callosum, which is a bunch of fibres that connect the left hemisphere of the brain to the right hemisphere. We have something called Split Brain Syndrome and have developed a dual consciousness, where you and I inhabit the same body.

'You, Ryan, are the right-brain, and I, Leonard, am the left-brain. You have the night, and I have the day. I'm sorry, I know this will be a shock for you, just like it was for me. But we need to work together, to find a way through this. Otherwise we're both going to end up in prison or a mental hospital for the rest of our lives. Ellen is here to help. She's my psychiatrist and she'll help us.'

The news dumbfounded Ryan. He remained silent, looking up at Ellen in a state of shock and confusion. His mind was racing at a hundred miles an hour. This revelation had far-reaching impacts and his current situation tied to a bed could easily land him in prison or, even worse, get him an appointment with the electric chair. He quickly understood that his priority was getting out of the ropes and off the bed. He had to find out how much Ellen knew about what he'd been up to.

'Oh, Ellen, I'm so confused!' cried Ryan. 'Is this why I've felt so lost and alone all these years? Why I've never felt myself in my own skin?

Because I'm inhabiting another person's body? Ellen, I really appreciate you trying to help me. I'm trying to process the fact that I'm actually Leonard, which is totally bizarre, but I don't understand why I'm tied to the bed.' Ryan turned on the emotion and tears welled up in his eyes at the very real fear that he could lose his life. A solitary tear rolled out of the corner of his right eye and fell to the pillow.

Ellen's heart melted as she saw the emotion on Ryan's face and felt again the intense connection they had shared just the night before. Not to mention the clouding effects of the bottle of whiskey she had polished off earlier. She just couldn't picture Ryan as a murderer and suspected that Leonard's story was a dramatisation, perhaps a way to make Ellen favour Leonard over Ryan in this Battle of the Brains, Left vs. Right.

Ellen reached down and held Ryan's hand, giving it a gentle squeeze. 'It's okay Ryan, I'm here for you, here to help you, just like I am for Leonard. The ropes are just a precaution. Leonard made some serious accusations against you, so I just want to get to the bottom of that before I let you loose.'

'Accusations? What do you mean? And why did Leonard talk about prison on his video?'

'Well, Leonard seems to think you're the Addict Killer.'

'What? That's ridiculous!' exclaimed Ryan. 'Why the hell would he say *that*?'

'I don't know Ryan, and to be honest, I'm not sure that I believe him. Nothing I've seen makes me think you could do those horrible things that the press have reported.'

'Did he explain *why* he thinks I'm some crazed killer? Since I didn't do those terrible crimes, he couldn't possibly have any evidence to prove it.'

'You're right, Ryan. He didn't show me any evidence that proves you're a killer. It's just something he said, and he seemed pretty convinced about it.'

'But I'm not a killer, Ellen, please. You've got to believe me!' pleaded Ryan. 'I just don't know what the hell's going on here, it's all too much,' he cried out, then closed his eyes and turned his head away from Ellen, trying to bury his face in the pillow but was stopped short because of his rope restraints. He was turning it on now, tears streaming from his eyes and his face contorted in anguish. He looked back at Ellen and begged her, 'Please Ellen, untie me and let me off this bed so we can talk. I want to understand what's wrong with me. Help me, Ellen, please.'

Ellen's empathy was getting the better of her. Tears welled up in her eyes as she saw the genuine emotion on Ryan's face. 'Can I trust you, Ryan?' she asked.

'Yes, Ellen. Yes, you can trust me. *Please* untie me,' replied Ryan.

The trusting Ellen got to work on Ryan's bindings. It took her a few minutes to untie the ropes and release Ryan from the bed.

'Thank you, Ellen, thank you for trusting me and believing in me, it means so much to me,' said Ryan, as he got off the bed and enveloped Ellen in an emotional hug, sharing his genuine relief at his release. 'Just give me a minute, I have to get out of these Grandpa pyjamas.'

Ryan disappeared into the bathroom, then went to the closet and came out to the living room dressed in his usual black jeans, shirt and boots. He sat down directly opposite Ellen and looked across at her.

'Thank you again, Ellen, for untying me. I really appreciate that. Now, can you tell me exactly what is going on here? Am I really Leonard? How the hell could I be me, but also be that wimpy nerd?'

'Like Leonard said, you had brain surgery when you were a kid, and you have Split Brain Syndrome, where there is no connection between the left and right sides of the brain. Leonard was the first personality, so he kept his consciousness, but then after the surgery, you appeared. Apparently, you used to come out at night. Leonard would go to sleep, then you would wake up in the middle of the night and talk to your mom. What do you remember of those days?'

'My long-term memory is very vague and cloudy. I remember little of anything from my childhood, which has always puzzled me. All my memories are recent. Basically, I wake up in this apartment, go to my studio to paint, or go out and get drunk, maybe spend some time with a lady or two, then come back here to the apartment and go to bed.'

'Have you ever been awake during the day?' asked Ellen.

'Not that I can remember,' replied Ryan. 'I like the night.'

'So, you mentioned your studio. How did you find that, and how does that arrangement work?'

'I got talking to a guy in a bar one night, said I needed somewhere to work, and he told me about his studio. It was close to the apartment, and the rent was cheap. He wanted cash to keep it off the books, didn't want a fancy lease or anything. We agreed on a price and I just pay him cash every month. Easy.'

'And the motorbike? How did you get your hands on that if you're so off the grid?'

'Won it in a poker game. Bet the farm on an enormous pot and got lucky. The guy was holding a full house, Aces over Kings, and he tossed the keys to his Harley in the pot. I wiped him out with a Four of a Kind. Poor bastard broke down in tears then ran off down the street crying. I had to get one of the players to show me how to ride the damn thing. I was shaky the first few times, but I soon got the hang of it. I love that colossal beast of a machine. I never registered it and don't have a licence.'

'And what about the letters to Leonard? Tell me about them.'

'That's something I remembered. I knew that was important. I recalled Leonard's name and address. Knew I needed to write to him. So, once I got settled in my studio, I wrote to him. It was comforting, you know. Like I had a friend. I mean, I've got some drinking buddies and had plenty of girls, but I'm basically alone. Leonard was the one person I could really talk to, through our letters. Even though he is a nerd with a superiority complex.'

'So how do you feel about all this now? Is it making sense to you? Is it adding up?' said Ellen.

'I guess it all makes some crazy sense. It's tough to argue with, even though it is one giant head-fuck. I guess I really am Leonard, as much as that concept seriously messes with my brain. There's only one thing that puzzles me.'

'What's that?' asked Ellen.

'Why you were stupid enough to untie me.'

Ellen's blood ran cold as she heard the hard edge to Ryan's voice and the cruel stare that had taken over his face. He looked and sounded totally different, like another person. She sobered up instantly and cursed her poor judgement at not calling the police, or at the very least not keeping Ryan tied up. Her disbelief of Leonard's story evaporated, and she knew she had made a terrible mistake.

All senses alert, she prepared to spring into action. Ryan just sat there, not moving a muscle, like a big cat ready to pounce, waiting for its prey to make a move. And move, she did, but not quick enough. She leapt out of the chair and made a run for the door, but had no chance of making it. Ryan sprang up from his chair with deceptive speed, thrust out his left arm and caught her high on the chest in a fierce clothesline block. Ellen's legs flew out from underneath her, with all the momentum of her upper body instantly transferred to her lower torso. Her legs swung wildly up into the air and her head whipped back ferociously and then she plummeted down to the floor in a violent impact of head, shoulders and back onto the floor like a body tossed out a window.

With the wind completely knocked out of her, Ellen struggled to stay conscious, with stars twinkling madly in front of her eyes. Ryan knelt down close to her, put his face right in close to hers and said in a menacing tone, 'Goodnight Princess Psychiatrist. See you in therapy.' And then he drew back his fist and pounded it into her eye, knocking her unconscious. Darkness descended quickly.

Ryan's mind was racing. He'd immobilised his target for now but needed a plan suitable for the Addict Killer. This was a chance to make a genuine statement for The Drunk.

He looked around the apartment with fresh eyes, intent on picking up clues that perhaps he hadn't noticed before. There! In a little porcelain bowl on the bookshelf was a set of keys with a Toyota badge, in a different place to where he and Leonard kept their keys for the apartment. Transport? Check.

He went to the bedroom and grabbed the ropes from the bed, then brought them back into the living room. He bound Ellen's ankles and wrists, then tied them together, forcing her body into the foetal position. He cut a length of material from a bedsheet and gagged her with it. Then he found an oversized, hard-shell suitcase in the closet, opened it and roughly jammed Ellen inside it. Hidden body? Check.

Then, Ryan spotted the empty whiskey bottle and crystallised his thoughts on the location to stage his latest performance. Kill site? Check.

Ryan grabbed the empty bottle, the car keys, and the suitcase with Ellen inside, wheeled it out of the apartment and down the hallway to the elevator, then hit the button for the carpark. Ryan eyed the apartment numbers on the car spaces and made his way to Leonard's car, emitting a loud groan when he saw the most boring, nerdy car in existence. A grey Toyota Prius. 'Jesus Christ Leonard, you are *such* a nerd!' he said, 'How the hell we are from the same DNA, I will never understand.'

Ryan unlocked the car, then lifted the hatch and heaved the suitcase with Ellen inside into the trunk. He got into the driver's seat, tossed the empty bottle of whiskey down on the floor and started the ignition. The drive down to Fredericksburg was a good sixty miles, so Ryan settled in with some hard rock on the radio. Surely the first time this piss-ant car had ever played that station, he thought with a grin. He kept the Prius to the speed limit for the entire trip, not wanting any cops to stop him and potentially discover what, or more correctly, who, he had in the trunk.

CHAPTER 58

Terror!

Primal, frantic, unadulterated terror charged through Ellen's body as she slowly returned to consciousness. She was in hell. The darkness was complete. Jammed into a tiny box, she was curled up in a tight ball with no space to move any part of her body. Legs bent, arms folded, back painfully constricted, head tucked forward in a somersault position; forced into a tiny space half her size, like some performing contortionist.

Panic!

She couldn't see. Her face was burning from Ryan's bashing. Every muscle in her body screamed in protest at the forced tension and torsion. The air was hot and stuffy; she felt she was suffocating, like there was no oxygen to breathe. The gag was tight around her mouth, and her nose filled with snot and fluid from the trauma. She snorted and felt the wet slime run down her face, mixing with her hot tears. Panic gripped her.

Screams!

Ellen screamed with all her might, but the sound got lost in the gag and then died further in her tomb. She tried to kick and bash against the sides of her tiny prison, but with no space to move, all she did was increase the muscle contractions of her entire body, bringing on a wave of cramps that sent fresh bursts of pain coursing through her every nerve.

The screaming, exertion, suffocation, panic, and pain all rushed in on Ellen in an enormous wave. The body's natural defence system shut down the non-critical function of consciousness to focus on survival. Ellen succumbed and mercifully faded once more into the black void.

CHAPTER 59

Virginia's history as the birthplace of American Spirits stretched all the way back to 1620. George Washington himself was famous for running one of the largest whiskey distilleries in the country after he retired from being America's first President. It was the perfect symbolism for Ryan's latest and greatest staging—The Drunk.

Ryan pulled into the Fredericksburg distillery that had been the source of Ellen's last drink, climbed out of the Prius and dragged the big suitcase out of the trunk. He grabbed the empty whiskey bottle and the tyre iron and walked around the back of the small distillery. There were no security guards, and the place was dimly lit. He stopped at the rear door, jimmied the lock and made his way inside, dragging the suitcase with him and hitting the light switch by the door.

The distillery floor was a dazzling collection of copper whiskey stills, pipes, vats, and barrels all over the place. It was a disorganised mess, just a small local distillery with low production volumes. But it had everything Ryan needed for his big statement. He laid the suitcase down on the floor in front of the biggest still and opened the luggage lid. He then opened the inspection hatch of the still and saw the corn and rye mash liquid in the bottom, ready to go for the next day's production run. He looked over at the control panel, which held a few basic buttons, switches, and gauges. Looked simple enough, he decided. Toss her in and press the button marked "Cook".

Light pierced through Ellen's eyelids. A delightful wave of fresh air washed over her, and a sudden feeling of space registered on her senses.

Consciousness returned. She opened her eyes and strained her legs and arms against her binding ropes. She lifted her head up out of her tiny coffin and looked around. The light receded in intensity as her eyes adjusted. She looked around, struggling to focus and then saw Ryan standing above her, staring down with an amused look on his face. 'Hey, Princess Head Shrinker, you're back with us! Look where you are—the source of the last drink you had back at the apartment. I thought you might enjoy another one.'

Suddenly Ellen remembered everything, and the terror returned. The night before with Ryan, the conversation with Leonard, the fateful decision to help him instead of calling the police, the whiskey, and the sheer stupidity of releasing Ryan from his bonds. Then the talking with Ryan and the chilling realisation of her terrible mistake and the sudden violence and imprisonment that had followed. And now here. Certain death. Part of Ellen's tortured soul immediately gave up, accepted and even welcomed what was to come. Soon, her suffering would be over, and she would reunite with her darling Dan and lovely Lucy.

All trace of resistance and struggle disappeared from Ellen's body as she sagged and went limp, flopping back down into the base of the suitcase.

'Now, now, Ellen. Don't be like that. Don't be sad. You're an alcoholic, aren't you? You should be in heaven in a place like this,' said Ryan with an expansive wave of his hand around the distillery. Ellen stared blankly up at Ryan through tired, blinking eyes.

Ryan pulled the switchblade out of his pocket, flicked it out of its handle, then reached down and cut the rope connecting Ellen's arms and legs together, but left her wrists and ankles bound. Ellen immediately stretched her arms and legs out of the confines of the suitcase, glorying in the sweet release of muscles unfurled and stretched. She rolled out of the suitcase and laid full stretch out on the concrete floor, relieved at her expanded range of movement.

Ryan let her enjoy her moment of relief, then bent down and removed her gag. Then he slid his arms under Ellen and lifted her up off the floor. As he carried her over towards the large copper still, Ellen understood what he was planning. Even though she had accepted her fate, her survival instinct kicked in and she struggled and screamed. Ryan shivered with pleasure as he saw her primal fear and the most basic of human instincts—survival.

Fighting against her bound hands and feet, Ellen thrashed around in Ryan's arms, but he was just too strong. He held on tight and carried her over to the still, right in front of the access hatch. Just wide enough to insert a shovel to load grain, it would be a squeeze if Ellen struggled too much. As Ryan inserted Ellen's head through the portal, her thrashing caused her to smash her head against the hard copper edging around the opening, stunning her into a momentary stillness. Ryan seized the opportunity and jammed her all the way through the hatch, sliding her through the opening and dropping her down into the liquid mash.

Ryan shut the hatch door and peered in through the glass inspection window, smiling at the scene of Ellen splashing around in the mash as she struggled to her feet. The whiskey still was a beauty, stretching a full twenty feet high, tall enough for Ellen to stand upright. Ryan gave her a wave through the glass and then went over to the control panel and pushed the heat button. Ellen resolved to stay silent for as long as possible, so as not to give Ryan the satisfaction she knew he craved, evidenced because he had removed her gag.

Ellen was in the eye of the storm. She felt the pulsing of the copper floor beneath her feet and the groaning of the metal as the steam made its way from the boiler to the still. Then it hit. Degree by degree, the temperature increased as more and more steam pumped its way through the still. Frantically, Ellen moved around inside the confines of the copper kettle, looking for a way out, or to elevate herself above the level of the liquid. But the safety designers had never considered the scenario of someone locking a person inside the still and cooking them to death, because Ellen came quickly to the conclusion that there was no way out.

The temperature of the mash rose through warm to hot and then burning, from forty degrees Celsius, to fifty and then on to sixty degrees. As the lower extremities of her legs started burning, Ellen started jumping up and down to try to get some relief. The air burned in her lungs as the heat rose further and further. Then her screams started. They erupted from her lungs involuntarily as she lost all control. Ryan shivered in ecstasy as he absorbed the frenzied scene through the looking glass and heard the muffled screams through the thick copper walls of the still.

The temperature rise continued relentlessly until Ellen finally gave up. She collapsed in a heap, instantly exposing her entire body to the intense, burning heat of the mash as it seared through layers of skin and made its way down to the flesh. Ellen's thrashing and writhing lasted just a few seconds before she passed out from the pain. Death followed swiftly.

Ryan left the heater on and the temperature continued to rise all the way to one-hundred degrees—the boiling point of water. The gaseous blend of steam, methanol, ethanol, and sulphides mixed with Ellen's bodily fluids to create a toxic concoction of vapour that made its way up the neck of the still and out through the condensation tube.

Ryan inspected the outpouring of the condensate liquid, fascinated at the thought that this was most likely the first ever distilled human. He collected the brownish red liquid and poured it into the empty whiskey bottle he had brought with him, smiling at the thought of Ellen ending up pickled in alcohol in a whiskey bottle. He screwed the cap on the bottle, then wiped it down with a rag. Then he looked around on the workbench, found a permanent marker and wrote on the bottle label. Ryan returned to the still, turned off the heat and placed the bottle on the floor in front of the still. The latest vintage of this Fredericksburg distillery was complete.

Essence of Ellen.

CHAPTER 60

The call came before dawn. This couldn't be good. I shook myself awake and answered, hearing Melissa's tired voice on the other end of the phone. 'Hi Simon. Frank just called me. Looks like it's the Addict Killer again. Another elaborate staging, this time with an alcoholic theme. It's quite a drive, so I'll come around to pick you up and we'll go down there together. I'll be out front of your apartment in fifteen minutes.'

'Okay, see you soon,' I said and hung up. I quickly freshened up, dressed and got myself out front just as Melissa pulled up. I hopped in the car, leaned over and gave her a kiss good morning. She responded with a kiss of her own and one of her bright, beautiful smiles, despite the ungodly hour.

We settled into our usual easy, relaxed conversation, and the sixty miles down to Fredericksburg went by in a flash. Dawn was just showing its first light at the distillery as we got out of Melissa's car. The local Virginia police were on scene, as was Delaney, who had been informed as a professional courtesy because of the connection with his DC murders. Delaney's crime scene guys pulled in just after us. He must have hit the phones hard in the early hours this morning to assemble his team so quickly.

We walked in the main entrance of the distillery building and the first thing we noticed was the pungent smell, like badly cooked meat. We walked over to Delaney, who introduced us to a pale-looking, white-bearded old man wearing a pair of tattered blue overalls. Delaney said, 'This here is Jim, one of the whiskey men. He came in early to start a batch cooking and he noticed something off straight away, so he called the local police. They had a look, put two and two together damn quick and called me. So, here we are. Jim, this is Melissa and Simon from the FBI at Quantico, they're helping us out on this case. Why don't you tell them what you told me?'

'Well, I came in real early, like. Around three a.m. I reckon. Had me a batch of mash in the still, ready to go. First thing I noticed someone had busted in the lock on the side door. Then I got my shotgun from my truck and carefully walked in to see what's what. Next thing I noticed was the smell, you know, like a bad barbecue. I looked around, didn't notice any folks in here. Then I looked over at my still and saw that bottle in front of it. It sure is one of ours, but we ain't made nothing that colour before.'

'Okay, go on,' said Melissa.

'Then I figured I should have a quick look, just to see if anyone needed any help, or anything. So… I had a look through the inspection window into the still. And I saw that poor person in there, all boiled and cooked up in the still like a meat soup. Darnedest thing I ever saw.'

'So, where did the liquid in the bottle come from?' I asked.

'All the alcohol and steam and whatnot evaporate from the still and goes out through the top tube, then runs down through a condensing coil over yonder. The gas goes back to liquid form as it cools and then comes out the end of the coil into the collection vat. They would have collected it from there, then put it straight in the bottle.'

'And what about operating the still? Would the killer have to have known how to use it, or have any experience in the business?'

'Nope. It's dead simple. Just push the heat button and you're in business. Nothing high-tech around this place.'

'Thank you, Jim, I'm sorry you had to go through that again,' said Melissa. 'Do you have any security system or video cameras on site?'

'No ma'am, we don't have nothin' like that. We're just a small distillery, mainly local supply. Never had much call for any of that fancy stuff. Generally, we're quiet down here in Fredericksburg, specially all the way out here.'

'Okay, thanks Jim. Is it okay if we go have a look around?' asked Melissa.

'Sure. Knock yourself out,' said Jim. 'I won't be doing any cooking for a while, anyhow. I don't feel so good. Think I might take myself on home if it's all right with you folks.'

'Yes, that's fine, thanks Jim. Just make sure you leave your number with the deputy, so we can get your official statement later,' said Frank.

'Sure thing. Bye, y'all,' said Jim, and off he went in his pickup truck.

Frank, Melissa and I all made our way further into the distillery, noting and observing as we went. We saw the lone whiskey bottle placed in prime position, right in front of a large copper still. The pungent meaty smell got stronger as we got closer to the still. We could feel the heat radiating from the copper surface as we approached.

The first task was to study the bottle. The contents were a noxious-looking, murky red and brown liquid. The killer had scrawled over the label in a permanent marker the words *Essence of Ellen*. Bastard. To reduce the poor victim of such a tortuous death to a cruel joke infuriated me. Memories of the horrific pain the Addict Killer had inflicted on Sally and of my pain in the aftermath of her death came flooding back to me.

We walked around the bottle to the side of the still and peered in through the looking glass. By the light of the room thrown in through the glass, we could make out what appeared to be a human corpse lying in the dregs of some foul liquid in the bottom of the still.

'Are you ready?' asked Frank as he grabbed the handle of the hatch. We nodded, though I wasn't convinced. We stood back as Frank opened it. A blast of air drafted out through the open hatch, heavy with moisture and the stench of death. All three of us immediately put our hands over our mouths and shielded our eyes from the noxious fumes.

After the initial draft cleared, we took turns looking in the still, shining a torch inside. Someone had suffered torture and a horrible death in the bowels of this enormous copper kettle. The arms, legs, and torso of the body contorted at odd angles, like the victim had been writhing in agony at the moment of death. Which, I had to admit, was consistent with what I imagine it might be like to be boiled alive. The horror of the scene and what the woman must have gone through in those last few hellish moments of her life was almost too much to process. I resolved to detach myself from what I imagine she must have experienced.

As I inspected inside the still, I noticed something just on the edge of the hatch and shone the torch on it. 'Hey Delaney, looks like we might have some blood and hair here, right on the edge. Make sure your crime scene boys get this.'

'Sure, will do,' responded Delaney in a tired voice. 'This psycho really is one sick puppy, isn't he? The goddamn press will eat this up.'

'Yep. Sure is. Hopefully, this evidence will help us identify the victim and point us in the right direction on this asshole,' I replied.

'We'll continue collecting evidence and then get the body out of the still somehow. You guys can head back now, I just wanted you to see the scene firsthand. We'll finish up here and let the techs do their thing. I don't hold out much hope of identifying the victim until somebody reports her missing. See you back at the station later,' said Frank.

Melissa and I got in her car and drove back to DC, going over the case as we went, picking through my notes as she drove, seeing if we'd missed anything and planning our next move.

CHAPTER 61

'Time for a showdown, Leonard,' said Ryan. After the night's exertions with Ellen and the long drive back to the apartment, Ryan was spent. But there was no way he would sleep tonight. He resolved to push through until daybreak. It was time for him to see the sun.

He cleaned up, showered, watched TV, ate some supper, drank some soda, looked through the apartment, even found his own letters that he had written to Leonard. It was so surreal! Whenever he started drifting off to sleep, he got up and walked around, even going outside for a few minutes of fresh air now and then.

Dawn broke. He went outside to watch his first sunrise, curious to see how this would play out. Would something magically trigger to make his consciousness disappear? He still couldn't wrap his mind around how this all worked. Couldn't really believe that he was *actually* Leonard.

After the sunrise, Ryan went back inside the apartment, feeling no different, with no sudden awakening or sense of Leonard's presence. Bit of an anti-climax, really. He continued to wait expectantly, but hope of any spectacular resolution diminished by the minute.

He was standing in the bedroom when the trigger came—the digital alarm clock blasting BEEP, BEEP, BEEP. He stumbled across the room and turned off the alarm, then returned and sat down on the bed, staring at the mirror.

Turmoil surged in Ryan's brain. He felt like someone had opened the top of his head and was stirring his grey matter with a giant spoon, mixing everything together. The turning and swirling inside his head built up further and further until it was like a raging, out of control washing machine inside his cranium.

Ryan reached up to his head and clutched both his temples firmly in his hands, trying to still the frothing maelstrom inside his skull. He looked at the mirror and saw his reflection crack and fracture like splintering glass. 'Argh!!' he screamed. 'What the FUCK is happening?!'

'I could ask you the same question,' came a quiet response.

Ryan stopped all movement. The churning in his head receded, and he felt a sudden clarity, a *knowing*. He felt the plasticity of his brain forming new pathways, felt the billions of neurons all firing together, forging a new link between the hemispheres of his brain. Somewhere from a hidden part of his mind, Ryan understood that something the neuroscientists called an *ectopic tract* had just formed, where the fibres that would normally cross the corpus callosum had found a different pathway and connected the two hemispheres together.

For the first time in his life, Ryan felt *smart*. He *knew* stuff. It brought with it a sense of calm.

'Leonard? Is that you?' asked Ryan.

'Um, yes, actually, it is me. Is that you, Ryan?'

'Hello, Leonard. Pleased to meet you, finally. I have to say, you're a handsome devil.' Ryan smiled at himself / Leonard in the mirror.

'Hello, Ryan. Well, this is certainly an odd sensation. I can feel… you, but at the same time, I feel… me. It seems our dual consciousness has now merged in awareness.'

'Sure looks that way, doesn't it? I know you're in my head too, I can feel how you feel. Your intelligence. How isolated and lonely you've been. I understand you. I remember your memories!'

'And I can feel you. Feel your passion, your creativity, your *rage*. And your memories. Oh, Ryan, what have you done?'

'What do you mean? Oh, your shrink, The Drunk.'

'I'm miffed and peeved that you killed Ellen.'

'Miffed and peeved? Who taught you to speak? How are we from the same brain? Don't worry about her. We needed to get rid of her, or she would have gone to the cops. She knew everything, and I mean everything. It's fine—you don't need her anymore, because now you've got me! Now that you know the truth and can understand what's going on, you don't need a damn shrink.'

'Well, what's done is done, I guess.' Leonard shrugged, realising that a lack of empathy was quite useful in this situation.

'Glad to hear you say that Leonard. Moving on, I have a question I'm hoping you can answer for me.'

'Proceed.'

'Why am I / we compelled to kill addicts?'

'Not hard to work that out, I guess. Our father died from a smoking addiction when we were way too young. That robbed us of a stable childhood and sent our mother into a pit of despair and pushed her into an addiction of her own—alcohol. And that addiction led to a horrible childhood, to her untimely death and the subsequent upheaval that pushed us out of our home and into the hands of a sequence of uncaring foster parents. Addiction was a source of much heartache and unhappiness for us. Becoming a killer of addicts is not an altogether unsurprising consequence of losing both our parents to addiction.'

Now it was Ryan's turn to shrug. 'Makes sense, I guess. I have to say, Leonard, that I already like having you around to explain things to me. Hey! Let's celebrate our meeting of the minds and go out for breakfast! I've never eaten a proper breakfast before, in the daylight. Take me out and show me your day life, Leonard. And then tonight, I'll show you my night life.'

Ryan was full of childlike enthusiasm about having fun with Leonard, which seemed so at odds with his murderous tendencies but Leonard shrugged it off. 'Okay, let's go. First question, what are we going to wear? Should we look like you, or me?'

'Leonard, you're a smart guy, but you dress like a faggot. We are not wearing slacks, a pastel shirt, loafers, and a cashmere sweater. I've seen your wardrobe, and it fucking *sucks*. From now on, I'm in charge of dress sense. Trust me, black is the way to go.'

They headed out of the apartment, both feeling their dual consciousness. They walked past the building manager who gave them a smug look and said, 'I see the black look is continuing, Mister Price. Bit of a change from the pastel wardrobe.'

'Mind your own fucking business, dipshit, or I'll be rearranging *your* wardrobe, and your face along with it,' snapped Ryan. The man recoiled, aghast, at this unexpected response from the normally painfully timid Leonard.

'Ooh, that felt good!' said Leonard as they exited the building. 'I've always wanted to make some cutting remark out loud to that imbecile, but never had the courage to do so. It's quite liberating.'

'There's gonna be some changes around here, Leonard. Get used to it.'

As they walked down the street, they looked at the world around them with fresh eyes, seeing everything through a new lens. Ryan was seeing things for the first time in the daylight and feeling Leonard's intelligence flooding his brain, like he was getting smarter by the minute. And Leonard was feeling Ryan's power, absorbing his confidence and invincible "fuck the world" attitude; like he could take on anything.

They feasted on bacon and eggs, pancakes, and coffee and then walked back to Ryan's studio to collect his Harley. As soon as they got on the big bike, Leonard felt his apprehension and fear disappear and Ryan's confidence take over as the engine of the big bike roared into life and they raced down the street.

Their first stop was to check out Ryan's post office box, followed by Leonard's. They laughed together at how they never knew all these years that each of them was just writing to himself! This day was such an awakening for them both. Right-brain Ryan now had logic and intelligence, and left-brain Leonard now had creativity and confidence. It was a powerful, intoxicating and dangerous combination.

Next stop was Leonard's workplace. 'Are you *sure* we should do this?' asked a concerned Leonard.

'Absolutely!' responded Ryan. 'You know you don't want to be stuck in this corporate prison anymore. It's time for you to get out of this shit hole. With our combined brains, we can do anything, make money anywhere. You don't need those assholes. Let's go tell that dickhead boss of yours where he can shove his damn job.'

Leonard leveraged Ryan's confidence to the max as he strutted into the foyer of the building, casually nodding to the security guard on his way to the elevator. As he walked into the lobby of his office floor, he was self-assured and ready for action. Even though it was Sunday, he knew his workaholic boss worked every weekend and sure enough, the light in his office was on.

Leonard walked straight into his boss's office and said, 'Harry, I thought I'd find you here, working on a Sunday. You really are addicted to your work, aren't you?' A menacing smile formed on his face and his mind started whirring with possibilities. 'Perhaps the next victim for the Addict Killer should be The Workaholic?' he thought to Ryan.

'I like where you're going with this, Leonard,' Ryan responded in their thought communication, with the mental equivalent of a nod and a wink.

Harry looked up from his desk, blinking through his squinty eyes, and saw someone who looked and sounded like Leonard, but without his wardrobe and timid manner. 'Leonard? What are you doing here?'

'I'm just here to tell you to stick your shitty job right up your fat, ponderous ass. I won't be working here anymore.'

Harry blinked furiously and said, 'Have you been drinking, Leonard? Are you all right?'

'Never better, Harry.'

'How about you sleep on it tonight and then we talk about it again tomorrow?'

'You won't be seeing me tomorrow, Harry. Or the next day. But who knows? We may run into each other one night after dark.' Leonard smiled cruelly and his eyes twinkled at the thought. Then he turned and strode out of his now ex-boss's office, caught the elevator down to the ground floor and exited the building.

'That was amazing!' exclaimed Leonard. 'I've wanted to have that conversation for so long, but never got up the nerve to go through with it! I feel so exhilarated.'

'Welcome to my life, Leonard, and your new life. We call the shots now, you and me. Nobody can tell us what to do, nobody is in control of how and where we spend our time anymore. The future is up to us.'

'Sounds good to me.' A feeling of invigoration surged through every part of their body.

They returned to the apartment in the early afternoon, finding it tidy after Esmerelda's visit, then fell into bed, exhausted.

CHAPTER 62

Ryan and Leonard had woken up together as one for the first time, both pleased to see that their new dual awareness was permanent. It was dark outside, already after nightfall. 'Strap yourself in Leonard, you're in my world now,' said Ryan as they strode out into the night and headed for Ryan's favourite drinking hole.

They walked into the bar like they owned the place. Ryan ordered a whiskey and a beer and Leonard enjoyed the burning sensation of the alcohol as it made its way down his throat and into his stomach, feeling the heat all the way down. Leonard even enjoyed Ryan's usual greasy burger and chilli fries, being such a change from the steamed chicken breast and stir-fried vegetables that were his common fare. After a few drinks and some casual conversation with the other patrons, Ryan said, 'Okay Leonard, dinner's over, now it's time for some action. Let's go, I know a great place where we can get you laid.'

Leonard felt a twinge of apprehension mixed with excitement at the thought of being with a woman for the first time, and said, 'Okay, but you'll have to step me through it, Ryan.'

'No worries, buddy, I got your back. Or should I say I've got my own back?' he said with a laugh.

They left the bar and walked off down the street when a man suddenly called out, 'Hey buddy! Got a light?'

'Sure,' said Ryan as they stopped, seeming casual but with all senses on high alert, instinctively scoping the scene and identifying three men, all likely threats. Ryan put his hand in his pocket and in the same movement as grabbing his trusty Zippo lighter, also palmed his flick knife.

'Well, well, well. Who do we have here?' sneered one of the men. 'I believe we met you a few days ago,' he laughed. 'Except you were crying like a little bitch and pissed your pants!'

'Leonard. Explain. Fast. This feels familiar, but the details are foggy,' thought Ryan.

'Shit. Two of these guys mugged me the other day. Let's go! We have to get out of here!' replied Leonard.

'Don't worry Leonard, I've got this. Watch and learn, my friend.'

Ryan faced the leader and shouted, 'Dude, I don't know what the fuck you're talking about, but I ain't no-one's bitch!' In a flash he flicked his knife across the bare shoulder of the leader, cutting a deep gash in the flesh.

'Fuck! What the hell?' shouted the man, holding his shoulder. 'Kill this prick right now!' he ordered to his compatriots.

The other two men sprang into action, one swinging a heavy steel chain and the other holding a short length of timber. Ryan sized them up and quickly went on the attack, stepping in towards the guy with the chain. He slashed at the arm holding the chain and struck the wrist, drawing a deep cut that reflexively opened the hand. Quick as a flash, Ryan grabbed the chain and immediately swung it around his head twice to build up speed and then followed it around with a full revolution of his body. Then, with the full force of the built-up momentum, he crashed it into the third man's skull. He watched in fascination as the chain wrapped around the man's head and the long tail of the steel links whipped him across the nose, spreading it over his face in a bloody mess.

Stunned, the three assailants looked at Ryan as they tried to process what had just happened. 'You're lucky I'm in a good mood. Now piss off out of here before I kill every one of you shitheads,' growled Ryan. And with that, they turned tail and ran off into the night.

The display of power stunned Leonard. So, this was what it felt like! All his life, he'd had the brains, but not the brawn. Now, he had both, and the confidence to apply it. With Ryan, he was superhuman!

'I have to admit, Ryan, that felt damn good,' said Leonard as they continued on their way.

'That's one of the best things in life, Leonard. Teaching jerks a violent, painful lesson. It's time for you to experience two of my other favourite things; getting drunk and getting laid.'

'I am in your hands, Ryan. Show me the way.'

They turned into another bar, this one with live music playing and a full dance floor. They hit the bar and slugged down drink after drink. Leonard had never been drunk in his life and before too long was feeling the effects of the alcohol. His inhibitions and sense of propriety and good behaviour flew out the window and he embraced the new, intoxicating feelings washing over him.

'Okay, Leonard. Batter up. I know from your memories you're still a virgin, so you get to choose our lucky lady tonight. You just point her out, and I'll do the rest,' said Ryan with a chuckle.

Leonard scoped out the room and spotted a tall, smoking hot, buxom blonde on the dance floor, wearing black knee-high fuck-me boots, with a short white miniskirt and big boobs busting out of a tight white tank top. A red flannel checked shirt tied around her slim waist completed the ensemble, topped off with lashings of bright red lipstick and pink eyeshadow. 'There. The tall blonde, dancing,' said Leonard.

Ryan let out a low whistle and said, 'Nice choice, Leonard. I approve of your taste in women. For a virgin, you sure are swinging for the fences.'

They made their way over to the dance floor and Ryan took control, first dancing nearby and then moving in closer and closer until he was dancing with the blonde. The woman gave the confident and charming Ryan a welcoming smile, and Leonard went gooey inside. After two songs on the dance floor, Ryan and Leonard took the gorgeous woman to the bar and shared two drinks. They went through the niceties of getting to know each other, and Ryan discovered her name was Bambi; he introduced himself as Leonard.

A slow song came on and Ryan put out his hand for Bambi to come to the dance floor for a close, slow dance together. Out on the dance floor, Leonard quivered as he felt, for the first time, the thrill of a woman's body pressed against his, and the deliciousness of his first passionate kiss. Ryan was guiding the plane, but Leonard was seeing and feeling it all from the co-pilot's chair. The make-out session continued, with Leonard and Bambi getting hot and heavy. Ryan stepped in and suggested they go to his art studio, which was just around the corner. Bambi agreed, and they made the short walk back to Ryan's place.

'Oh, this is *such* a cute place!' cooed Bambi. 'Are you really an artist? Did you really paint all these pictures?'

'Yep. Sure did, Bambi. That's all me,' replied Ryan. 'Do you want a drink? Maybe some music?'

'Yes, please. Vodka tonic for a drink. And some music would be nice. My favourite band is Simple Minds,' replied Bambi.

'How appropriate,' thought Leonard.

'Shut up, Leonard,' thought Ryan. 'The last thing we care about tonight is her intellect. In fact, the dumber the better. We're going to screw her, not debate her. Now, tonight is all you buddy. I'll be there with you, helping you along, but you call the shots. This is your first time, so you go for it. I'll just be along for the ride, like a mental threesome.'

Leonard poured the drinks, put on some quiet music and then returned to Bambi, who had settled on the couch, with her long, luscious legs stretched out in front of her, resting on the coffee table. Leonard handed over the drinks and said, 'Bambi, you really are smoking hot, you know that?'

'Well, thank you Leonard, you're not so bad yourself,' she said with a laugh as she took the drink and downed half of it in one gulp. 'Come over here and give me some loving.'

'You got it, babe,' said Leonard, and stretched out beside her on the couch. Leonard was nervously waiting for all this to unfold. He had by now accessed Ryan's memory bank of sexual experiences but had never felt it firsthand and was bursting with the anticipation of it all.

Leonard gently reached across to Bambi's cheek and turned her face towards him. They kissed passionately, tongues exploring each other's mouths.

'Touch her boobs,' instructed Ryan. Leonard obliged, slipping his hand under Bambi's tight tank top and feeling her voluptuous breasts and erect nipples beneath her bra. He slipped his hand behind her and, accessing Ryan's technique from his new memory bank, expertly unclipped the bra with one hand, eliciting a nod and a smile of admiration from Bambi at his dexterity.

Leonard brought his hand back around under Bambi's top and slipped it under the loose bra. He gasped at his first ever touch of a woman's naked breast, a feeling he had resigned himself to never experiencing. Tonight was the most exciting night of his life—he had already felt for the first time the adrenaline of violence, the confidence of drunkenness, and now his first sexual encounter!

Leonard continued exploring Bambi, delighting in the sensuality of her body, the feeling of her flesh responding to his touch, the arching of her back as he continued kissing her and caressing her breasts and tickling her nipples, gently at first and then more urgently. Bambi was groaning under his touch, so Leonard took the next step and ran his hand down Bambi's chest, across her tight, flat stomach and over the surface of her clinging miniskirt. She arched her groin up to meet his touch as he reached under her skirt and felt a lace G-string beneath. He pulled down her panties all the way past her high black boots.

Leonard's heart was in his throat and his erection was straining at the zipper of his jeans. He drank in the sight of Bambi arching back on the couch, absorbed every touch, sight, sound, taste, and smell of this complete experience. He ran his hand up Bambi's leg to the inside of her thigh, gently stroking and exploring as he went higher and higher. As he reached the junction of her thighs at the pubic bone, he felt no hair; she was completely shaved! Leonard gasped as he felt ready to burst. 'Easy, tiger, easy. Calm down, take it slow,' whispered Ryan in his head, calming Leonard and bringing him back from the brink.

Fingers exploring, Leonard's touch went up between Bambi's legs and inside her. 'Third base!' thought Leonard, 'First time at third base.' He explored Bambi's delightfully warm, wet depths and started groaning in response to Bambi's panting pleasure. Bambi reached over to Leonard, pulled his shirt up over his head and started running her hands over his chest and sucking his nipples. Leonard responded by pulling Bambi's tank top up over her head and taking down her miniskirt. He gasped at her glorious beauty; she was stunning! She was shining like a supermodel, stark naked except for her knee-high black boots.

Bambi reached over to Leonard and pulled down his black jeans. 'Hey, let's both leave our boots on, it feels real sexy,' she said in a soft, throaty voice. Leonard smiled and helped her pull off his jeans over his boots. Leonard had gone his entire life without a woman other than his mother ever seeing him naked, and here he was for the second day in a row in his birthday suit in full view of a woman! Except this time, he got to enjoy it.

Leonard looked down at Bambi, who was staring hungrily at Leonard's throbbing erection. She laid back on the couch and spread her legs in front of him, giving him a full view of her glorious depths, open and ready for him. Leonard couldn't wait any longer. He moved over to Bambi, reached down and kissed her on the mouth, then feverishly licked both nipples, igniting her desire even further. She reached down, grabbed hold of him and guided him inside her. Leonard gasped again as he felt

Bambi's warmth envelop him completely, in a moment of pure delight that for so long he had thought would never arrive.

Leonard pushed himself into Bambi and she responded with a deep thrust of her own, then drew back. Again, he drove in and again she responded with passion. Their rhythm continued, driving harder and deeper with every thrust, both getting lost in the moment, panting and groaning with desire, breathing faster and faster, until they were both at their peak. Suddenly, Bambi arched her body up in pure ecstasy, away in her own world. Leonard felt her vagina contract around his penis, holding it tight in the moment of climax, and that triggered his rush too. For the first time in his life, he came inside a woman.

It had *actually* happened! Thanks to Ryan, Leonard was no longer a virgin.

CHAPTER 63

The morning light woke Leonard and Ryan from their slumber on the couch as the sun streamed through the window of the studio. They were alone after ditching Bambi the night before.

'Okay, Leonard,' said Ryan. 'We've got you drunk, got you laid, told your boss to jam his job up his fat ass and beat up some creeps who were harassing you. I think we both know the next big thrill you need to feel.'

The statement hung heavy in the air as Leonard contemplated his response. 'You mean the Workaholic? Kill my boss? I'm not so sure that's a good idea. Someone will miss him immediately, and those damn cops will see the connection between the two of us and make a beeline straight for me. It's too close.'

'Yeah, you've got a point there. But we do still need to pop your cherry in the killing department. Is there another addict you can think of that deserves to die but has no genuine connection to you?' asked Ryan.

'Hm… now that you mention it, there is a particularly irritating individual who has raised my ire on a few occasions. He's a Gamer. Totally addicted to gaming. He sometimes walks around the halls of the apartment block with his goddamn Virtual Reality headset on if you can believe that! He's bumped into me twice and was extremely rude when I protested. He is rather irksome.'

'Ire? Irksome? Jesus Christ, Leonard. You are a smart bastard, but your intellectual drivel kills me sometimes,' said Ryan. 'So, what do you think? Shall we spend today planning and setting up your first kill and then take him out tonight?'

A shot of adrenaline pumped through Leonard as he contemplated the thought of taking a human life. Looking back, he could admit now that he had enjoyed the thrill of planning the kills for Ryan but would never have had the nerve to carry them out himself. Ryan's confidence and cockiness were intoxicating. Leonard had never felt so alive; it was like Ryan's presence was supercharging his own personality, driving him to a recklessness and free abandon that he had never dreamed possible. He felt that embracing Ryan's bloodlust would be the ultimate symbol of breaking the chains that had bound him his entire life.

'The fact he's in my apartment building is a risk, but mostly he keeps to himself, locked away in his apartment playing his games. So, nobody will miss him for quite a while, I'm sure. Let's do it. I'm in,' said Leonard quietly. 'I'll need my notepad; we've got lots of planning to do and we'll need time to set everything up.'

Leonard knocked sharply on the nondescript apartment door. The light of the streetlamps peering in through the window of the lift lobby punctuated the darkness outside. There was no movement in the corridor and no sound coming from the other apartments, which was unsurprising given the lateness of the hour. The adrenaline pumping through Leonard's system threatened to send him into overdrive and on into meltdown, until Ryan's voice whispered quietly in Leonard's head, 'It's okay, you got this. I'm with you every step of the way; I won't let you fall. Just breathe.' The soothing tones helped to calm Leonard's jangling nerves.

'Who the hell is that?' came a loud voice from inside the apartment. 'I didn't order no pizza!'

As the apartment door swung open, Leonard wondered at the sight of a slovenly twenty-something wearing a stained white singlet, boxer shorts, and a red silk robe adorned with Chinese dragons. A large Virtual Reality headset strapped to the man's head completely obscured his eyes and half his face from the rest of the world. His pale skin looked like it hadn't seen the light of day for months, and his pimply, blotchy complexion suggested a diet dominated by junk food. The Gamer's hands furiously worked the controllers he held in his hand. Still mid-game, he hadn't even paused the action to answer the door.

'Well, what is it, dickhead? What do you want?' came the irritated voice from the doorway.

Leonard calmly reached up with a taser and thrust it into The

Gamer's neck, instantly turning the man into a twitching, convulsing mess who immediately dropped the game controllers and collapsed on the floor, writhing in pain.

Leonard stepped into the apartment and closed the door behind him, feeling the surge of power upon completion of the first step of the plan. He went to work on the limp form on the floor, administering the small tranquilliser dose from the syringe he'd carried in his pocket. He grabbed the V.R. headset and controllers, then stood the man up and draped an arm over his shoulder. The short, thin young man was a comfortable weight for Leonard to drag around, which in the case of unexpected discovery would allow him the flexibility of explaining his victim's unconscious state as a stupor induced by drugs and alcohol.

Leonard opened the apartment door and glanced down the corridor. Coast clear, he dragged the limp form of The Gamer down the corridor and into the fire stair. One flight of stairs down to the carpark and the body was soon in the boot of Leonard's Prius.

Leonard flopped into the driver's seat and took a deep breath. All was going according to plan. He was excited, nervous and twitching in anticipation of what was coming next. 'Am I really going to do this?' asked Leonard.

'Absolutely, you'll do this Leonard,' responded Ryan. 'You know he deserves it and you know you want to do it. He's got it coming.'

Leonard nodded and replied to himself, 'Yes, you're right, Ryan. This is *exactly* where I want to be and what I want to be doing.' He steeled his nerves once again, hit the starter and drove calmly into the street.

The fifteen-minute drive to the abandoned railway siding and maintenance yard passed quickly. Leonard cruised quietly into the parking lot, comfortable with the layout of the site from the hours he had spent through the day setting up the kill zone. He climbed out of his car, went around the back and opened the boot. Moving quickly, Leonard subconsciously observed that even though he still felt like himself, this activity was Ryan's domain and he could feel he was taking on more of Ryan's physicality in his movements, and his skill and ability working with machinery and equipment.

Leonard reached in and grabbed the body under the arms and pulled it out of the boot, letting the feet drop heavily onto the ground. He moved into the enormous abandoned workshop and placed the body on a chair in the middle of the cavernous space. He reached down and clamped his victim's ankles into the steel manacles that he had bolted to the floor that morning, noting again the sharp metal edges around the top of the shackles.

Leonard looked around the space, illuminated by the glow of his battery-powered work lights. He observed the five large mechanical levers, each a five-foot length of hardened steel formerly connected to old railway switches. Leonard traced the ends of each of the levers, noting the alternate paths he had created.

Everything was ready.

Leonard retrieved the adrenaline shot from his bag, then plunged it into the thigh of The Gamer. The response was immediate; the man's head snapped back, his arms shot up and his mouth sprang open in shock. 'Whoa!' shouted The Gamer. 'What the hell's going on?' He jerked his hands up to the V.R. headset strapped around his head and then shrieked in pained surprise as he smacked himself in the face with his game controllers. Leonard had bound The Gamer's wrists together with heavy gaffer tape and strapped a game controller to each hand, heavily restricting the man's movement.

As The Gamer reached his hands up more carefully to his face to try removing the headset, Leonard said in a menacing tone, 'Leave it on, dipshit. You're going to play a little game.'

'What do you mean?' whined The Gamer, shocked and confused at what was going on in the real world around him, trying to get his addled brain back into some order after the Taser shock, tranquilliser, and adrenaline shot, all with the V.R. game still running through his headset. 'Who are you, what do you want and where am I?'

'Well, since you're such an addict, I thought I would give you a chance at recovery. You're going to play a little game I created for you, called Four Ways to Die.'

'What? Did you say *Die*?' quivered The Gamer, as the reality of his desperate situation started making its way into his consciousness. 'Why are you doing this? What did I ever do to you?'

'You're a symbol of everything wrong in this festering world, which needs to be taught a lesson!' snapped Leonard, his mood rising to a fever pitch. 'You people on your goddamn phones and screens, wandering around the streets bumping into innocent bystanders, falling off buildings and getting hit by cars from walking in the street. Jesus Christ, you people can't even take a piss without staring at your phone. You spend your life glued to screens and obsessed with some electronic fakery make-believe world constructed by computer programmer nerds. It's a disgrace! You're a blight on humanity!'

'But, but,' stammered The Gamer, 'I just like playing games, what's the problem?'

'When your addiction impacts *my* world, that's when it's a problem,' snarled Leonard, as he pressed the muzzle of Ryan's handgun against the throat of The Gamer, hard against the Adam's apple. Intrigued, Leonard could see the pulsing of the blood flowing through the bulge of the throat as his victim's tension rose with every moment.

'Now, here's how it will go—you like games, right? Stand up slowly out of your chair. You can feel something cold and hard pressed against your throat right now. As you've probably guessed, it's a loaded gun. If you don't play this game, I *will* pull the trigger and blow your head right off your neck; that is for damn certain.'

'Alternatively, you can play this game and try to "beat the boss" I believe is the term for you Gamers, and you might just come out of this alive. Here are the rules; you'll feel by the shackles around your ankles that you cannot move from this position. In front of you are five levers. Four levers will cause your death, in a manner of your choosing; I'm sure you will appreciate the randomness of this. But one of those levers connects to the shackles and will set you free. It's all very simple, although unlike one of your electronic games—you only have one life to lose.'

The Gamer had been quivering since Leonard had jammed the cold steel of the gun muzzle against his pulsing throat; now he started shaking like a leaf in a windstorm. He put his bound hands up to his chest as if in prayer and begged, 'Please, I don't know who you are or why you're doing this, but please don't kill me! I'm only young, I haven't even started living my life yet; I've done *nothing* with my life. Please give me a chance.'

Leonard smiled at the pleading response and said, 'I *am* giving you a chance; play the game right and you can beat the boss and come out of this with your life. It's more than you deserve—you've already had your chance at life, and you pissed it away in your V.R. world. Now, enough jibber-jabber, it's time to play.'

'NO!' shouted The Gamer. 'I won't do it! I don't want to play.'

Leonard forced the gun even harder against the throat of his victim, watching as the harsh end of the muzzle formed a ring of red in the skin, displacing the flesh underneath as it compressed the cartilage of the windpipe. 'I promise you; I *will* pull this trigger and you will die if you refuse to play this game. If you play, you have a chance. Isn't that what your games are all about? The thrill of not knowing the outcome, of taking on the game and beating it? Well, here's your chance; the biggest chance of your life.'

As the gun pressed harder and harder into The Gamer's throat, he heard the resolve in Leonard's voice and felt his air supply dwindling. The choice was no choice at all. His shoulders slumped as the resistance left him. He would try his luck with the game.

Recognising the moment of decision, Leonard eased off the pressure on the gun and said, 'Very good. I'm glad to see you'll play. I'll step back now to give you some room. In front of you are five levers. You can't see them because of your ridiculous headset, but you can reach out and touch them.'

Leonard watched in fascination as his victim reached out his bound hands together in front of him to feel the levers one after the other. A shiver of anticipation ran through Leonard as he looked at each of the old railway switch levers and visually traced their individual path of death.

Leonard had rigged Lever 1 to an overhead crane directly above The Gamer. Suspended overhead was a one-tonne block of concrete that had been a temporary foundation stone used during construction work. Pulling the lever would release the load and crush the man standing beneath.

Lever 2 connected to a powerful sixty-four-volt locomotive battery that Leonard had found earlier in the day and then charged using a generator. One terminal of the battery was wired to the handle of the lever, complete with a salt-laden gel to increase skin conductivity. The other terminal was wired to the metal manacle around The Gamer's left ankle, forming a complete circuit. A nasty electrocution would result from this option.

Lever 3 connected to a nail-gun, positioned directly in front of The Gamer and pointing straight at his head. Leonard smiled at the thought of the mess this one would make.

Leonard scowled as he looked at Lever 4, which he'd hooked up to a quick-release mechanism on the ankle chains that would spring open if pulled. Leonard hoped The Gamer didn't choose this one, but he felt it was important to have this option in the spirit of this new adventure. Although, he thought suddenly; he wasn't certain he could let The Gamer go with his life if his victim chose this option.

Leonard smiled at Lever 5, his favourite. His gaze followed the mechanical path from the lever to a pulley suspended from a heavy lifting beam directly above the Gamer. A long chain ran from the pulley across to a high platform on which was a train bogie; a section of train undercarriage with four heavy train wheels, axles, brakes, and coil springs.

An immense force waited for release at the pull of Lever 5.

Transfixed, Leonard watched The Gamer run his fingers across all the levers, as if trying to divine their secret meaning and game his way to freedom. His hand stopped at the electric shock lever and felt the sticky conductive gel; instantly suspicious, he moved on. The searching fingers stayed long and hard on the life-saving Lever 4, and Leonard held his breath as he willed his victim to move past it.

Suddenly, The Gamer got spooked, changed his mind and moved on to Lever 5, the Bogie, as Leonard had christened it, enjoying the wordplay relating it to the mythical Bogeyman. Smiling, Leonard was shouting in his head, 'Yes! That one—pull that lever; pull it now!'

The Gamer obliged.

The long, powerful switch gear lever engaged the chain block, and the Bogie slowly and quietly rolled the two inches to the edge of the gantry, ten metres up in the air and ten metres away from The Gamer. Slowly, gracefully, the Bogie rolled majestically on its steel wheels and then tipped over the edge.

Leonard watched in fascination as five tons of hardened steel fell from the high platform and swung in a long arc faster and faster down towards The Gamer who was standing stock still, silent and listening intently, waiting for what was to come.

The scene unfolded before Leonard as if in slow motion—the Bogie swung down on the chain, trading its gravitational potential energy for the horizontal movement of kinetic energy as it reached the bottom of its pendulum swing. The Bogie appeared to linger because of its massive bulk, but it gathered enormous momentum with every millisecond of travel on its wide ten metre arc.

As the Bogie flattened out at the base of its curve, it was travelling at top speed on a horizontal path and the chain groaned at the maximum strain as the beam above flexed under the load.

The Gamer was immobile, still not knowing the outcome of the handle he had pulled, whether he would go free, or how he might die.

Leonard held his breath as he watched the scene reach its climax.

The Bogie whipped past Leonard's line of sight and disappeared in a flash. So did The Gamer.

Leonard stared at the emptiness where The Gamer had been standing just an instant before. Then he looked down at the manacles. A pair of old grey sneakers was all that remained. Leonard smiled when he realised this was the only remains of The Gamer after the Bogie had done its work. Then he did a double-take and looked closer; the shoes still held a pair of human feet, with bloody stumps poking out their tops. The sharp edges of the steel manacles had neatly sheared the man's legs off at the ankles as the five tons of steel had slammed into him at a velocity of over ten metres every second.

Impressed, Leonard looked up to see the Bogie approaching the peak of its upswing. The limp body of The Gamer, folded in half at the waist by the fierce impact of the front axle of the Bogie, launched like a catapult up towards the roof. Leonard noticed impassively that there were no feet at the end of the legs and blood was gushing out of the fleshy mess at the ankle stumps.

The elegant slow motion of the Bogie's travel stopped at the peak of the long pendulum swing and it hung suspended, motionless for a split-second before it started its journey back toward the floor. This was in stark contrast with the path of The Gamer, whose body was still flying through the air. Then, it too reached its vertical peak and started to descend as gravity took hold.

Leonard flicked his view from one to the other, as the Bogie came racing back down towards him and The Gamer flew away from him. In a delightful moment of synchronicity that appealed to Leonard's sense of order, the Bogie flew past him at the bottom of its arc just as The Gamer hit the floor some thirty metres away across the expanse of the enormous workshop. A sickening thud emanated from the limp form as it smashed into the hard concrete. Leonard smiled as he noticed his victim's V.R. headset still firmly strapped around his head, and the game controllers still strapped to his hands. The symbolism of the kill was intact; the signature of the Addict Killer was clear.

Leonard searched his feelings. He felt no remorse, no regret, only the thrill of elation at the outcome of his plan. He had now officially joined Ryan as a killer—a taker of human life.

And it felt good.

CHAPTER 65

'Bingo!' exclaimed Delaney. 'We've had a missing person report just come in, for a woman named Ellen. Could be our poor whiskey woman. You know, the damn press has already labelled that victim The Drunk, because of how AK killed her, even though they have no clue who she is. You two go check out the missing person report. Her name is Ellen DeMarco. She's a psychiatrist in DC.'

Melissa and I made our way to the address of the missing woman and arrived at the reception desk. We noted a small waiting room looking busier than it should. There were four very agitated patients, who were not looking very patient at all.

The flustered receptionist looked up and said, 'Are you from the police, already? That was quick—I only just called in the report.'

'Yes, Miss. We're from the FBI. I'm Special Agent Melissa Munro and this is my deputy, Simon Winter. Do you have somewhere quiet we can talk?' replied Melissa.

'Come through into Ellen's office. We can talk in there,' responded the receptionist, in a worried tone. 'My name's Lily,' she continued as we walked.

'So, tell us Lily, how long has Ellen been missing?' asked Melissa.

'Since yesterday. I've been with Ellen for five years, and she's never missed a day of work without calling me. I called her phone, texted her, emailed her, rang her home phone, messaged her on Facebook, everything. Then I called her neighbour, who is Ellen's emergency contact, and asked her to go knock on her door and see if she was home.

She called me back shortly after and said Ellen wasn't at home and that she hadn't seen her all weekend, which she said was very unusual. So, it seems like nobody has seen her since Friday night when I left the office at the end of the day. I let it go all day yesterday to see if she would turn up, because I wanted to give her twenty-four hours, but there was still no sign of her this morning.'

'Does Ellen have any family?' I asked.

'No. Her parents are both dead and she has no brothers or sisters,' replied Lily.

'What about a family of her own? Any husband, boyfriend, or children?'

'No, sadly not. It was a terrible thing. She told me once that she'd been married before, but one of her patients killed her husband and daughter in a murder-suicide a long time ago.'

'I'm sorry to hear that. It must have been difficult for her,' I said. 'I'm sorry, but I have to ask you a tough question. It's a very delicate matter, and we *will* keep the answer to ourselves, but it is extremely relevant to the case, otherwise we wouldn't ask. Is Ellen much of a drinker?'

Lily looked highly embarrassed and reluctant to reply, even looking around guiltily and shuffling on her feet, like she didn't want to betray a trust or confidence. We waited patiently, letting the silence fill the space. Finally, she relented and said, 'Well, she does keep a few bottles of her favourite whiskey in her office, and she is a regular at a bar down the street. Plus, I have seen her drunk quite a few times, so I guess that could classify her as someone who enjoys a drink from time to time.'

Melissa and I looked at each other with a worried expression. Things were certainly pointing towards Ellen being our victim. Lily noticed the look and said, 'What is it? You look worried. Has something happened to Ellen? Please tell me.'

'We're concerned, Lily. We discovered a woman's body, and we have reason to believe her name is Ellen. We're not saying it's her, but after what you've just told us, we think it could well be Doctor DeMarco,' said Melissa.

'Oh, my God!' said Lily as she put her hand over her mouth and leaned against the desk. 'Please, no! That's terrible.'

'Now, we don't know for sure, Lily, so don't panic or say anything just yet. But I think it would be best for you to cancel all her appointments for today.'

'Okay, I'll do that as soon as we're finished here,' said Lily, who was collecting herself and seemed glad to have something that would keep her busy.

'Great, thanks. And if it's not too much trouble, it would really help if we could get a sample of her DNA. Does she have a hairbrush here at the office, by any chance?'

'Sure, she keeps a hairbrush in the bathroom, I'll go get it for you. Is there anything else I can do?'

'Well, we know there are lots of rules around this, but if we could just see a list of Ellen's current patients, that would be an incredible help. We don't want a copy of the list, or any details at all, we just want to see if anything stands out relevant to our current investigation,' I asked. 'Perhaps a list of current patients might be on Ellen's desk while we're in here talking?'

'Um, okay, I know it's against the rules, but if it can help Ellen at all, I'll do it. But you mustn't copy it, or I could get in a *lot* of trouble,' she said.

Lily left the room, then came back a moment later holding a hairbrush and a single sheet of paper with a list of names on it. Melissa and I ran down the list together and both noticed one name that leapt off the page.

Leonard Price.

CHAPTER 66

We walked down the street away from Ellen's office, following Lily's directions to Ellen's favourite bar. We went inside and spoke to the manager, checking the roster for the previous Friday night. We got lucky and found one of the bar staff on shift had been working then.

'Hi, are you Suzie?' Melissa asked the barmaid.

'Yes, that's right. What can I do for you?' she replied.

'We understand you were working last Friday night?'

'Yes, I was. What's this all about?'

'We're just following up on a routine inquiry about a woman who we understand might be one of your regular customers. Her name is Doctor Ellen DeMarco. Her rooms are just down the street,' explained Melissa.

'Oh, sure, I know Ellen. She comes in here a few times a week. And she was in here last Friday night, she really tied one on. Has something happened to her? I hope not, because she's a cool lady, and a *great* tipper.'

'We're not sure yet, we're just making our inquiries now. Did she get talking to anyone that night?'

'Yeah, there was a guy here, a stranger who I'd never seen before. I noticed he came into the bar just after Ellen. He sat down at the end of the bar and was checking her out. Then he offered to buy her a drink, so I set that up. Then Ellen invited him over and they got talking and really seemed to hit it off. They both got plastered and then walked out together. I think they might have taken off on a motorbike, because I heard a big bike go past a few minutes after they left the bar.'

Melissa and I looked at each other. This was sounding promising, a good solid lead and a possible ID of the Addict Killer. 'What did the guy look like? How was he dressed?' I asked.

'He was around twenty-five, I guess. Tall, maybe six feet. Solid, maybe two hundred pounds. Dressed all in black. Jeans, boots, T-shirt, jacket, tousled dark hair, sunnies, the works. Looked like a real bad-boy, but charming, you know? Obviously very confident with the ladies.'

'Thanks very much, Suzie. That's an excellent description. You've been a great help. I don't suppose you got this guy's name, did you?'

'Yeah, I did. The dude's name was Ryan.'

CHAPTER 67

'Dammit! It's those FBI agents again!' said Leonard as he looked at the intercom video screen from the apartment. 'We've got to get rid of them. I need to take charge of this. It worked last time.'

'Okay,' said Ryan. 'This clever shit is your department, genius boy. Go for it.'

Leonard pressed the talk button and said, 'Give me a few minutes. I just got out of the shower. I'll buzz you when I'm ready.' Then he went to the closet and quickly changed into Leonard's standard garb, slicked down his hair and put on his glasses, transforming him back to the pre-Ryan nerd. Leonard prepared himself internally, taking over the personality traits of what he and Ryan now collectively thought of as their 'host body'. He changed his gait and his speech pattern back to Leonard-mode and then pushed the remote door lock button to give the agents access to the apartment.

CHAPTER 68

Once we reached Leonard's apartment, I knocked on the door, which Leonard opened immediately.

'Hello, again. To what do I owe the pleasure of a second visit from you two?' asked Leonard in a sarcastic tone. This guy was still a real jerk.

'We have some follow-up questions, Mister Price. May we come in?' responded Melissa.

'If you must,' sighed Leonard, and stepped aside to let us in.

We settled at the table and Leonard asked, 'So, what is this regarding?'

'We understand you are a patient of Doctor Ellen DeMarco,' said Melissa.

Leonard's eyes narrowed, and he said, 'And exactly how, may I ask, did you become aware of that highly confidential piece of information, and what possible relevance does that have to do with anything of your concern regarding our previous conversation?'

'We are investigating a missing person's report on Doctor DeMarco. While in her office, we happened to observe, simply in passing, a list of current patients on the doctor's desk. Your name was on that list, Mister Price,' replied Melissa.

'That's *Doctor* Price, I remind you again. You would do well to remember that,' said Leonard with a touch of annoyance in his voice as he looked over his glasses at us like some university professor with a superiority complex. 'So, you just *happened* to see the patient list, did you? Seems rather convenient for you, not to mention a dereliction of duty by her practice. And I ask again, what possible concern is it of yours?'

'Well, you see, Mister, sorry *Doctor* Price, Doctor DeMarco is missing. Nobody has seen her since Friday night. Can you account for your whereabouts this past weekend?' said Melissa.

'If Doctor De Marco is missing, shouldn't it be *her* whereabouts you need be more concerned about, rather than mine?' sneered Leonard in response.

God, this guy was such a smartass, he was really getting on my nerves.

'We're simply following a line of inquiry, Doctor Price,' said Melissa.

'Well, are you talking to any of her other patients?' he asked.

'Not as yet. Because none of *their* names were left at a crime scene,' I replied quickly.

Leonard shrugged his shoulders and said, 'As we have discussed previously and as you can see, I live alone, I have no family and let's just say I prefer my own company to that of the unimaginative and unintelligent populace. I spent the weekend alone, mostly in my apartment.'

'We'll be checking your story with the building manager tomorrow. Unfortunately, he's off sick today.'

'Suit yourself, it's your time.'

'Don't worry, Doctor Price, we will. One last question. Do you know a man named Ryan, by any chance?'

This last question looked like it touched a nerve. Leonard displayed a minor facial tic in response, showing he might know something.

'No. I don't know anyone named Ryan. Now if you will excuse me, I have better things to do with my time than waste it on your blathering. Goodbye.'

And with that, Leonard ushered us out the door.

CHAPTER 69

My phone rang just as we left Price's apartment. It was Delaney with the news that the Addict Killer may have struck again. The frequency of the kills was increasing at an alarming rate. DNA evidence had only just confirmed Ellen DeMarco as the latest victim, and now here we were just a few days later, potentially on the way to another kill site.

Melissa and I pulled into the gravel carpark of the abandoned railway siding and saw the flashing lights of the police cruisers out front. Apparently, a jogger had run past this morning and noticed some movement through one of the large windows; knowing the place had been abandoned years before, he'd looked in through the window and then called the police. We could see a man in running gear talking to one of the beat cops, so decided he would be our first stop before going into the building.

'Good morning Sir, I'm Special Agent Melissa Munro from the FBI and this is my deputy, Simon Winter,' said Melissa to the jogger, who had the rangy build of a true long-distance runner with thin, sinewy legs poking out of the bottom of his high-cut running shorts and thin but strongly defined shoulders and arms sticking out of his singlet.

'Hi, I'm Arnold,' replied the witness as he glanced at his watch. 'Look, I'm sorry, but will this take much longer? I really have to get to work.'

'Just a few more minutes, please Arnold,' said Melissa with a smile. 'We'd just like to hear your story direct from you and then you can be on your way. We'll follow up later with a formal statement, so you can get on with your day. We really appreciate your help.'

'Okay, sure, I understand,' said the jogger. 'I was on my regular morning run and as I ran by that big window, I saw a large shape slowly swing past. I know they abandoned this place years ago, so I thought it was strange. I went over to the window, peered in and could tell straightaway that someone had been messing around in there.'

'What made you think that?' I asked.

'Well, there was an enormous set of train wheels hanging from a chain and slowly swinging and spinning around, and red splashes on the floor, which looked like they could be blood. Plus, I could see a shape on the floor over on the other side of the workshop, which I thought might be a body. So, that's when I called you guys. That's it, really. Nothing else to tell.'

'Did you see anybody around or notice anything else out here in the carpark? Anything at all?' said Melissa.

'Nope. That's it. Nothing else to report,' said Arnold, wanting to get things done and move on with his day.

'Okay, thank you Arnold, you've been a great help, we really appreciate you taking the time to call this in instead of just ignoring it,' said Melissa. 'You can go on your way now. We'll be in touch if we need anything else.'

As Arnold turned and ran off into the distance, I turned to Melissa and said with a note of apprehension, 'Shall we?'

Melissa nodded and headed inside the old warehouse in silence, both of us feeling the weight of potentially discovering another AK victim, so soon after the horror of poor Ellen DeMarco.

The morning light was streaming through the windows of the old workshop in bright beams, lighting up dust particles doing a hypnotic dance in the air. The incongruous beauty of nature's display struck me, set against this backdrop of human brutality.

We were greeted by the odd spectacle of an enormous chunk of fabricated steel dangling on a chain suspended by a pulley mounted from a lifting beam overhead. It was a train bogie, slowly swinging and spinning in the air. A lurid splatter of red was splashed across its top.

'That sure looks a lot like blood,' said Melissa.

Feeling slightly numb, I nodded in silent response as I continued to look around and under the bogie. Spotting something on the floor directly underneath it, I crouched down and peered at what looked like a pair of old sneakers with red socks stuffed in their open tops.

The gag reflex was on me before my conscious mind recognised what my subconscious had already identified. The saliva flowed, and the bile rose in my throat, feeling that immediate sickening head rush and stomach heave that signified an imminent vomit. Catching myself at the last second, I quickly turned away and gagged but kept my breakfast where it belonged. Just.

'Simon, what is it? Are you okay?' asked Melissa, concerned at my reaction.

'Yeah, I'll be okay,' I replied. 'I just need a minute to process that. It caught me completely off-guard. It's not every day you look at a pair of old sneakers topped off with a set of bloody stumps in them. There are goddamn feet still in those shoes!'

Steeled for the sight, Melissa carefully examined the sneakers and shook her head in disbelief. 'This certainly looks crazy enough for AK. Let's see what else we can find.'

We examined the large steel levers that were sitting next to the suspended bogie. Carefully, we checked each lever, visually tracing the path and discovering what would happen if someone pulled each of the levers, but careful not to touch anything. We quickly identified three other potential causes of death, and what looked like a fifth option, which would have freed the victim. 'Looks like the killer gave the victim a fighting chance this time; we haven't seen that before,' said Melissa.

'Hmm… not much of a chance, one in five,' I replied. 'And who knows if he would have let him go, anyway.'

We turned away from the deadly levers and the slowly spinning bogie. Heading across the room was a vivid trail of dark red streaks along the floor, bearing the unmistakable markings of blood spatter. Spread-out splash marks and an angled trailing pattern showed the blood had fallen from a significant height, from a victim travelling at speed. We followed the trail, observing the initial strong gush in a concentrated zone leading directly from the sneakers and then spreading out in a wider pattern as it went, indicating an increasing height.

The bloody shoes and trail of blood showed the killer shackled the victim to the floor and the swinging bogie cut him off at the ankles. The incredible force of the impact folded the man in half, smashing his head down on top of the bogie. The momentum of the bogie swept him up in its arc, with blood gushing out from the open ankle arteries at the bottom of the severed legs. The force of the blow combined with the pull of gravity and a heart pumping at full power would have created a geyser of blood spewing out from the base of the legs.

We walked a good thirty metres across the room, still following the trail of blood. It ended at the crumpled form of a body lying on the floor, with the torso and all four limbs resting at an unnatural angle. Somehow, the body had stayed together under the force of what was obviously a tremendous impact. But it had folded sideways; the spine appeared to have snapped in half. Arms and legs were splayed all over and the body took on a surreal appearance, missing as it was the feet that should have been at the ends of the legs.

'At least he didn't suffer. I guess it's some consolation,' said Melissa. 'Death would have been instant from an impact of that magnitude.'

'Yep. Still, the poor bastard would have known something was coming, being strapped to the floor like that.'

We examined the body and found a massive head wound where his head had caved in because of the impact with the hardened steel of the top of the bogie.

Besides the elaborate staging of the scene, the thing about the body that implicated the Addict Killer was the V.R. headset strapped to the victim's head and the game controllers taped to his bound hands.

'The Gamer, I presume?' I said to Melissa.

She shrugged in response and said, 'I guess so. Plenty of young men are addicted to computer games, so it looks like he fits that profile. We'll have to find out who he is and where he lives before we can say for certain, but it sure looks that way.'

'Looks like he played the biggest game of his life and lost it big-time. No extra lives for The Gamer this time,' I said.

Once the crime scene guys turned up, we headed back out to the car and made our way back to the station, quietly lost in our own thoughts, wondering what fresh hell the Addict Killer would unleash next.

CHAPTER 70

'They're getting close!' snapped Leonard. 'They know your name and the building manager saw me with Ellen on Saturday morning! You shouldn't have killed her, goddammit!'

'Take it easy, Leonard. What can I say? Planning's not my strong suit,' replied Ryan in a contrite tone. 'I acted on impulse. You pissed me off when you left me out in the cold, and I wanted to punish you by killing your shrink. It made sense at the time, but in hindsight I agree it probably wasn't the best move. And speaking of poor decisions, I'm sorry about planting the envelope with your name on it at The Hoarder crime scene. They wouldn't be sniffing around here if it weren't for that. I wouldn't have done it if I'd known who you were. That is, me! All I ended up doing was incriminating myself. A real fuckup, actually.'

'You can say that again,' admonished Leonard.

'So, what now?' asked Ryan. 'Now that we've got the team back together, we're invincible! With your brains and my balls, we can get through this.'

'Well, as I see it, we have two choices. Option one—we run right now. Option two—we kill those two FBI assholes and then run.'

'I like Option two,' said Ryan with a smile.

'Okay, it's settled then. Let's get to work,' said Leonard.

First, they called the DC police headquarters and asked to speak to Melissa Munro and were immediately put through, but hung up before being connected, thus establishing the whereabouts of their target. They quickly drove across town to Police HQ in Leonard's nondescript Prius and waited discreetly down the block, keeping a constant vigil on the comings and goings. After an hour lying in wait, they spotted the two agents leaving in a black SUV. Leonard followed a few cars back, unobserved, all the way to a house in the suburbs of Arlington. They watched as the Munro woman got out of the car and ran to an enthusiastic greeting from a small boy. Presumably, this was her house, and the child her son. 'Good leverage,' said Ryan.

'Agreed,' said Leonard.

They continued to observe as Winter left the vehicle and received a delighted welcome from the little boy, then he entered the house with the woman and her son. The babysitter left a minute later, and Winter stayed on in the house. They could see movement through the window on what looked like dinner preparations. 'Looks like our two agents are playing house, getting very cosy. Interesting,' said Leonard.

'So, what's the plan, maestro?' asked Ryan.

'Well, we know Winter's past as a druggie from when you killed his junkie girlfriend. I'm thinking he has a relapse, shoots up, then kills the woman and her son in a drug-fuelled rage, and then overdoses. Bam, bam, bam, those three little piggies go to market. Job done, heat's off us, we take a few days to get our things together and then we leave this shit hole forever.'

'Man, I love your work. You really are a genius, buddy. It's great to have you back again. Let's go score some heroin, get some supplies and make it back here quick so we can do the job,' said Ryan.

CHAPTER 71

'Babe, that was one delicious dinner, thank you,' I said with a satisfied smile. 'How about you read Bobby a bedtime story while I clear the table and do the dishes?'

'Sounds good to me. And then we can go ahead with that thing we discussed,' she said with a cheeky grin and a wink.

That was the signal! We were on for tonight. We had discussed me sleeping over for the first time and had agreed that we would only do it if Melissa felt right, if she were comfortable after we'd had dinner. And she'd just given me the green light that we were on for tonight. My heart skipped a beat as I stood there in the kitchen.

I felt conflicted, but the happiest I'd ever felt. I now cared more about someone else than I did for myself. My heart was full of love for Melissa and her son; I was really falling for her. Our ten-year age gap didn't bother me. The fact she was a mother didn't matter to me. I felt genuine passion for Melissa and was drug-free for the first time since college. It had been months since Sally died, and I'd been with no other woman since then. I knew I was ready, and this was the right move for me.

Melissa was extremely emotional when we talked about sleeping together. I would be the first man she's been with since her husband died; in fact, the first time she's been with *any* other man—she and her husband were high school sweethearts. But she'd said the time felt right to move on. Right for her and right for Bobby.

I felt like a schoolkid again, on a promise for prom night. It's not lost on me what a big deal this is, for both of us.

Just as I finished up the dishes, Melissa came down the stairs after reading to Bobby. I turned from the sink to her and she flashed me a coy smile. She turned her head slightly to hide her face as her hair fell over it; her eyes sparkling with promise. The effect was mesmerising, and I felt my stomach fluttering with butterflies. I was so nervous!

'Did Bobby go to sleep okay?' I asked.

'Yes. My sweet little darling negotiated three bedtime stories out of me tonight. But that's okay, I wanted to make sure he was completely asleep, plus I wanted to get out of doing the dishes!' she said with a laugh.

I chuckled in response and reached for her to come to me. She crossed the room in a few quick steps. I loved the way she moved, like an athlete, a cross between a dancer and a fighter. She melted into my arms and I enveloped her in a warm embrace. We stayed like that for minutes, just resting in the comfort of our growing love for each other, both knowing that tonight we would need to take it slow. We both needed tenderness to deal gently with the past pain we had suffered.

Finally, Melissa turned her head and looked up at me, and a single tear ran down her cheek. My heart melted at this show of fragile emotion. I wiped the tear away and said, 'Are you sure you want to do this tonight? We don't have to; we can wait if it's too much right now.'

'Yes, it's okay. I want to. This is a combination tear, happy and sad. Sad because I'm farewelling an old love, but happy because I'm welcoming a new love into my life. I want you, Simon,' she said, and then got up on her toes and kissed me, a delightfully warm and soft touch on my lips. I responded to her kiss, just as gently. I rested my butt down on the table to drop my height for her and make it more comfortable. I drew her closer to me and we kissed long and hard, making out like teenagers, exploring each other's bodies through our clothes.

When the time felt right, I picked her up and carried her out of the kitchen then quietly went upstairs to the bedroom, still kissing her as we went.

We undressed each other slowly, drinking in the tender sensuality; kissing, touching and deeply feeling that delicious thrill of a lover's first touch. We made the sweetest love I had ever experienced. Everything felt so right, so clean, so pure. There was no fumbling and bumbling like my school years, no casual detachment like my college years and no drug haze like my time with Sally. It was perfect. Our tender, emotional lovemaking complete, we fell into a blissful sleep in each other's arms.

Neither of us realised that Melissa had been so distracted she forgot to turn on the alarm for the first time since the installation.

CHAPTER 72

From their vantage point in the Prius out on the street, Ryan and Leonard, dressed in a full black outfit complete with ski mask and gloves, observed the goings-on in Melissa's house. They saw the downstairs light turn off and a soft light, perhaps from a bed lamp, go on upstairs. Sometime later, all trace of light in the house was gone. Everything was dark.

They got out of the car and went around to the rear of the house to check for entry points. They discovered a heavy reinforced door and toughened windows fitted with deadbolts. Security was tight.

They tried a common weak point in many houses—the cellar door. An expertly applied crowbar got them in. They quietly crept through the basement, up the stairs and into the house. All was quiet.

But not for long.

CHAPTER 73

The euphoria of our amazing night together was still running through my brain and I'd been having a sweet, dreamless sleep. I felt content, relaxed and happy. As my senses slowly came to awareness, I wondered what had woken me.

Then I felt it.

A cold, hard cylinder pressed firmly into my temple. My system suddenly flooded with adrenaline as the fight-or-flight reflex kicked in. Sensing danger, it took all my control not to cry out and suddenly leap out of bed.

Staying totally still, I slowly opened my eyes. Moonlight washed faintly through the curtains, just enough for me to see an outline of a person standing over me. From the corner of my eye I made out the sinister shape of a gun barrel.

As my senses continued to process the chilling scene, my hearing kicked in and I noticed a quiet whimpering coming from the other side of the room. A sickening dread hit the pit of my stomach because I knew what I was about to see as my gaze slowly drifted over to the source of the noise. In the corner I saw poor little Bobby, bound and gagged, hunched in the corner in his pyjamas, his entire body shaking and heaving with sobs of sheer terror.

This was too much! My rational mind could no longer exert control and the fight-or-flight reflex took over. I convulsed into action and reached up for the hand holding the gun to my head but found my attacker well prepared. His other hand flashed, and he hit me with a hard fist of iron. My head exploded like a firework burst, then fell back to the pillow. As I cried out in pain, I felt Melissa stir beside me. Stars still flashed in my head and then the visual assault continued as the figure stepped over to the door and flicked on the bedroom light.

I turned to Melissa. I saw terror on her face as she registered the situation, and then total panic as she saw her little boy cowering in the corner. Oblivious to the danger from the hulking figure in the room, her maternal instinct was too strong. She leapt out of bed and rushed over to her son. 'Bobby, Bobby, are you okay? Oh, God, not again!' she cried breathlessly as she gathered him in her arms and smothered him in a hug. Bobby immediately buried his head into her silk nightgown as the sweet relief of his mother's embrace settled his fear.

An ominous chuckle came from the corner of the room and Melissa and I turned to the sinister figure, dressed all in black including a black ski mask, and pointing a gun at us with a steady hand. The detached processor part of my brain registered the gun as a Smith & Wesson .38 Special. The figure reached up and removed the ski mask, revealing a broad smile of twisted, sick enjoyment.

'Leonard Price? Is that you?' I asked, incredulous. While the facial features were remarkably similar, I couldn't accept that this was the same wimpy, scared and superior nerd that we had interviewed twice.

'Well… that depends on how you define a person, doesn't it?' came his response. 'You could say I'm the new and improved Leonard. There's another aspect of Leonard called Ryan, who in the past only came out at night. Thanks to a special psychiatrist, whom I believe you met recently, we now cohabitate in this mortal vessel. Instead of the cumbersome Leonard / Ryan label, how about we do that cool paparazzi thing and put our names together? Hmm… "Renard" just sounds like a retarded Chinese guy saying Leonard. How about "Lyan"? Hey, you can call me Lion! I'm the King of the concrete jungle, the supreme hunter. Seems kind of appropriate really, I like the sound of that.'

Jesus Christ, this was so fucked up! I couldn't believe we had this guy twice, could have taken him in, but ignored the signs and the evidence because the damn profile didn't fit! But we hadn't allowed for two distinct occupants of the same mind. This was so much to process.

It suddenly dawned on me just how serious the situation was and how much danger we were in. The man pointing a gun at us was not the nerd we had met previously, but a sick, brutal serial killer who had already killed at least eight people. I turned to look at Melissa and Bobby and realised with horror that this wasn't their first time in this situation—only recently one had lost a father, the other a husband, in *exactly* this situation, in this very room. I had to get us out of this!

I was just in my jockey shorts, with no weapons nearby. I thought if I could get to my shaving kit in the bathroom, I could try for my cutthroat razor, but success in that attempt was unlikely.

"Lion" looked at me with a smile and said in a disturbingly quiet, sinister tone, 'It's funny how easily I can read people now that I've connected my left-brain logical intelligence to my right-brain emotional intelligence. I can read you like a book, dickhead. I can see the wheels turning, the gears grinding in that tiny mind of yours. I know what you're thinking, testing the options, looking for a way out. Well, you can fucking forget it, *pal*!' His voice rose in intensity as he jabbed the gun in my direction to emphasise his words.

The muzzle of the big handgun glared at me ominously like some demented black eye, standing as it was between our assailant and the safety of those who had come to mean so much to me.

'Now don't worry, Mister FBI Agent, or should I say Mister Junkie? I don't really know what to call you now,' said Lion. 'Imagine our surprise when our consciousnesses connected and we realised that the FBI man who had knocked on the door of our apartment was the same filthy scag dope-fiend who we saw crying and wailing like a bitch after I killed his smackhead girlfriend! The sweet irony was priceless! So, don't worry, we've come up with a worthy plan to end you. We'll be re-introducing you to your friend, the White Lady. Or you'll get a bullet right between the eyes after you've watched me have some fun with your new woman and her snivelling little turd offspring.'

My stomach dropped like a stone as I realised what Lion was talking about. He would send me back to heroin hell. Suddenly my brain faced a conflict—my conscious mind dreaded the thought of going back into the pit of despair from which I had just escaped. But my primal, lizard brain flooded with excitement at the prospect of the massive rush and intense high to come. My heart started beating faster, my eyes widened involuntarily, my breath rate increased, and blood flushed to my face. The physical responses were uncontrollable, none of which escaped the home invader.

'Ha-ha-ha-ha! Look at the junkie! Panting like a bitch in heat at the chance of a shot of heroin! Well, I guess that answers the question of who's in control here, doesn't it?' sneered Lion. 'The FBI man is back in the dugout and the drug addict steps up to the plate. Ready to knock it out of the park, *buddy*?' he said with an unmistakable tone of derision in his voice. He reached into his pocket and took out a baggie filled with white powder and held it between his fingers, letting it sway hypnotically.

I looked desperately at the evil little baggie that was a symbol of everything bad in my life. Then I looked over at Melissa, who had been silent through the entire exchange, desperately trying to shield her fragile son from everything that was happening, doing all she could to protect him. Her eyes wide, with tears of sadness and terror running down her cheeks, she silently mouthed the word, 'No' and shook her head slowly from side to side.

Seeing her and little Bobby there, so fragile and desperate, I knew there was only one thing to do, for I knew exactly what would happen if I didn't. I decided to sacrifice myself to give them a chance to live.

I turned to Lion and nodded my head, without saying a word.

CHAPTER 74

With a wide grin on his face, Lion swept everything off Melissa's dressing table and laid out the works. I had to give him credit—he'd done his homework. Everything I needed was right there, from belt to spoon, syringe, cotton ball, lighter, citric acid, and water. The only thing missing was the alcohol swabs, but I'm sure he figured that was a pointless gesture, since catching some unwanted disease from unsterilised gear would not exactly be on top of my list of concerns at this point.

The entire process had a surreal, other-worldly feel to it. One half of me was watching, fascinated at the ritual of it all. Like many mainlining drug users, the ritualistic process of laying out the works and preparing the gear was a key part of the thrill of heroin injection for me. The other half of me was thinking, planning, calculating, strategizing and wondering how the hell I would get out of this alive and keep Melissa and Bobby safe.

Melissa could see everything going on, with the drug paraphernalia laid out on the table and my eyes glistening with anticipation. She broke her silence for the first time as she called out, 'Simon, NO! Don't do it! Not after everything you've been through—you can't go back into that hell!'

'Shut up, bitch!' snapped Lion, and he strode across the room in a flash, gun pointed in front with his right hand as he drew back his left, clenched his fist with brass knuckledusters and clouted her across the cheek. Her head snapped back and twisted around.

'NO! Motherfucker! Get away from her!' I shouted as I leapt off the bed and raced towards him, but he immediately swung the gun around and pointed it right between my eyes, stopping me in my tracks.

'Melissa! Are you okay?' I asked as I looked over at her sprawled on the floor, blood welling and spilling out from the wound on her cheek. Bobby's bottom lip trembled, a fresh set of tears welled up and he started bawling, the trauma all too much for the poor little boy.

'Shut your damn mouth kid! Shut the fuck up!' shouted Lion, face purple with rage and spit flying from his mouth as he drew back his left hand again.

'NO! Wait, it's ok, I'll settle him down,' mumbled Melissa out of her swollen face, thankfully still conscious, the threat to Bobby's safety bringing her back to awareness. She wrapped Bobby up tightly in her arms and quietened him down.

Calm again, Lion quietly said, 'Now, where were we? Ah, that's right, watching the junkie destroy himself by shooting up heroin, I believe.' This little display from Lion had convinced me beyond any doubt that I had to cooperate with him, that there was no way out. He was callous, brutal and completely without mercy.

I went over to the dressing table, with Lion covering me intently with the gun. I looked down at the works laid out before me and started my ritual. I shook the heroin out of the baggie onto the spoon, deliberately spilling as much as I could and leaving as much as possible behind in the bag. These were both cardinal sins that I wouldn't have dreamt of doing back in the day, where every grain of H was sacred.

I added a small amount of water and citric acid on to the spoon and then lifted it up with a hand that was, as always during my drug ritual, steady as a rock. But I faked a twitch and spilt some solution off the spoon. Then I clicked the ignitor on the stylish Zippo lighter and watched trancelike as the flame burst forth. I applied the flame under the spoon and held it there much, much longer than usual, cooking and smoking away as much of the heroin as I could, trying my best to dilute the mix. I stopped when Lion called out, 'Hey! What are you doing? Is it supposed to be making that much smoke?'

I flicked down the cover of the lighter to extinguish the flame and placed it on the dressing table along with the spoon. Then, I placed the cotton ball in the heroin solution, inserted the needle in the mix and drew back the plunger, stopping it well short of a full draw, again a grave sin for any self-respecting heroin user. I left behind as much of the mix on the spoon as I dared, hidden as it was by the cotton ball. With all my shortcomings in the preparation, I figured I had a hit that was less than half my usual strength. I prayed that it would be weak enough for me to still function and do what I needed to do once it was inside me.

'Okay, Junkie,' snarled Lion, aggressive and hyper-alert. 'Now inject it. All of it. I'll be watching to make sure you don't skimp on it.'

'Wait. We have a deal, right? I do this, and Melissa and Bobby go free, unharmed.'

'Yes, you have my word,' said Lion solemnly. I didn't believe him for a second but had to play along with the charade.

I looked down at my bare arms, still with scarred veins. I decided to inject behind my right knee this time. I looked over at Melissa, who couldn't possibly know what I was thinking or planning. All she could see was her new boyfriend about to mainline heroin in her bedroom.

After what had just happened to her after the last outburst, Melissa wisely stayed quiet. Her cheek was purple and bleeding, the eye already closing. She looked like she had serious facial injuries from the powerful blow that Lion had landed on her delicate face. Tears were streaming down her cheeks and she was pleading with her eyes for me not to go through with it. But for this crazy plan of mine to work, both Melissa and Lion had to believe that I would check out on a massive high.

I stretched out my leg so that Lion could see what I was doing and then reached the syringe down behind my knee. I quickly inserted the needle and the primal part of me felt the instant rush that accompanied that piercing of the skin. I looked over at Melissa, said, 'Goodbye Melissa, I love you,' then closed my eyes and drove the plunger home.

The rush was instant. It had been months since I'd last used, and I wasn't ready for the intensity. But I could tell it was a weak mix, having felt the full blast of a powerful hit so many times before. I acted out the heroin high, rolled my eyes back in my head and then closed them as I laid back down on the carpeted floor of the bedroom.

I fought the high instead of giving in to it, grasping at reality as urgently and strongly as I could to maintain my connection with Melissa. I focused my senses to retain my grip on reality and my connection with the physical world. I could see coloured flashes, hear muffled voices, feel soft carpet and smell fear. This clutching at awareness was the total opposite of the escape from the world that I had sought in the past when on drugs.

With enormous effort, I concentrated all my attention to force myself to awareness. I cracked my eyelids open just a touch and saw Lion crouched on his haunches. The gun rested casually on his knee, pointed directly at Melissa, with his entire attention on her. My limp body had left his awareness as he focused on his next victim. I strained to hear what they were saying, and finally my brain deciphered the sounds.

'So, are you ready to have some fun?' came Lion's sickly smooth voice. 'The question is, what are we going to do with this boy of yours? Is he going to interrupt us, or do I need to keep him quiet?'

'No, no, he'll stay quiet, I promise. Let's put him in his room so we can have the space to ourselves,' said Melissa.

Lion shrugged and nodded his agreement. They all left the bedroom together to put Bobby in his room and I saw Lion pull a rope from his pocket as he walked out, perhaps to restrain Bobby or lock the door.

As soon as they left the room, I looked around at the mess on the floor from the dressing table and noticed the bottle of nail polish remover lying next to me. I forced my muscles into action, unscrewed the lid, inserted the syringe and drew back the plunger, filling the entire syringe with the toxic acetone. As quickly as I could manage, I screwed the lid back on and laid back down in the same position I had been when they'd walked out, again with eyes open just a crack.

Melissa came back in the room first, followed by Lion, still with the gun trained on her. He ordered her to lie back on the bed, then looped a length of rope around each ankle and tied them to opposite corners of the bed, pulling her legs apart. 'Remember to behave, or your little boy will pay the price,' he said, in a threatening tone, then tied her left wrist. This was too much! I felt I wasn't strong enough, but I had to move now, while he was distracted and facing away from me before he did anything unspeakable to Melissa.

I opened my eyes fully and prepared my muscles for action. As Lion bent down to pick up another length of rope, I made my move. I staggered up from the floor, wobbled unsteadily over to Lion and hammered the syringe deep into his neck, puncturing the wall of his carotid artery. I desperately drove the plunger all the way home, injecting the full dose of poisonous acetone directly into his bloodstream.

Lion's head swivelled around, eyes wide open in stunned disbelief. He clutched at his neck and mouthed the single word, 'Motherfucker!'

But the nail polish remover wasn't acting fast enough. Lion drew his hand up and levelled the gun at me.

It looked like it was all over. The situation was hopeless.

But then behind Lion I saw Melissa reach down beside the bed with her free arm and take a mighty swing with a small aluminium baseball bat. She smashed it into the side of Lion's head with a sickening thud, caving it in like a watermelon hurled against a brick wall.

Lion's eyes rolled back in his head at the impact. The momentum of the fierce blow snapped his head sideways so hard that it bounced back off his shoulder and then lolled and bounced as his legs buckled and his body crumpled beneath him. He flopped to the floor and gave a few involuntary twitches and then was still. The combination of poison delivered directly into his artery and the concussive blow to the head had done its work. He was dead.

Stone cold.

<h1 style="text-align:center">CHAPTER 75</h1>

The enormous effort of resisting the heroin hit took its toll on my body, along with the blow to my face and the sheer terror of what might have been. I collapsed to the floor, struggling to maintain my connection with reality.

'Simon! Stay with me! Hold on, don't leave me,' called Melissa from the bed.

I could sense the fear and the urgency in her voice and knew I needed to stay strong. I looked up at her, still on the bed as she worked at the bindings with her free hand. I nodded and forced myself to stay in the present. I focused all my attention on Melissa and forced out some stilted words, 'It's okay Melissa, I'm still here, I'm with you. I just can't stand up right now. Get yourself free and then go see Bobby.'

Melissa frantically worked herself out of her ropes, leapt off the bed and ran out of the room, then returned a few minutes later. She'd comforted Bobby and left him in his room, obviously not wanting to expose the poor little boy to the bloody mess on the floor.

'Are you okay?' asked Melissa in a worried voice.

'I'll be fine,' I replied. 'I just need to sleep it off now, but I want to get out of this room and away from that bastard.'

I forced myself to stand up and put my hand on Melissa's shoulder for support. Then we walked to Bobby's bedroom, and I said, 'Hey Bobby, I'm super tired and need to go to sleep for a while. Can I use your bed?'

Bobby ran to his mother and looked at me with wide eyes. He nodded his head slowly and then buried his face in Melissa's neck. I collapsed on the small bed, totally spent. The last thing I saw was Melissa taking out her phone to call the police, still cuddling her terrified little boy.

CHAPTER 76

'Special Agent Simon Winter,' came the announcement from the stage.

As I made my way up to receive my graduation certificate, I was struck by the circuitous path of twists and turns that had led me to this moment. I looked at Melissa standing in the crowd, with Bobby sitting on her shoulders, both smiling and madly waving at me.

I felt such gratitude for my life, for the lessons I had learnt and the person I had become. Recovering from serious addiction, losing a loved one, finding redemption and then making amends. Reconnecting with family and friends, cheating death, finding a new love and experiencing the joy of being a father figure. All these things combined to make me the man I am today.

Less than two years ago, I had stood in this very spot, imagining this graduation day, only to have it taken away from me by a stupid accident in Hogan's Alley. But as I looked back on the chaotic and torturous times that came after that fateful day, I was grateful for everything and can say with absolute certainty that I wouldn't change a thing, because it brought me to this moment. By the toughest of lessons, I had learned two of the most basic and important human traits—humility and respect.

I swore at that moment that I would embody the motto of the FBI in my professional life—Fidelity, Bravery, Integrity.

And in my personal life I would follow my rule; Simple Simon says be happy and embrace love in your life.

-- THE END --

ABOUT THE AUTHOR

Mike Dowsett lives in Melbourne, Australia with his wife Liz; they are the proud parents of three adult sons. Mike's other titles include his business book *Engineer Your Business* along with fictional works *Chernobylite* and *Odessa*. You can find out more about these and Mike at www.mikedowsett.com